Chapter 1

KARL

She dipped her hand in the barrel of ice-cold water and held it down, watching the hairs rise on her forearm. Her fingertips tingled, then the stinging faded away until her hand felt like it was just meat, throbbing in the enveloping, relentless cold – but she held it still, forcing herself to form a bowl as slowly as she could. Drawing a deep breath, she looked at her fractured reflection. A young woman stared back at her, eyes narrowed in determination, high cheekbones and a set jaw forming the impression of a descending bird of prey.

'Helga!'

She exhaled and splashed her face with the cold water. 'Coming!'

When she rounded the corner of the barn the land opened up around her. She could see over and through the treetops, all the way down to the longhouse by the river. The old barn was just visible, but the other houses were all hidden by the trees. Following the river she watched the Ren Valley open up, the dark browns and rich greens of forest giving way to patches of painstakingly

1

cleared land. Late one night, when the ale had settled in him, her father had said that he was the ruler of all he could see. Some might have argued that the valley wasn't his by any rights, but she had yet to meet anyone who saw Unnthor Reginsson sitting in his high seat with axe and bow within reach and wanted to argue.

'Are you done?' Einar's voice rang out. She could picture him, down by the foot of the hill, standing by the side gate. Even at twenty-five winters, he still had the face of a boy. She knew he must have changed since the day she first came to the farm to stay with Unnthor and Hildigunnur, eleven winters ago, but it didn't feel like it. She remembered watching him run past, chasing Unnthor's daughter and trying to splash water on her. Even though she'd not seen him chase girls since Jorunn left to be married, he'd always be that boy to her. She smiled to herself.

'Yes,' she shouted back. The hay was stacked where it needed to be and a path had been cleared for the sheep. They'd be going on round-up in a month or so, but the longer they left it, the messier it got. *Deal with things quickly and effectively.* Her mother had taught her that.

She skipped down the path from the new barn, drinking in the air while it still held a bit of the night's cold. The thick trunks towered over her. In the winter they shielded her from the winds coming up the valley from the southeast; now they gave her a nice bit of shade from the morning sun. As the ground levelled, she could see her foster-brother below, moving towards the gate.

'Don't you dare check my work, Einar Jakason,' she muttered under her breath, and he must have heard her because he stopped and just watched her, waiting patiently. Thinking of something

KIN

Helga Finnsdottir Book 1

SNORRI KRISTJANSSON

Jo Fletcher

BOOKS

First published in Great Britain in 2018
This edition published in 2019 by

Jo Fletcher Books
an imprint of Quercus Editions Ltd
Carmelite House
50 Victoria Embankment
London EC4Y 0DZ

An Hachette UK company

A CIP catalogue record for this book is available
from the British Library

PB ISBN 978 1 78429 809 8
EBOOK ISBN 978 1 78429 808 1

10 9 8 7 6 5 4 3 2 1

Typeset by CC Book Production
Printed and bound in Great Britain by Clays Ltd, Elcograf S.p.A.

To Morag, who taught me to appreciate murder mysteries.

KIN FAMILY TREE

The Family

Unnthor Reginsson m. Hildigunnur Heidreksdottir

Karl Unnthorsson
m.
Agla Gunnarsdottir

Ormar Karlsson   Gyda Karlsdottir

Bjorn Unnthorsson
m.
Thyri Agnarsdottir

Volund Bjornsson

Jorunn Unnthorsdottir
m.
Sigmar Kolbeinsson

Aslak Unnthorsson
m.
Runa Geirsdottir

Bragi Aslaksson   Sigrun Aslaksdottir

The Staff

Jaki
|
Einar

Helga Finnsdottir

funny to say, probably. Helga smiled. He regularly tried to get one over on her in their war of words, but so far he'd been unsuccessful. She might not be Hildigunnur's daughter by blood, but she was a quick learner and she'd caught plenty enough of her adoptive mother's sharp tongue.

When she cleared the trees, Einar was still there waiting, a coil of rope around his shoulder. 'What took you so long? Were you snacking on the hay?'

'Girls don't eat hay, Einar,' she shot back. 'Which means whoever's saying she's your girl these days is probably a horse.'

As soon as she came close enough, he swatted at her with the rope. 'You're a witch,' he said.

'Am not,' Helga said. 'If I was I'd have turned you into something passably attractive.'

'Pff,' Einar said, grinning.

His father Jaki, broad-shouldered and silver-haired, stepped out of the longhouse and shouted, 'Get a move on, you two – they're all coming today!'

Einar rolled his eyes. 'Yes, Father,' he shouted back, then he turned to Helga. 'Come on, we need to sort out the old cowshed.'

'Why?' Helga asked, not moving.

'Apparently Bjorn and his lot are staying there.'

'Is this to keep the brothers separated?'

'It is,' Einar said. 'Why d'you think the big man went east while Karl went south? Apparently they used to fight every single day – Karl beat up his brothers again and again, until Bjorn got strong enough to stop him. Hildigunnur got a lot better at healing wounds that year.'

'We're in for a great time, aren't we?' She sighed.

Einar shrugged and pushed off the fence. 'It'll be all right,' he said as he walked off. 'I'm sure the old 'uns'll keep them reined in.'

The inside of the old cowshed smelled faintly of animals and stale hay. Sunshine seeped in through cracks in the wall where the wood had warped, but most of the space was draped in a pale light somewhere between dusk and shadow, except for a bright cone spreading from the open door which showed the skeleton of a once-functional building littered with an assortment of tools, lumber and broken farm-stuff. A stack of planks the height of a man sat in one corner, next to some broken rods and unfinished hides strung on warped old frames. A solid rune-covered stone pillar stood in another corner, nearly hidden in the shadows.

'It's so small,' Helga said.

'They only had four cows back then . . . Hildigunnur's been on at Unnthor to do something about it for years, but there're always more important jobs that need seeing to,' Einar said. 'They can't make up their mind whether to tear it down or turn it into something else.'

'I don't know if I've ever been in here,' Helga said, looking around curiously. 'The smithy's your father's den, and this has always felt like it belongs to Unnthor.' She kicked a piece of wood and it bounced into a corner. 'So what do we need to do?'

'First thing is to carry all of this out, I think – we need to clear the floor so we can build beds for Bjorn and his family—'

'*What?* Why—?' Helga was looking distinctly unimpressed.

'The stories are mostly true, you know. He stopped fitting in any of the bunks in his twelfth winter. And young Volund is his father's son.' Einar thought for a moment. 'Oh, right – you've never met them, have you?'

'No,' Helga said, 'I've never met Bjorn, or Karl. I think they were all supposed to come five years ago—'

'—but Karl was away and Bjorn's family was ill. I remember. You know Aslak, of course.'

'How could I forget? He brought two small children and a dragon of a woman with him. Will she be coming as well?'

''fraid so,' Einar said.

Helga shuddered. 'I'd rather deal with an angry bear.'

'I know what you mean,' Einar said.

'And then there's Jorunn and Sigmar. I remember her, I think, but I haven't met him.'

'No,' Einar said, busying himself with a cracked beam, suddenly less interested in talking.

Helga grabbed a spade with a broken handle. 'I don't remember having seen this one.'

'They're all old things,' Einar said, shifting a plough with one handle out of the way. 'Unnthor's been meaning to repair 'em for a while now, but d'you know what I think?'

'You *think*?' Helga said, feigning surprise.

'Shut your mouth,' Einar said over his shoulder, lumping the old plough towards the door. When he came back he was practically twinkling with mischief. 'I think the old man is so happy at how the farm is going that he *allows* himself to own broken tools – so he just leaves 'em where they break and Father drops 'em in here.' He looked around at the debris. 'The hoard of a brave warrior, this.'

'Hah,' Helga said, 'I find *that* hard to believe.' She thought of Unnthor, her adoptive father, who'd taken her on eleven winters ago – at his wife's urging – just as the farm was emptying of children. Picturing him being easy with his hard-earned riches was almost impossible. Back in the day there'd been rumours that he'd come back from his raiding in the west with a hoard to equal anyone's, but the old bear always flat-out denied it. With the ever-present Jaki's help, he'd sent back most of those chancers who'd come to look. The rest were buried just beyond the fence to the west. Eventually word had got out and the locals, seeing how hard Unnthor worked his farm, reasoned all those rumours were just that, fireside stories, and soon enough those in search of quick and easy profits found other places to look.

'I find that hard to believe,' Helga repeated, then added with a smirk, 'Hildigunnur wouldn't let him!'

'Maybe,' Einar said, 'but she's kept the old bear company for so long . . . I reckon she knows when to fight and when to look the other way. They're each as stubborn as the other, those two.'

'Probably why they've stayed married,' Helga said, shifting a couple of broken sledgehammers. 'In time my mother's story will feature "The Legend of the Taming of Unnthor".'

'It'll be a good story, though. Just like Unnthor has "The Wooing of Hildigunnur". I still like it, even though I've heard it at least once for every summer of my life.'

'So in your case that'd make – what, twelve?'

Einar made a face at her and bent to find the grip on a big

cracked whetstone. 'Unnthor Reginsson went to find himself a wife. He wanted Hildigunnur but her father, old Heidrek, was part troll . . .'

Helga strained to shift a stack of planks out of the way. 'Only part? The old men can't have been far into their drink when they told you last time. I thought he was—'

'Nine feet tall if he was an inch. And the bastard filed his teeth,' a gruff voice said from the doorway: Unnthor of Riverside, chieftain of Ren Valley and ruler of all that he saw, blocked out most of the light. His shoulders weren't that far from touching either side of the doorframe, his grey hair was still thick enough to plait and his neatly trimmed beard was full. At sixty-two summers he still struck an imposing figure. 'He used to kill bears for fun, that one.'

'And you strode up to him,' Helga said.

'And smacked him in the head with the thigh-bone of an ox,' Einar said.

'Not quite,' the old man said. 'I opened my mouth to speak, and *he* hit *me* – knocked me back four steps and cracked my jaw good and proper. *Then* I hit him with the bone, and down he went. When he came to I asked him if he gave me his permission to marry his daughter.' He joined them in shifting tools towards the door.

Einar smiled. 'And he said—'

'—the crusty old troll laughed and said, "Go right ahead. She hits harder than I do." And he wasn't wrong,' Unnthor said. 'No – leave that.'

Einar stopped just short of touching the stone pillar. 'Why?'

'It would be bad luck to move it. It's been there since the day we settled. The gods would disapprove,' he added. 'Just leave it.'

Einar shrugged and moved towards the pile of timber. 'I need you to get started on the beds for Bjorn and Thyri – oh, and little Volund as well,' Unnthor said. 'Stack the planks over there,' he added, pointing at the corner of the cowshed furthest from the door.

'Little Volund is now twelve winters,' Helga said, 'and he hasn't been little for a while, Mother says.'

Unnthor dismissed her with a huff and a hand-wave. 'He's little if I say he is,' he said. 'Einar, go and get your father's tools. We'll build the beds where you're standing.'

Einar nodded, dropped the planks on the ground and left. The rest of the debris of farm life that had been tucked away in the old cowshed was now neatly piled up outside by the fence and the empty space was filled with silence.

'My own flesh and blood is coming for me, Helga,' Unnthor said quietly.

'What do you mean, Father?'

The old man turned to look at her. In the half-light he seemed very tired. 'My own flesh and blood,' he said, 'with darkness in their hearts. I saw it in a dream.'

She opened her mouth to speak, but the rattle of metal on metal warned of Einar's approach. Unnthor heard it too, and in a blink the tired old man had disappeared, replaced with the fearsome chieftain.

Despite the heat, the hairs on Helga's arms rose.

*

8

At noon, Jaki's voice boomed across the grounds: 'Riders!'

Helga felt a surge within. Unnthor's odd behaviour in the shed had stuck with her, but she did her best to ignore it. *Something's going to happen.* While the safety of the everyday was comforting, there was a *pull* to this: the world was coming her way. She ran to the main gate, where there was an unhindered view down the valley. Jaki and Einar were already there.

'They're not sparing the horses,' Jaki pointed out.

'When did Karl ever spare anything?' Einar said.

The stocky man grabbed his son by the arm, none too gently. 'You will watch your mouth,' he growled. 'Do you understand?'

'Yes, Father,' Einar said, trying not to wince at the grip.

Jaki let go. 'Just – if you can, say nothing.' He glanced at Helga. 'That goes for you too, girl,' he said.

Helga nodded. 'Of course.' She stared down at the riders. She could just about make out the shapes . . . 'Are there three of them?'

'Too far for me to tell,' the old man mumbled.

'Maybe . . .' Einar looked puzzled. 'But who have they left behind, then?'

From a distance, Hildigunnur's voice rang out across the yard. 'Helga? A little help—'

With a last look at the approaching riders, Helga turned and ran towards the longhouse, an imposing structure with walls almost twice the height of a man. The woman in the back doorway looked like a twig in comparison, but Helga had quickly learned not to judge her by her size. Hildigunnur, the woman who'd become her mother, was tougher than most men. She might not be either tall or wide, but she moved with an ease that belied her fifty-five

9

summers, and she could still run for half a day without stopping. As impossible as it might seem, she was Unnthor's match in all ways. For the last thirty years they'd been at the heart of their valley, and the next over, and the one after that. Women travelled for days to seek Hildigunnur's advice; most thought her firm but fair – and those who didn't at least had sense enough to keep silent and tell stories about witchcraft when they were *well* out of earshot. Like her or not, everyone agreed that her wisdom ran deep.

'Shift it, girl,' she shouted. 'I'll grow a beard waiting for you.'

'And if you did, Mother, it would look great.'

'Flattery will get you nothing but trouble,' Hildigunnur said, smiling. 'Pots await. The travellers will need feeding. So you've been building beds – is that all done?'

'A while ago,' Helga said. 'Einar was pretty quick.'

'Oh, he's a good 'un,' Hildigunnur said. A glint flashed in her eye. 'And not bad to look at, either.'

'Mother!' Helga said. '*Ugh!* Really?'

'You may see him as a brother,' Hildigunnur said, leading Helga into the longhouse, 'but people see things differently.' She glanced over her shoulder before she closed the door. Unnthor had joined Jaki and Einar at the gate.

When the riders were close enough for the three men to get a good look at the horses, a deep silence spread among them.

Jaki finally spoke. 'I see Karl has done well,' he said.

Unnthor grunted in response.

The horses were running at full gallop, muscles bunched, necks stretched out with the joy of speed. The riders, hunched over, were shouting encouragement and urging their mounts on. One of the riders inched ahead of the other two and continued to stretch the lead.

The men at the gate could make out shapes now. A mastiff was bounding alongside the racing trio, tongue lolling. 'Karl's not winning this one, though,' Unnthor said with a note of satisfaction.

The rider on the leading horse rose up in the saddle and punched the air, then reined in the mount, slowing the beast until the riders behind followed suit. The hood fell away to reveal long blonde hair and rosy cheeks flushed with excitement.

'Grandfather!' the girl shouted, and beside her the dog barked in response, a big, throaty sound.

'Gytha!' Unnthor shouted back as the horses closed the distance. 'You ride like I'd taught you!'

'Better, I should think,' growled the larger of the two trailing riders. Karl Unnthorsson was built solid: thick across the chest and shaped like a tree trunk. A patchy black beard stuck out from his jaw like a badly wired brush and his left cheek bore the scars of battle. Thick eyebrows gave his face a perpetual scowl. He wore a leather strap around his neck and the top of a silver Thor's Hammer was resting on his collarbone. 'She don't hold back.' As he dismounted smoothly, the dog padded over and nudged his hand.

'Karl,' Unnthor said. 'Welcome home.'

'And I'm invisible, am I?' The third rider dismounted swiftly. A tall but slim woman, quick of movement, threw her hood back with a flick of her wrist. A blonde braid lay over her right shoulder, richly inlaid with silver thread. There was no mistaking the look of mother and daughter.

'Welcome, Agla,' Unnthor said. 'You are ever a treasured guest in my house.'

'You lie like you dance, old bear,' the woman said, 'awkwardly. But it is good to see you.'

Jaki swung open the gate and the three riders walked their horses in.

'Magnificent animals,' Unnthor said.

'They're good,' Karl agreed, 'but I need a stronger one for me. They're all from the same breeder and they carry similar weights. Gytha won because she's lighter.'

'Did not,' the girl shot back. 'I'm just better than you.'

'The spirit of youth,' Karl said. 'I'll teach you a lesson soon enough.'

'You'd have to catch me first.' Gytha danced away from her father's reach.

'You'd better keep moving, then, or I'll snap your pretty neck when I do,' Karl said.

'And then I'd kill you in your sleep,' Agla said.

Karl's laugh was short and sharp.

'Einar, take the horses,' Unnthor said. 'I'll bring our travellers in for some food.'

Karl looked around. 'This is new,' he said, nodding towards the stables.

'Built it six years ago – six?' Unnthor looked at Jaki.

'Seven,' Jaki corrected him.

'It's been a while,' Karl said.

12

'Leave the horses. Your mother has some food on.' Unnthor ushered the quibbling family towards the longhouse.

Once they were out of earshot, Jaki glanced at Einar. Beside them, Karl's mare snorted and stomped her foot. 'I told you,' the old man murmured, 'if you want to keep all your bits attached, say nothing.'

Helga watched the smile slide onto her mother's face. Then she heard the approaching voices, and a moment later the door opened. The grey-haired woman glanced at the pot and Helga took the hint. She focused on the wooden spoon, stirring the stew in steady circles.

'Wife,' Unnthor bellowed, 'we are given the gift of guests!'

'Agla! Gytha!' Hildigunnur walked swiftly across the longhouse floor and swept the two women up in a hug. 'Welcome, my loves.'

'Thank you, Grandmother,' Gytha said as her mother extricated herself from Hildigunnur's arms. 'You look as young as ever.'

'Oh, *psh*,' Hildigunnur said, 'I am old and weak, and so are my bones.'

'Didn't feel like it,' Agla said, rubbing her shoulder. 'If that's how you hug your husband, no wonder he's known for his foul mood.'

'Whereas Karl is a right little lamb,' Hildigunnur said, eyes twinkling.

Gytha laughed. 'Hah! The old bitch has some bite still!'

'GYTHA!' Karl's voice cracked the air like a whip. 'Come here, *right now*—'

The girl pursed her lips and bit down on words that seemed to be pushing to get out. 'Yes, Father,' she finally managed to mutter. She walked up to where Karl stood next to Unnthor.

The dark-haired man was all angles, shadows and fury. 'You will bring honour to my name when you are a guest in another's house.'

'But—'

'But *nothing*,' Karl growled.

'I thought it was quite funny,' Hildigunnur said.

'Mother,' Karl said between clenched teeth, 'stay out of this.' He turned to Gytha. 'Go and see to the horses' – he stopped her in her tracks with a vicious glare – 'and *behave* yourself.' At the far end Helga worked hard to attract no attention whatsoever. Moments later the door slammed as Gytha left.

For a moment, no one said anything.

'Well,' Hildigunnur said, breaking the silence, 'at least we know she's not a changeling.'

Karl's scowl melted into an almost-smile. 'She gets it all from her mother.'

'Does not! She's as stubborn as a stone, and I'm not. I'm very reasonable,' Agla said.

Behind Karl, Helga watched Unnthor swallow a laugh.

'No, you're not,' Karl said. 'You'll argue about anything.'

'No, I won't!'

'Yes, you will.'

'Shut your mouth, old man – I am *very* reasonable!'

'Karl, stop teasing,' Hildigunnur said. Helga's heart sank as her mother turned towards her, followed by Karl and Agla's gaze. It did not feel pleasant.

'Now, I need to introduce you to our girl Helga – she's lived with us since about two years after you left, and she could just as well be your sister, except that she's smarter and better-looking. We're keeping her here as long as we can.'

Karl bowed his head once in greeting.

Agla gave her the once-over, like she would a horse, and appeared to find her uninteresting.

And just like that, Helga was invisible again.

'Would you two like a bowl of something to eat, or are you about to start arguing again?'

Despite the humour in Hildigunnur's tone, Agla still glared at her husband, and though Helga searched for a tell-tale twinkle, a smile or any sort of affection in the woman's face, she found nothing.

'Yes, thank you,' Agla said, and Hildigunnur turned her gaze Helga's way, which was as good as a snapped command. Hands working automatically, she plucked out wooden bowls from their place under the side benches and filled them with stew. The steam played around her hands, heating her skin. She adjusted her grip and hurried out to the table, where Agla had sat down next to Unnthor. Hildigunnur had disappeared, but Helga didn't need to see her mother to know she'd be working somewhere she knew the girl would pass by. She'd stop her for an exchange of words, then there'd be the tilted head, the raised eyebrow – the surreptitious glance to ensure that the two of them were the only ones sharing the joke – and moments later Gytha would be swallowing a chuckle, eyes sparkling at her grandmother's spirit. Helga could almost hear her mother's voice, throwing wisdom over her shoulder. *A well-placed word can save you a lot of trouble.*

Without realising, she found she was standing near Karl, sitting silently by the table. 'Here you go,' she said, stumbling over her tongue.

He stared straight up and at her, brown eyes twinkling, smiling wrinkles forming. *He's struggling not to lick his lips*, she thought. *Like a wolf.* 'Thank you. Thank you very much,' he said, smirking at her.

'Thank Mother,' Helga said, more sharply than she'd intended. 'It's her stew.'

Instead of recoiling, however, the dark-haired man's smile just widened. 'It looks . . . good enough to eat.'

She could feel his eyes on her long after she'd retreated to her place in the shadows.

Einar led the newcomers' horses to the far end of the stables. He had thought for a moment about using the stalls near Unnthor and Hildigunnur's own mares, but the animals' laid-back ears and snorting quickly convinced him that that was a bad idea, so in the far end they went. He started with Karl's horse, brushing down her flanks with smooth, even strokes. He quickly realised the big black mare had a fierce temper and he'd have to be on his toes if he was to avoid being bitten.

'*Ssh*, girl,' he muttered, 'you'll feel better once I'm done.' The horse tossed her head angrily and snorted, but didn't snap at him again. 'That's it,' he whispered, 'just a couple moments more and you'll be rid of me.'

'What makes you think she'd want rid of you?' Gytha asked

from the doorway, making Einar jump back, just a moment before yellowed teeth were snapping at his hand. He shifted out of the way of the mare's stamping hooves before turning to the girl. He looked at her, but didn't speak.

'She's all right,' she said, and as she moved towards him, the mare responded to the familiar presence, snorting once and rolling her head. 'Here. Give it to me,' Gytha said, holding out her hand for the brush.

Einar passed it over without saying a word.

Gytha started grooming the horse, falling into an even rhythm. 'You've done this well,' she remarked.

'Why do you say that?' Einar said.

'Because you still have your fingers.' Gytha smiled at him. 'That means she likes you.' When Einar didn't respond, she frowned. 'Would you like me to look after our horses?' she said.

'I . . . um . . . if you want,' Einar said.

Gytha looked at him for a moment. 'Why won't you talk to me?' she said.

'I'll be outside if you need me,' Einar said, slipped from the stall and out through the door. He closed it behind him.

The mare snorted at Gytha.

'Don't you start,' the girl said. 'You wouldn't have done any better.' She drew the brush firmly along the animal's back. 'But he looks fun, and I have three days.' Stroking the mare's head gently, she whispered in the horse's ear, 'We'll see who gives up first.'

Chapter 2

BJORN

Unnthor sat by the riverbank, elbows on knees. His silent stillness blended with the gentle sounds of the river and birdsong from the bushes on the other side. By his feet, sunlight set the surface of the slow-moving water glittering like a cascade of gold. The old man watched as a figure approached from the direction of the longhouse, his stride even and purposeful.

'Here we go,' Unnthor muttered.

When he was close enough, Karl saluted. 'Mother said I would find you here.'

'Something shifted upriver last year. This has become quite a good spot,' Unnthor said. He reached for the fishing pole and pulled on the twine until the hook emerged from the water. 'I thought I'd see if I could grab something extra for the pot.'

'They'll bite soon enough,' Karl said.

'They usually do,' Unnthor replied.

'You're well.'

'I get by.'

'How are things in Glomma?'

Unnthor turned and looked west, towards the mountains that separated them from the Glomma Valley. 'The usual,' he said. 'The odd neighbourly dispute. They still come to me to settle, or when they think they want to know what the gods think about this, that or the other. I never tell them what *I* think.'

'Which is?'

'That the gods are most likely busy doing something much more important than caring about who shags whose daughter.'

Karl smirked at that.

'We had a cattle thief two years ago.'

'Really?'

'Traveller from down south. Thought he'd find some simple country folk, pick a couple of easy farms.' Unnthor smiled. 'He was not a wise man.' The shadow of the same smile crept up on Karl's mouth, and for a moment the two men looked remarkably similar. 'How about you? I keep hearing stories from the south, but I never know what to believe.'

'We've done well,' Karl said. 'I got on a boat with a bunch of hard bastards, captained by a man called Sigurd Aegisson.'

Unnthor whistled. 'Even up here we've heard of him,' he said. 'One of Skargrim's old crew? Hard as the rocks, that one.'

Karl smiled. 'As hard as he needed to be. We took everything we could in the land of the Saxons, which was a lot – enough to buy me a big farm down south.'

'I'd heard something about that, but—'

'Twenty-four head of cattle,' Karl interrupted.

Unnthor went quiet. 'Twenty-four,' he said. 'That's ... that's impressive.'

'And forty head of sheep. Four workmen, two of them with wives.'

'You've done better than me, then,' Unnthor said.

'Because I didn't bury my treasure,' Karl said.

'I believe a man should earn what he has in life,' Unnthor snapped. 'And don't tell me you believe that old wives' tale still?' He stared at his son. 'There is no hoard,' he said slowly.

Karl stared back at him, but he did not speak. After a moment, he looked away, down the stream. 'I thought as much,' he muttered. 'Just a tale, anyway.'

'That's right,' Unnthor said. By his feet, the fishing line drifted with the current, slack and lifeless.

The knife sliced into the meat with precision and force as Hildigunnur guided the blade slowly, deliberately, skilfully into the lamb, finding the sinews that held muscle and bone together. An arm's length away, Helga peeled turnips and tried to be invisible.

Behind them, Agla sighed and continued her complaining. 'I just don't know what to do with her. She acts—'

'Exactly like you did when you were young?' Hildigunnur said, not unkindly.

'Yes,' the blonde woman said, deflating onto a pile of furs. 'And I worry she's going to make all the same mistakes.'

'Mistakes aren't so bad,' Hildigunnur said, yanking off the leg with a twist. 'That's how you get to be wise.' She turned and winked at Agla. 'Like us.'

Agla sighed. 'Yes. Maybe. I just wish she could ... I don't know ...'

'Be easier to manage? Softer. Kinder.'

'Yes.'

And where would she get that from? Helga thought.

'That is sometimes the way with young women,' Hildigunnur said. 'They're horrible, mistake-making, man-eating monsters. Like Helga,' she added.

'What? Am not!' Helga exclaimed.

'Oh, I bet you are.' The blonde woman laughed. 'Bet you've got them lined up, sword in hand.'

'A whole row of them,' Hildigunnur said, 'fighting for the honour.' She added a hip-swing that suggested exactly how Helga's imaginary suitors might duel. Behind them, Agla cackled with delight.

'Very funny,' Helga said, 'but too accurate. I think you speak from experience, Mother.'

'Oho,' Agla exclaimed, 'you're raising a fine one of your own there!'

'I know,' the older woman said, smiling at Helga. 'She is a fine one indeed. I have run out of puzzles to pose her, and I cannot teach her more about the gods because she knows it all already. She's got a nose for curing herbs, too. But now we should stop this talk of strapping boys or she won't sleep tonight for excitement and thoughts of swordfights – of various shapes and sizes. Tell us news of the world, Agla: what's happening in the south?'

As Karl's wife started recounting news of politics and war, Helga snuck a look at her mother and thought of all the times she'd seen Einar wrangle particularly stubborn mares into submission. Mother had a similar look of contented achievement about her.

'Keep working,' Hildigunnur said under her breath as Agla prattled on behind them. 'Food won't prepare itself.' The older woman's knife cut swiftly through the lamb's neck.

It was Jaki who spotted him first. 'That's got to be Bjorn.'

'Where?' Einar said. He leaned against the gate for a moment, wiping sweat from his forehead.

'There – down by the bend.' Jaki pointed, and sure enough, about a mile down the road, two riders walked their horses while a third, trailing behind the walkers, sat slumped in the saddle of the last beast.

'Do you think he's ridden at all?' Einar said.

'I hope not, for the sake of the poor animal!'

The person on the left, of average height and build, was moving at a calm, even pace. The man on the right was a good head and a half taller, broader and bigger in every sense, making the horse next to him look more like a pony. A dog walked by his side.

'He's in no rush,' Einar said.

Jaki sighed. 'He rarely is, our Bjorn.'

'Do you miss them?' Einar said after a while.

Jaki thought for a couple of breaths before answering. 'The place is quieter without their shouting, that's for sure.'

'But didn't Bjorn and Karl—?'

'Eh,' Jaki said, dismissing Einar with a wave, 'they weren't the best of friends – but they were brothers. A little bit of age and distance cures that kind of nonsense. But all four of them are dangerous in their own ways, and I've felt a cold in my bones of late.'

'What do you mean?'

'There's trouble coming,' Jaki muttered.

'Oh now, old goat! Am I finding out that my father has turned fishwife in his old age? What's next – dream signs?'

Jaki turned to look at Einar. He didn't say anything, but his face looked carved out of stone.

After a moment the young man looked away, and saw Helga approaching.

'Why are you two lazy sods hanging out here by the gate?' she called.

'Bjorn's coming,' Einar said, nudging her towards the road.

'First time back,' Helga said. Beside her, Jaki raised an eyebrow. 'He had just left when I got here.'

'*Hm*,' Jaki said, 'that sounds about right. Which is—'

'Eleven winters,' Helga said. 'I think.'

The old man looked stricken. 'What? *Eleven*? Where does the time go?'

'Well met!' a deep voice boomed; they were now close enough for everyone to make out faces. The big man waved and called, 'Jaki – is that you?'

'Who else?' Jaki shouted, smiling.

Helga could sense Hildigunnur as she came up behind them.

'Well met, son!' Hildigunnur shouted. 'Stew's in the pot!' Behind her, Agla and Gytha came out of the longhouse and stood behind the old woman. *They know their place already*, Helga thought.

'That's good news to weary travellers,' Bjorn said.

As he closed in, Helga couldn't help but stare. Everything about Bjorn Unnthorsson was big: his face was coarsely hewn, his hands were like shovel blades. Blond hair and beard gave him the appearance of some kind of hill giant; even the wolfhound by his side, a huge dog in its own right, looked like a puppy by comparison. *Nine foot tall and filed his teeth*, Helga thought. If Karl at his best was like Unnthor at his worst, Bjorn must trace his looks to Hildigunnur's side of the family. Bjorn's wife Thyri almost disappeared in the shadow of the big man as they reached the gate. A woman of average size, in sensible clothing, she seemed to drift along in Bjorn's wake. Her light brown hair was bound in a traveller's bun and tied with a leather strap. Helga glanced at the elfin Agla next to her. *Such a difference*, she thought – then her attention was caught by the awkward dismount of the boy on the horse. Though almost the size of a man, and a big one at that, he had the soft face of a child and all the grace of a newborn deer. While Bjorn and Thyri exchanged greetings with the other women, Helga found herself staring at the boy. Minded by no one, he just stood there, clearly not sure where to go or what to do. She saw in him the shadow of her younger self, lost and ignored, and her feet moved before her brain caught up.

She slipped in between the horses. 'Are you hungry?' she said quietly, by his shoulder. The boy looked at her with watery blue eyes. His lips pursed, but he stopped short of saying anything. Instead, after a moment, as if processing her words, he nodded. Helga smiled. 'Come with me,' she said, winking conspiratorially. After another moment's hesitation he led his horse on after her.

'Volund!' Bjorn snapped, and Helga felt the boy tense up.

'Don't worry,' Hildigunnur said, 'Helga will look after him.'

'Boy's a halfwit. He needs a clip 'round the ear more'n he needs looked after,' Bjorn grumbled.

Helga looked back at the newcomers. Bjorn took up so much space that she couldn't even see Thyri any more. 'Lead the horse through here,' she said to Volund, pointing to the stables. 'Einar will take care of him. Did you have a long trip?' The boy nodded and looked down, then peeked up at her, chin still on his chest. Helga smiled. 'Do you like lamb stew?' The boy nodded again, more enthusiastically, and Helga's smile spread. 'Then let us go and raid the pots!' She marched off, feeling an unfamiliar sense of satisfaction when she heard the boy falling in behind her. He dragged his steps a little, but he was following. They were rewarded with the rich smells of cooking meat as they entered the longhouse. Helga walked over to the big pot, grabbed a ladle and dished up a generous portion, and the boy immediately sat down, hunkered over the bowl and started shovelling the food in his mouth. 'You might want to be . . . um – careful—' Helga started, but too late: Volund was already in the process of spitting the food back into the bowl.

He looked up at her, surprised and betrayed. 'It's *hot*!'

Helga couldn't help the grin. 'Yes, it is. Blow on it, like this.' She took the bowl from him and blew gently on the top. Volund looked at her, eyes full of distrust, but he accepted the bowl again and took a small spoonful, pushing it carefully past his lips. Moments later his face lit up in a radiant smile. Frowning, as if trying to remember something, he stuck his spoon in, lifted it up and blew on it with all the care of a master craftsman.

'That's it,' Helga said. 'Just like that.'

Volund beamed and continued to eat as his parents came in, chatting with Agla and Hildigunnur.

'—been a kind winter,' Agla said, craning her neck to speak to Bjorn's face. 'We've got ourselves into a good situation down south. How are things on your side?' The door closed behind them.

'Oh, the valleys are hard work, no doubt,' Bjorn rumbled, 'but the Svear keep to themselves and we stick to our end.' The big man lowered himself onto a bench that creaked ominously. 'We sometimes trade with them. This one time I managed to get three wagonloads of—'

'BJORN!' Einar's shout was almost drowned by an unholy brangle of barking and growling. There was a blink of an eye inside the longhouse when no one knew what was going on – and then the big man was up and, for all his bulk, moving surprisingly swiftly towards the doors. Helga, still vaguely aware of Volund cowering over his bowl of stew behind her, found herself pulled in his wake, following the rest of the family.

By the time she was through the side door of the longhouse, Bjorn was already halfway across the yard. The big grey wolf-hound was poised, teeth bared, over Karl's mastiff. Blood was streaming from a cut on the white dog's square muzzle. Its head was close to the ground but powerful legs were pushing for purchase, preparing to spring at its slim grey opponent. 'Breki,' Bjorn shouted, *'here!'* The wolfhound hesitated for a moment and the mastiff barrelled into it, maw opening wide and clamping down on the grey dog's neck.

'NO!' Bjorn waded in and levelled a savage kick at the white dog.

'What the fuck are you doing to my dog?' Karl shouted, charging across the farmyard towards the fighting animals, but Bjorn ignored him and kicked the mastiff again, catching it squarely in the ribs. The big dog howled and released its grip on the wolfhound, who retreated, head down but eyes fixed on the mastiff, still focused on the attack.

Karl grabbed his brother from behind with both hands, planted a heel on the back of his knee, pushed and twisted, and Bjorn hit the ground with a scream.

'Stay away from my dog!' Karl growled as he leaped over the big man and lunged for the mastiff's collar. The dog growled at him, but did not snap. 'Calm down, Erla. Calm down,' he said, and the mastiff whimpered in response.

Karl turned on the big man, who had managed to rise to his knees. 'Why did you set your fucking dog on him, you big bastard?' he snapped. 'What's wrong with you?'

'I didn't set anything on anything, least of all your mutt,' Bjorn growled. 'Einar shouted, and I came out.'

'And I'm supposed to believe that?' Karl said. 'You did this on purpose—!'

'I did not!' Bjorn shouted. 'No such thing – and if I did, you know I'd tell you right to your face, rather than attack from behind like a fucking coward.'

Karl's fists were clenched and his weight had started to move from his back foot to his front when Unnthor's voice cracked over their heads like a whip. 'If you two whelps don't stop this *right now* I will treat you both as you deserve,' he snarled, striding towards where the two men had squared up. '*Back off.*'

'But he started—' Bjorn began.

'NOW.'

Helga watched from the longhouse doorway as the giant and the warrior somehow *deflated* into six-year-olds being told off by their father. Karl spat on the ground and turned to see to the mastiff, which had slinked off and crawled under a cart.

'Why were the dogs loose, anyway?' Bjorn growled as he knelt by the bloodied wolfhound, soothing it with gentle strokes while he examined the wounds.

'They must have slipped their leads,' Unnthor said, standing over him. 'Out to cause trouble, like their owners. Now, am I going to need to watch the two of you all day, or are you going to act like grown men?'

'I won't do anything,' Bjorn said, adding under his breath, 'I never do.'

Unnthor snorted. 'At least you haven't learned to lie since you left. Don't be a fool.' With that he walked over to the other side of the farmyard, where Karl had coaxed the mastiff out from underneath the cart. The big dog favoured her side and whimpered as the dark-haired man touched its ribcage.

'Any breaks?'

'No, no thanks to him,' Karl growled. 'You can't just kick someone's dog like that—'

'*Shut up,*' Unnthor said. 'You should have made sure yourself that your dog was tied up properly in the first place. As should he,' he added when Karl made to protest. 'But I need to know that you've both grown up and stopped this stupid rivalry – just for the next three days. Then you can go your own way and do whatever you do. But while you are on *my* land, you show me respect. I can still give either or both of you a thrashing.'

Karl turned to look up at his father. 'Did you summon us here to shout at us?'

'No.' Unnthor glanced round at Hildigunnur. 'We asked you here to see you – to see *family*. We haven't met up for a long time, and I thought we should. I got tired of your mother telling tall tales about your successes. I thought I could hear it from your own lips.'

Karl looked around quickly. The women were heading back to the longhouse and Bjorn was busy with his dog. The words tumbled out of him. 'Father, I need help – I borrowed to extend the farm and then sixteen of mine got the rot – and I can't . . . I can't pay it back.'

Unnthor frowned. 'Sell some of your cattle. Get rid of workmen. It's not complicated.'

'That won't be enough.'

'How much did you borrow?'

'Too much,' Karl said. 'I thought—'

'Well, you shouldn't have. Never borrow,' Unnthor snapped. 'Work. Sell the farm if you have to. Start a new one.'

'Why would you not want to help your own flesh and blood?'

Unnthor looked Karl up and down, choosing his words carefully. 'Because I think any offspring of mine should be able to help themselves. And they should not seek to hold more than they can carry.' With that, he turned around and walked away.

'Don't turn your back on me, *Father*,' the dark-haired man muttered. 'You won't live for ever.'

By his knee, the mastiff whimpered.

Einar closed the door to the smithy behind him and looked around. His father's workshop was simple but effective: a workbench nestled up against the wall with a row of well-worn tools above it. He reached for the hammer and put the bent pegs on the table. The first blow covered the sound of the door opening softly.

'Weren't you supposed to look after the dogs?' Gytha said behind him.

Einar twisted around. 'You have a knack of sneaking up on people,' he said.

'I'm sorry. I didn't mean to.'

'Don't worry,' Einar muttered.

'What are you doing?' Gytha said, closing in.

'Just straightening some pegs,' Einar said.

'Can I help?'

Einar frowned. 'Help? Uh, no. It's a one-man job.'

Gytha leaned in, touching shoulders with Einar. 'Can I watch, then?'

Einar turned and looked at her for the first time. The breath caught in her throat and her eyes twinkled with anticipation.

He reached out and grabbed her shoulder firmly. Then he marched her towards the door, opened it and pushed her out. 'No,' he said.

Gytha stumbled backwards, taking three steps to gain her balance and avoid a fall.

By the corner of the smithy, Bjorn, bent over his wounded dog, looked up. Within a blink, he smirked. 'Oh – what's going on here? Did the little princess not get what she wanted?' The wounded animal on the ground by his feet whimpered.

'Shut up, Uncle!' she snapped. 'He's a – he's a *jackass*!' With that Gytha stomped away.

The big man grinned as Einar firmly closed the smithy door, but the smile faded when he saw Karl heading towards him from the longhouse. The dark-haired man stopped ten yards away.

'I didn't set Breki on your dog,' Bjorn said.

Karl looked at the horizon, then at the trees. 'Sorry I kicked you,' he said.

Bjorn shrugged. 'It's no matter. Got me to the ground quick enough, I suppose. Good move.'

'Had to fight some big bastards out west,' Karl said. 'Knee's the best bet for someone my size.'

Bjorn smiled. 'I'll remember that – and plant it in your face next time.'

Karl smiled back. 'You're an arse.'

'A bigger, better and hairier arse than you, Brother,' Bjorn said. Unnthor stepped out of the longhouse and glared at them, but the big man waved. 'Don't worry, Father. Karl was just explaining to me how he was wrong in every way and how he'll give me the farm after you go sailing on the burning boat.'

'Who says it's his to give?' Unnthor said. Standing between them, Karl stiffened for a moment, then he laughed. A smile crept up on Unnthor as well as he walked past his sons. 'I suppose I'd better treat you like the dogs you are and take you out for a run around.'

'What do you mean?' Karl said.

The old man ducked into the smithy. The brothers exchanged glances, but neither spoke.

When Unnthor came back out, he held three spears. A bow was slung over his shoulder and a quiver hung at his waist. He threw a spear to each of the brothers. 'We're going hunting.'

'—caused quite a stir!' Agla said. The midday sun's rays were lancing into the longhouse from the open vents, casting a yellow glow on the four women.

'I can imagine,' Hildigunnur said, whittling a small piece of wood. In time it would be a sitting dog or a horse or a bull, whatever she wanted. The blade moved smoothly, the tiniest of cuts doing exactly what she needed them to. The way her fingers closed around the polished reindeer-horn handle, the slim blade seemed to be almost a part of her.

Like a claw, Helga thought as she watched from afar. She was trying to busy herself with some stitching, but the bloody needle wouldn't go where she wanted it to. What had in her mind been a sumptuous vine stretching from the hem of her skirt up along her leg looked more like the trail of a drunken crow. She frowned, ripped out the stitch for the fourth time and started again.

'All we know, though, is that after they ran out of food she got caught stealing. I didn't hear from where or what, but no one spoke to her for weeks.'

'Awful,' Hildigunnur murmured.

'Isn't it? You have to question what women like that learn – and how they get their husbands.'

'Oh, I can think of a couple of ways,' Hildigunnur said.

Agla giggled. 'It's so good to have someone to talk to,' she said.

'It is,' Hildigunnur said. 'How about you, Gytha? What do you think about this woman?'

Gytha was sitting sullenly next to her mother; she'd not said a word for ages. For a moment she stayed silent, then she spat, 'She's a cow – was a cow, is a cow, will always be a cow.'

Agla sputtered, but Hildigunnur interrupted her. 'If all your mother says is true, that sounds like a fair assessment to me.'

Gytha snorted and clammed up again, but Helga couldn't help but notice the angles of the young woman's elbows and shoulders softening just a little bit. Not much, not much at all, just the tiniest bit. Hildigunnur shot the girl a smile and continued listening to Agla.

Gytha drew a deep breath and sighed, loud enough for everyone to hear, but before anyone could react, the door flew open and Bjorn's wife stumbled through.

'Well met, Thyri,' Hildigunnur said. By her side Agla fought and failed to hide her annoyance.

Thyri shook her head quickly, flustered. 'Forgive me, Hildigunnur. I – uh, I – thank you for inviting us. I come as a guest – uh – I can't find Volund,' she said, her voice shaking. 'He's never— I don't—'

Hildigunnur was on her feet and halfway across the floor before Helga understood what had happened. Her voice was no longer laced with a smile. 'How long since you saw him?'

'Uh – a little while?'

'Agla and Gytha – river. Helga – stables.' Hildigunnur put a hand on Thyri's shoulder. 'We'll take the road.' She clapped her hands twice, hard. 'Move.' The command in her voice had the women out of their seats before they'd even realised it.

The sun hit them as they stepped outside. The shade of the longhouse had made Helga forget about summer for a little while, but the warmth of the morning had been replaced by the oppressive heat of midday. She thought of Volund as she walked out into the yard, watching the backs of the older women. Going to the stables felt wrong, somehow. What would the boy do? *I'm in an unknown place*, she thought. *I'm hot and uncomfortable. I'll go to the river . . . no – because despite the body I'm in, I am still a pup, and I'm bored. There's more to play with . . .* As Hildigunnur guided Thyri to the main gate and Agla disappeared down towards the river with Gytha in tow, Helga looked at the stables, made a decision and turned left, towards the side gate.

The echoes of Volund's name being called out followed her as she made her way towards the new barn. The shade of the trees made the heat a lot more bearable. 'Clever boy,' she muttered, breathing in the scent of the pines, looking around, searching for – *there*. A dark circle where someone had overturned a rock; a line suggesting someone had poked the beetles underneath with a stick. Her heart beat a little faster as she hurried on. A broken branch, some torn moss – the signs were small but consistent: someone had gone up the path, picking at things that took their fancy. She kept checking for trampled grass or even footprints where he'd veered off as well, but she could find nothing.

A bend in the path, and the new barn loomed above her, the sun shining on the east wall. Helga peered around the corner and saw Volund lying outstretched in the shadow, motionless, fast asleep in the shade.

A giggle escaped her lips and the boy stirred, but he didn't wake until she nudged him with her foot. 'Come on, lazy-bones.' She smiled at him. 'Your mother is worried.' Volund opened his eyes and looked dully at Helga. 'Come on, *up*!'

The boy rolled over and pushed himself clumsily to his feet. 'I – I fell asleep.'

'That happens to the best of us,' Helga agreed, 'but now we're going down to the farm and Einar – the nice boy who tends to the horses – will find you something to do.'

Volund nodded, face serious. 'That sounds good.'

Helga stifled a grin. 'Good. Let's go.' She walked off back towards home, Volund trailing behind for a bit, then catching up and walking happily by her side.

'Volund!' Thyri's voice rang out the moment they cleared the treeline and Helga saw the woman running a few steps towards the side gate, then stopping, as if catching herself. Hildigunnur, behind her, walked briskly towards them.

The boy beside Helga slowed down. 'Come on now,' she said, forcing as much happiness into her voice as she could. 'We're going to find you something to do, remember?'

But Volund's head was down and his feet were dragging. "'m in trouble,' he mumbled.

'Maybe,' Helga said, cheeks hurting from maintaining the smile, 'but trouble only lasts so long, and then you'll be free to do fun things. Maybe we can go fishing in the river.'

A quick glance from the boy. 'In the river? Promise?'

This time, the smile needed no forcing. 'Promise.'

The steps picked up ever so slightly.

Thyri was waiting by the gate, almost as if afraid to leave the safety of the farm. 'Why did you run away, you stupid boy?' she shouted. 'I was so afraid!'

'Wanted to go and look around,' Volund muttered.

'You don't *ever* do that without telling me where you're going!' As soon as the big boy was close enough to grab, Thyri reached for him and hauled him bodily through the gate. 'You're coming with me and sitting where I can see you.'

As he was being dragged off by his mother, Volund twisted his head to look over his shoulder at Helga. He looked unhappy.

Promise, she mouthed and got a half-smile in return.

When mother and son had disappeared, Hildigunnur asked, 'Where did you find him?'

'At the new barn,' Helga said. 'He'd gone to play in the woods and fell asleep in the shade.'

Hildigunnur smiled. 'That wasn't where I told you to look, was it?'

'No,' Helga admitted.

'Good. That's as it should be.' The old woman sounded pleased.

'You have good instincts, girl. Trust them. And now I'm going to go back to my workbench and try to make sure young Volund doesn't get mothered too hard.'

Helga praised her own mother-luck as she watched Hildigunnur follow Thyri and the boy into the longhouse.

The forest was quiet, and awash with green light filtering through the leaves. Karl ghosted forward, spear in hand, eyes trained on the prize: a seven-point stag grazing contentedly a hundred or so yards away.

Suddenly the animal's head shot up, every muscle in its body tensed and its nostrils quivered.

Karl, grunting, sprinted headlong towards it, crashing through the undergrowth – but in the blink of an eye the stag was off, pushing away on powerful legs. The spear whistled through the air and sank deep into a tree trunk, inches away from the animal's neck.

'Well done, Brother,' Bjorn said behind him. 'Maybe it tastes nicer if you scare it to death.'

'Shut up,' Karl spat. 'It probably smelled you.'

'It didn't,' Bjorn said. 'If it had it would have come towards me for a cuddle.'

Karl strode away from his brother, grabbed the spear and yanked it free. 'Where's Father? We need to tell him the stag got away.'

Bjorn turned around. 'He was behind me just now. He had the bow, didn't he?'

An arrow thunked into a tree trunk a couple of yards to their left. 'He did,' Unnthor said, some distance behind them. 'And since it is only fair to divide the labour, because I killed the stag' – the old man emerged from the trees where the stag had disappeared, grinning – 'you get to gut and carry it.'

Without a word Karl tossed the spear to the old man. 'Fine. Where is it?'

Unnthor gestured behind him, and now they could see the trail of blood. Karl pushed the branches of a bush aside and moved out of sight.

'When did you drop back and circle round us?' Bjorn asked his father.

'About half a mile ago,' the old man said.

'How did you know where it would be – or where it would go?'

'They used to be your woods, but they were my woods first.' He smiled and ducked into the bushes behind Karl, who was standing over the carcass of the stag. Two arrows were buried in its neck, one of which had gone right through and was sticking out the other side.

'Not bad, old man,' Bjorn said. 'He must have passed right by you.'

'Near enough,' Unnthor said. 'Sometimes you have to take the shot, even though they're too close.'

'You haven't seen fit to get started, Brother?' Bjorn smirked.

'You were always better with a knife – at least when the target wasn't moving,' Karl said.

'That's because he paid attention when I taught him,' Unnthor grumbled. 'And if you wait any longer to get started, the forest will skin it for you.'

Flies drawn by the smell of blood and death were already buzzing around the corpse. 'Right,' Bjorn said, 'let's get this done. Ullr, hear our prayer. We thank you for the bounty you have given us. Yours is the blood of the beast. The hunter salutes you.' He knelt by the stag's exposed throat, tilted the neck and slit it, his movements precise, practised. Rich, dark blood flowed away from him and sank into the forest floor.

The dogs smelled them first and set off baying to the sinking sun. The noise sounded otherworldly inside the longhouse, like something happening far, far away. Jaki's disembodied voice drifted in after the dogs. 'They're back,' he announced unnecessarily.

'About time,' Hildigunnur said, putting away her knife and dropping the wooden piece into a little cloth bag.

Agla was up already, stretching her legs and rolling her shoulders. As she moved towards the door, Thyri cleared her throat. 'Uh, you don't think . . . ah . . . could we maybe avoid telling Bjorn that Volund went missing?'

Helga glanced at her mother, whose face was carefully composed. A gentle frown emerged. 'Volund? Missing?' She smiled. 'My grandson was with me the whole time.'

Bjorn's wife exhaled and beamed at Hildigunnur. 'Thank you,' she said quietly.

'*Psh*. It's nothing. Now just sit tight. They'll be here soon enough. My old bones tell me we'll have something nice roasted tonight.'

Thyri settled down again, and Helga tried to pair her up in her mind with big, boisterous Bjorn and failed. Since she'd brought Volund back, the woman hadn't managed to string three words together. There needed to be a balance of sorts in a marriage, she knew that, but she hadn't seen a marriage like this before now. Unnthor and Hildigunnur were maybe a little different, size-wise, but Bjorn and Thyri? How could that woman stand up to a man the size of a mountain bear and twice as loud? She turned back to her sewing, trying to find that nice, comfortable mind-place where the fingers just got on with it and worked of their own accord. Try as she might, though, she couldn't shake the uncomfortable feeling she'd had when Karl had looked at her earlier. She'd heard her mother counsel young women on avoidance, and in some cases, where best to plant an elbow or a knee, but this was different: the men they came to her to complain about weren't her sons.

Voices came from outside, almost drowned out by the dogs' frenetic barking.

'They're very loud, aren't they?' Helga said.

'And why shouldn't they be?' Hildigunnur said. 'They're simple creatures, and there's blood in the air.'

My own flesh and blood. With darkness in their heart. They're—

A short, sharp pain punctured her thoughts. Helga looked down at the needle: it had gone smoothly through the cloth and straight into her finger. The drop of blood was bright against the black thread.

Chapter 3

ASLAK

Looking around the room, Helga felt dizzy. Her new place at the far end of the table felt uncomfortable and strange, much like the new faces all around her. Although they could probably fit in another thirty or forty guests, the longhouse felt stuffed full of people. Gytha sat next to her mother, across the table from Jaki. Her father's right-hand man seemed quite happy, unlike his son; Einar, sitting beside him, was looking very uncomfortable. Karl and Agla were just off the corner, by his father's right hand. Old Unnthor and Hildigunnur sat at the head of the table, looking down towards where Bjorn sat with his family. When she walked by with her plate, Helga narrowly dodged an extended arm as she got the full force of his storytelling.

'—but the wolves didn't know that they were supposed to get killed, right? So my friend Arnthor wades into the snow to get this one he thought he'd wounded – and another ten come out of the bushes!' Bjorn slapped his thigh for emphasis. 'The look on his face when he turned and tried to run, crying' – a mime followed: red cheeks, puffed out with panted breaths – *'help me! Help!'*

'And then what happened?' Gytha asked, riveted.

'They got 'im, of course,' Bjorn said. 'Jumped him in the snow. Luckily I was close enough, so I' – Helga just caught a glimpse of Thyri sighing, as if to say, *Here we go again!* – 'whipped down my breeches and pissed on 'em!' Bjorn's raucous laughter almost swallowed the words. 'They hate the smell,' he explained when he'd recovered, noticing Gytha's bemused look, then added, 'Arnthor did, too!'

Agla smiled at him, then looked at Thyri. 'Tell us about what's happening in the east. Is it true Harald Fair-Hair threatened to invade?'

'*Pff,*' Bjorn said, 'that big old girl wouldn't dare. He'd have to walk it. The land would have half of his men.'

Helga thought Bjorn suddenly didn't seem quite so friendly any more.

'Stop this talk of war,' Hildigunnur said firmly. 'Be quiet and eat your meat.'

'Not likely, with the troll-child at the foot of the table,' Karl said.

'Shut up, squirt,' Bjorn said. 'I'll say what I want, when I want.'

'That seems to be the problem,' Gytha said.

For a brief moment, everything stopped. Glances bounced around the table – and then Bjorn guffawed. 'Hah! The only person around this table with a big set of balls is a girl!' As Gytha grinned, he added, 'The way she's going, she'll have Farmboy's too, before the night is done—'

As he nodded towards Einar the smile instantly vanished off Gytha's face. She threw down her spoon, stood up and went storming away from the table.

'Gytha!' Karl roared after her, but to no avail.

Agla drew a deep breath. 'Go easy on her, Bjorn,' she started. 'She's young—'

'Young?' Bjorn interrupted. 'She's been chasing the stallion over here all day long – ain't nothing young about what she wants to do to 'im, I reckon.'

Einar's face went bright red as he stared down at his platter.

'Bjorn!' Thyri snapped.

'What?' the big man said. 'Everyone can see it.'

When Helga looked at Hildigunnur, she glanced towards the door. The command was clear: *Find her*.

The air was cooler outside, the long shadows easing into twilight. The dogs knew her scent, so they didn't bark. She quickly checked the few buildings, although she was sure they'd be empty, then in her head she worked through the routes Gytha could have taken. After a moment's thought she turned right, towards the river.

She found the girl sitting in the grass, head buried between her knees, shoes an inch from the water's edge. 'He's an arse,' Helga said as she approached the hunched form.

'Who?' Gytha said, head down, voice cracking.

What would her mother say? All the conversations she'd listened to in the longhouse came back to her. 'Do we need to pick one? All of them, I reckon.'

That got a short, sharp laugh. 'You're not wrong.' Gytha turned to look slyly up at her in the fading light. 'Have you had him? Einar?'

'What?'

Irritation flashed across Gytha's face. 'Have you *had* him? Had a ride—?'

'Oh – oh!' When she finally understood, Helga giggled and sat down. 'No. No, I haven't. I wouldn't – I've known him so long, he's more like a brother.'

'I like him,' Gytha said. 'Or, well, you know. I think he'd be fun.'

People see things differently, Hildigunnur whispered in her head, and Helga bit down on her first thought. Sympathy was what was needed here. 'Who knows, though,' she said. 'I've not seen him with any girl for a long time. I don't think he's promised to anyone.'

Gytha's face brightened. 'Really? Well, that's good . . .'

In the distance they heard one of the dogs barking, followed by muttered voices.

The girls shared a look, and Gytha twisted round and crawled up to the edge of the riverbank on her stomach. She looked down at Helga. 'Two, with two small children. Two horses. A dog. They don't look armed.'

'Aslak is here,' Helga said.

And then there were three, she thought.

The first knock was drowned in Bjorn's forceful recital of 'The Farmer's Daughter and the Handsome Bull'. The second was louder and firmer, and everyone in the longhouse fell silent as the door inched open and a young man stepped in, his slim frame wrapped tight in a well-worn cloak. 'Four road-weary travellers seek guests' rights,' he said, 'and maybe some stew?'

'ASLAK!' Bjorn roared. 'You little shit!' Even Karl raised a mug and smiled. The young man looked up at them and was about to speak when two blond blurs pushed past at hip-height, one on either side.

'GRANDDAD! GRAMMA!' Charging across the floor, Bragi and Sigrun leaped on their grandparents, hugging as hard as six-year-olds could. A woman entered and took her place beside Aslak. She might have been a head shorter than him, but she stood tall. Her eyes were little slits of flint. Bjorn's blurred grin stretched even wider. 'And Runa! Wel—'

'Welcome to my house,' Unnthor said, firmly and loud enough to be heard over the big man.

'We have food for you,' Hildigunnur said, moving around the table with Bragi attached to her leg. 'Come on, little bear,' she said, ruffling his hair. 'Let Gramma go or you'll starve to death.' She glanced at the child's bony frame, but said no more.

Bragi's sister had already pushed her grandfather down into the high seat and sat herself on his knee. 'Do you know what a fox is?' she began.

'Yes,' Unnthor started, until she looked at him sternly. The old raider faltered. 'Um, I think so?'

'Well,' she said self-importantly, 'a *fox* is an animal with a big tail. But it is not a wolf, because wolves are bigger.'

'Oh, is that so?' Unnthor said. 'I am glad someone is here to tell me these things.'

'Yes. Now be still so you can learn,' Sigrun said, crossing her arms in the way of mothers through the ages. The old man nodded solemnly, not alone in working hard to contain his mirth.

'So, Aslak – why so late?' Karl asked, interrupting his niece's lecture on the difference between wolves and foxes. 'You live just half a day's ride away, don't you?'

Aslak winced. 'We were late to start, I guess. I—'

'We had things to see to,' his wife said.

'It must be difficult, running your farm,' Karl said, smirking.

'Yes, it is,' Runa said, eyes flashing, 'but we do well enough.'

'Good to hear—'

But Runa was already on her way to the pots, where Hildigunnur was standing ready with her ladle.

'Father – stew!' Bragi carefully passed up a bowl.

'Thank you, Son,' Aslak said.

'Gramma says I can be a Viking when I grow up,' Bragi announced.

'Does she?'

'Yes, and I can grow Viking carrots and hunt animals and get Viking furs and sail with them in a ship and sell them to someone like Vikings do,' Bragi said.

'Don't tell your father about Vikings, boy – he knows nothing. Come and sit next to your Uncle Karl.' The dark-haired man patted the bench next to him and Bragi was there in a flash. 'My son Ormar, your cousin, is away a-Viking right now,' Karl said. 'Seventeen winters old, free to roam, just him and the sea.'

'Don't fill the boy's head with nonsense,' Agla remonstrated. 'Ormar is probably starving hungry and freezing cold and soaking wet right now – and I certainly hope he's doing his best to stay out of the way of spears and axes.'

'Vikings get spears and axes too?' Bragi's eyes were wide open in awe.

'They sure do,' Karl said, grinning. 'Tomorrow I'll teach you to fight. But we'll start with a beating stick.'

The boy was out of his seat in a blink. 'Mum! *Mum!* Uncle Karl is going to teach me to fight! With a stick! A – a – a beety stick!'

'Is he, now?' Runa's voice was cold.

'Yes! Can I, Mum? Can I? *Can* I?'

Runa, thin-lipped, walked over to where Karl was sitting. She leaned over and whispered in his ear.

'But the boy needs to—' Karl began.

Lightning-quick, Runa caught his wrist in her hand and slammed it on the table, leaning on it with all her weight, as she continued to whisper. Moments later, her point made, she retreated, smiling. Karl watched her move off, discreetly rubbing the soreness out of his wrist under the table.

'Of course you can,' she said to her son. 'I was just explaining some things to Uncle Karl about young boys and stories and how I know where he sleeps.'

'Hooray!' Bragi said, diverted almost immediately by the spoonful of stew she held out to him.

A bellowed laugh from the other end of the table interrupted their exchange and they both stared at the old man, who sat, all smiles, with a frowning Sigrun in his lap.

'It's *not* funny!' the little girl said again.

'No – no, you're right – that's exactly what the fox says. Now go and get yourself some of your gramma's good stew, yes?' Big hands gripped under Sigrun's arms and Unnthor rose quickly, sweeping her way up in the air, much to her squealing delight, before setting her down gently on the ground. The little girl scarpered to her grandmother immediately, hands outstretched for a bowl.

Gytha and Helga stepped inside, and Hildigunnur beckoned them over and ladled out the hearty stew. A heaped pile of dirty bowls told the tale of a meal well received. 'Did the fresh air do you good?' she asked, looking searchingly at Gytha.

'It did,' the girl said. For a moment her lower lip quivered, but then the mask was back on.

'Good,' Hildigunnur said.

Helga leaned in and whispered, 'I think I saw more people coming.' She watched her mother scan the interior of the longhouse. Bragi and Sigrun had abandoned their meals to play with the bag of old bones Hildigunnur had got out ready for their arrival; they were ensconced in a corner, deeply immersed in some complicated game of farmyard management. Volund had drifted silently in their direction and was watching wistfully from a distance. The three brothers had gathered together and Bjorn was in the middle of telling another long, involved story; the wives, ignoring their exuberant menfolk, were still at the table, exchanging their own less brash and boastful stories. Einar and Jaki were nowhere to be seen, likely slipped out to see to the beasts.

Hildigunnur sighed. 'That'd be Jorunn, then.' She shook herself, as if to shake off her mood, and winked at Helga. 'Right, daughter of mine. I hope one day you get a family of your own. I wouldn't want you to miss out on all the joys.'

She turned around and cried loudly, 'Everyone – *get up!* We have visitors at the gate and this time they're not taking us unawares. We're going to go and meet them. *All* of us.'

Chapter 4

JORUNN

When they left the longhouse, the first thing that drew Helga's eye was the flame, leaping hungrily at the rapidly darkening sky from high above the gate. Jaki was standing beneath the mounted torch; the flickering firelight caught on all the angles of his face.

Shadow of a different man. The idea danced in front of Helga's eyes, but as soon as she could focus on it the light shifted and he was back again: friendly old Jaki, just as normal. Unnthor walked up to him, little Sigrun sitting proudly on her granddad's shoulders, and took up his own place by the gate. Side by side, Unnthor and Jaki looked like brothers. Helga caught a flurry of words as Sigrun tried to explain to them both why birds liked flying instead of walking.

The families took up position on either flank, like warriors. In the twilight they could just make out the shadowy figures of two riders making their way slowly towards the farm.

'Get a move on, girl,' Bjorn shouted. 'Aslak's growing a beard waiting for you!'

'Shut up, you lumbering meat-sack,' a woman's voice shouted back. 'That's not happening any time soon!'

Karl smiled. 'So it doesn't look like marriage has softened our beloved sister.'

'She always had a mouth on her,' Bjorn agreed.

Beside Helga, Einar muttered something, too quietly for her to hear. 'What did you say?' she whispered.

'Nothing,' Einar said, rolling his shoulders slowly, working out the tension. 'Nothing,' he repeated.

The riders were obviously in no hurry as they rode their horses at a walk towards the farm. Helga had instantly picked out Jorunn, even from a distance: straight-backed and slim, her figure was almost identical to Hildigunnur's. A long auburn braid hung down past her breast. The man next to her was of average height and build. The firelight caught on keen eyes that scanned the assembled people, but he held his tongue as he and his wife dismounted smoothly.

'Welcome, daughter,' Unnthor said. 'It makes my old heart proud to see you.' He looked at Sigmar. 'You're welcome too, Sigmar: you are no less of a son to me than this lot—' He gestured to Karl, Bjorn and Aslak.

'Thank you, Unnthor,' Sigmar said. 'I should have visited your house sooner.'

'That you should,' Unnthor said. 'Now, come along. There's food.'

The family walked towards the longhouse, but Helga noticed Einar was hanging back.

'What's wrong?' she said, once they were out of earshot, but Einar was shaking his head.

'Nothing,' he muttered, refusing to meet her eye.

'Well then,' she said, grabbing him by the elbow, 'come on then. You don't want to stand alone out here like a boil on a horse's arse.' She could feel a little bit of pull, but then he gave in and let himself be led towards the light coming from the longhouse door.

When they entered, Jorunn was already comfortably ensconced by her father's side and chattering away.

'—we're heading south afterwards. But we wanted a good break here, give me a little time off from Sigmar driving us onwards all the time,' she added with a smirk.

'Fair enough,' Unnthor rumbled. 'What about food – your mother's stew is rich and warming – or have you eaten already?'

'We ate on the road,' she admitted with an apologetic look at her mother.

'Good – so settle down, then. We were about to put the children to bed – just like we used to do with you, remember?'

Inside, the long table had already been folded up and placed up against one wall, and the families had arrayed themselves in a large semicircle. Karl, Agla and Gytha sat together by their beds, Karl and Agla chatting quietly while she re-braided Gytha's bright hair. Aslak was sitting next to Runa, although she had her back to him and was bent over two small forms. Bjorn sat alone on the other side of the long room.

Hildigunnur had pulled up a chair and placed herself in the middle of the half-circle. At her side Unnthor was relaxed and comfortable in his great carven chieftain's seat.

'I wanna hear the story,' Bragi protested sleepily, cocooned in his blanket.

'Shush and listen, then,' Runa said.

Helga led Einar over to the corner by the workbench, where they pulled up stools. She caught Gytha glancing in their direction, just for a moment, but didn't react. *People see things differently.*

'Right,' Hildigunnur said. 'You lot take up quite a bit more space than you used to,' she added, grinning.

Behind her, Thyri snuck in, Volund in tow, and walked over to Bjorn. She leaned in and whispered something that made him nod.

'But you always used to like a good story. This one is about brothers and honour.'

'Story,' a high voice piped up behind Aslak, and he turned with a smile to quieten his daughter.

Finally, peace settled on the longhouse.

Hildigunnur cleared her throat. 'Back in the time of kings and the age of heroes, one man rose above the others in valour and prowess. His name was Starkadr, and none was his match. He had a sworn brother, Vikar Haraldsson, who was raised by his father's murderer. Vikar swore vengeance, and Starkadr helped him become the King of Agder and the Western Fjords. He and Starkadr fought many battles, and none surpassed Starkadr in the arts of war. Then, one day—'

'There was a monster!' Bragi piped up.

'Shush,' Runa said, 'that's not this story. Listen well, because you need to hear this.'

'—one day,' Hildigunnur continued, as if nothing had happened, 'they were sailing when the wind left Vikar's sails. Their god-speaker was an old man named Himli. He read the bones, throwing them again and again, but the darned things kept saying that the king must be sacrificed. When the men revolted, Starkadr stood between his king and a whole ship full of raiders and said they'd need to take him first. When no one did, Vikar said they should row to shore and decide upon the will of the gods at home.

'The night before they settled Vikar's fate, Starkadr's foster-father, a man named Grani Horsehair, took him for a long walk. He led Starkadr across a bridge that shimmered in many shades of grey in the moonlight and arrived at a secret council, where Grani threw off his hood and turned out to be Odin in disguise.' Hildigunnur winked at Helga. 'The All-seeing praised Starkadr for his loyalty and bestowed many gifts upon him – and Odin also decreed that Starkadr should live for the duration of three lifetimes and have three-fold fortune in each one of them. The warrior got riches beyond belief, guaranteed victory in battle with the best weapons, respect from people in power – and the gift of skaldic poetry to go with it.'

Helga heard the murmurs of affirmation echo around the long-house; it was right that the gods reward the good and loyal.

But Hildigunnur hadn't finished. 'So, when he heard Odin had elevated Starkadr to a place almost as high as the gods them-selves, Thor became furiously jealous,' she went on; there was an edge to her voice now. 'He cursed Starkadr, now his own brother: Thor compelled him to commit a horrible crime for every lifetime he lived, banished him from fatherhood and put a geas on him: that every time Starkadr took ownership of a house, a farm or any bit of land, it would be ruined and destroyed within a week.

'But Thor was not done: Starkadr would feel that his fortune was never enough; he should never go through battle without the most painful of wounds, he would be hated by commoners, and he would always forget the poems he spoke.

'So, blessed and cursed by the gods, Starkadr walked the earth for thrice sixty years after that, the most fortunate and the most unfortunate Viking that ever there was. He could never live for long in one place. He lost all his friends to death – and he had to endure lesser skalds reciting his works as their own. He would have lived to this day if Thor hadn't made him an offer: that he kill his best friend's grandson with a magical spear. The moment Vikar's son's son died, the Viking who couldn't die would find peace. In the end, Starkadr the Mighty was a pawn of the gods, and he lost who he was.'

She looked each of her children in the eyes before she finished. 'So remember,' she said, putting the full weight of her gaze behind her words, 'Thor was poisoned by jealousy and there was no honour in what he did to Starkadr. Who you are is not to be measured in wealth or fear, but in the weight of your name. You are the children of Unnthor Reginsson, and I command you to hold his name high with your deeds.'

The low-burning fire cast a reddish glow along the floor of the longhouse; the people were little more than shadowed outlines. Helga watched as the biggest of the shapes stirred.

'Time for bed,' Bjorn rumbled as he rose, and Thyri got up and pulled a sleepy Volund to his feet. Muttered goodnights followed them out the door. Karl's family made their way to the far corner of the house and settled onto their beds and soon all

Helga could hear was slow, rhythmic breathing, interspersed with gentle snores.

But her mother's voice still rang in her ears: *He was a pawn of the gods, and he lost who he was.*

Sleep did not come quickly to her.

Chapter 5

PREPARATION

The first rays of the morning sun crept over the hill, giving colour and life to the half-light and turning the trees around the field from grey to green. Shuffling backwards, Helga dragged her broken plough-blade through the grass, all the while staring at her bent knees and the mark she was making.

'Aaand – stop!' Einar commanded.

She did as ordered. 'This is *heavy*,' she said, rubbing her aching arms. 'Why aren't you doing this bit?'

'Someone has to watch the line. Now, turn to your right.' He pointed helpfully, ignoring her scowl.

She looked down at her feet then at the straight line between her and Einar, grunted, and twisted the plough-blade. 'Like this?'

'Good – now drag it in that direction until I say so.' He pointed to his left.

'You're enjoying this,' Helga muttered as the ground at last started giving way to the blade, a line forming between her retreating footsteps.

'Stop and turn!'

She did as she was told, dragging the line back towards Einar. When she got to where he was standing and joined the third line to the first, she was sweating. 'What is this *for*?' she asked, catching her breath.

'Don't you remember the last one?'

'Let's assume I don't,' she said, sharper than she'd intended.

'Oh,' Einar said, 'that's right, we said. That was eleven summers ago now. Sorry. Anyway, this is for the stone throw.' He gestured at the long triangle Helga had drawn on the ground. 'The one who throws the furthest wins, but they have to stay inside the lines. Then they'll go to the next stage, over there' – he pointed to where a knee-high barrier had been erected in front of three targets, the closest twenty yards away, the furthest a hundred – 'to chuck axes and spears, then it's bow and arrow.'

'All on the same day?!'

'Then there's the foot-race.' Einar was on a roll now. 'They'll go down that way' – he gestured airily towards the north end of the field, where a stake had been driven into the ground – 'round the stake and over to the next' – another stake, driven into the ground to the far east of the field – 'then down past the third and home.'

'And then they're done?'

'Oh no.' Einar grinned. 'The old bear insists that there's going to be a game of Tafl too, but he didn't say any more than that.'

Helga frowned. 'Why?'

'He has his reasons, probably,' Einar said. 'He usually does.' In the distance they could hear the roll and clatter of a cart. 'Oh shit! I forgot! The stones—'

'*Which* stones?'

Jaki came into view, leading a horse and cart at a slow walk half a mile down the path. Einar looked around, head swivelling. 'Where's the axe?'

Helga stopped and thought, retracing their steps. 'Over there,' she said, 'where we left our food.' The axe was propped up against a long log just perfect for sitting on for a bite of lunch. *It's good to know what's important in life*, she thought to herself and smiled.

Einar walked over to the big axe and hefted it. 'Good,' he said to no one in particular. Then, with a mighty swing, he brought the blade down on the trunk, twisting it on impact and sending a sliver of wood flying as the blade sliced into the wood. His strong arms yanked it free immediately and sent it airborne again and again, the edge of the axe biting ever deeper into the wood. Helga watched the muscles in Einar's back knotting and releasing, knotting and releasing, as he swung the axe again and again in a visual song of strength and rhythm. Soon enough, a four-foot-long portion of the trunk fell off, sharpened at one end, flat at the other. Einar inched a toe under the log and kicked it to one side, then moved up and started again.

Helga turned, half listening to the rhythmic sound of metal thwacking into wood, and looked for Jaki. The old man was closing in on them, but he was taking his time, leading the horse gently towards the site. When he saw her, he waved, and the cart rumbled on, coming to a halt just as Einar delivered the final blow.

'Are you just finishing this now, boy?' Jaki said.

'Forgot, Father. Sorry. I've spent most of my time trying to get Helga to work.'

'What?' Helga spluttered. 'You have not, you sheep's arse!'

Einar grinned. 'She can be terribly difficult sometimes.'

'Oh, go talk to someone who wants to listen to you,' Helga said. Then she paused to think. 'No – wait. That's no one.'

'Don't worry,' Jaki said, 'I know which one of you is a lazy bum.'

Einar picked up one of the logs. It was all he could do to wrap his arms around it. 'Where do you want them?'

Jaki looked around. 'Good work, both of you,' he said. 'This is all where it should be. We'll drop the stones over there.' He pointed to the centre of the field.

With Helga following, Einar lugged his log to the spot Jaki had nominated. And while his father led the horse over, Einar turned the piece in his hands and drove it down into the ground until the stump formed a nice, stable circular platform. He measured it by his hip, then put all of his weight on it.

'That looks steady to me,' he said to Jaki.

The old man shuffled over and prodded the log, then pushed it a couple of times before pronouncing himself satisfied. 'It'll do. Get the other two.'

'Feel free to help,' Einar told Helga as he collected the next chunk of wood.

She glared at him, then bent down and picked up the last log, willing her face not to show any strain. Instead she inclined her head at Einar and said, smiling, 'Lead the way, lazy bum.' She tried not to wince as she dropped it to the ground, but couldn't stop herself grimacing at the ease with which the old man grabbed it and hefted it into place. Einar took the other, and soon they were both driven deep into the ground, where they formed an evenly spaced line.

'Done?' Einar said.

'Not quite,' Jaki said. 'Let's not forget the bastard stones.' He walked over to the cart and slid the back panel aside. Three great stones lay on the cart bed. *No one could shift those!* was Helga's first thought: the smallest of them was a slab the size and shape of a sheepdog's body, while the biggest looked more like a ball – one that would reach Helga's knees.

Einar whistled softly. 'Is this—? Can we even do this?'

'Requested by the old man,' Jaki said. 'These three *specifically*.' There was a hint of a smile on the foreman's face. 'No idea why. He said they were in the cart already, so why not use 'em.'

'Right,' Einar said with a sigh. 'Okay, so let's get to it.' He leaped up into the cart, bent his knees and, with a grunt, pushed the smallest stone until it started shifting, reluctantly scraping along the cart bed.

'Careful . . .' Jaki stood by the edge, callused hands ready to catch the edge of the stone as it approached. 'Let's get it right the first time.'

'*Sounds . . . like . . . a good . . . idea,*' Einar grunted between clenched teeth.

The moment the stone hit the edge Jaki's hands were clawing at it to get purchase, then pulling it forward. 'There,' he muttered, 'come down now . . .'

Einar was off the cart in a flash and standing shoulder to

shoulder with his father. Together, they lowered the big stone gently down to the ground next to the first pillar.

'That one is just about doable, I reckon,' Einar said after they'd caught their breath.

'Just about, yes,' Jaki said.

'How about this beast?' Einar said. The second stone looked like someone had lopped the roof off a longhouse: it was almost triangular, but wide and long in the wrong places.

'Have to be careful of the grip on this 'un,' Jaki said. 'Do it wrong and the stone's five times heavier. I am not as good at this as he is.'

Helga stayed well out of their way as Einar moved in beside him. Grunting and cursing, they managed to inch the huge stone towards the edge of the cart-bed, then jumped down and took the weight in their arms. Breathing hard, they staggered over to the second pillar. They bent their knees, slowly lowering it, but when the stone was still a foot off the ground Jaki winced.

'Drop it—' he hissed, red-faced.

Einar was only too happy to comply.

'—but watch your toes,' the old man said after the stone landed.

'*Thank you*, Father. *Very* caring,' Einar said. The two men stood together, chests rising and falling, hands on hips, staring at the stone.

'That was an absolute bastard,' Einar eventually said.

'You're not wrong,' his father agreed.

Helga watched as Einar's shoulders set. 'Right,' he said, 'let's get the third one off the cart and have it done with.'

'We're not touching that thing,' Jaki said, walking slowly towards the horse.

Helga's skin tingled. She watched as the animal's ears perked up; she could only catch the occasional half-heard word, the odd sound of Jaki soothing and coaxing the beast, but the horse snorted and tossed its head, and when Jaki took the bridle it didn't try to move away.

'What's the plan?' Einar said.

'Age and wisdom,' Jaki said, 'that's the plan.' Tugging gently on the reins, he urged the horse into a walk and the cart lurched into movement behind it. Jaki muttered to the horse, which stopped. The old man moved past the animal's front legs and put a leathery hand on its back leg. Then he reached for the reins and pulled them gently towards him, while pushing on the straining muscle. The horse whinnied in protest but did as it was told, inching towards the old man. The harness shifted, but eventually the cart rolled to the left.

Comprehension dawned on Einar's face and he took up position behind the cart, yanking to shift it out of the wheel tracks. The rear end swung towards the third pillar. 'That's enough,' he called.

Jaki moved along towards the horse's head and let go of the reins. 'Good girl,' he muttered, 'good girl.' His hand went into his pocket and a bright green apple emerged. The horse nudged him; lips peeled back, she went for the treat.

Einar was already at the horse's side, loosening the straps that held the cart's shafts in place. 'Ready,' he said.

'Ready,' Jaki said, reaching for the straps.

The smooth sound of wood on leather as the shafts rose out of their fastenings was joined by the scrape of stone on the cart-bed. A chunk of mountain the size of two full-grown rams tumbled off the cart and hit the ground with a dull *thunk*, sinking two fingers deep into the ground.

Free of its ballast, the cart rocked wildly on its wheels, then fell jerkily back into place.

Einar stared at the stone. 'He requested *that*?'

'He did,' Jaki said.

Helga could see Einar thinking, working something out, but then he shook his head as if to get rid of a fly. 'Is that it?' he said.

Jaki shook his head. 'Nope. He wants two seats and a table. Helga, you can sit for this one if you want, and then we'll all walk back.'

'Thanks,' Helga said gratefully, and as Jaki and Einar started debating sizes and angles, she walked over to where they'd left their rations. Hildigunnur had insisted she take a piece of cured deermeat as big as half a fist to gnaw on and right now her stomach was thanking her mother profusely. Since her log had been demolished, she scouted around for something else to sit on and soon found the perfect tree stump with just the right amount of shade. She settled down, smiling at Einar and Jaki. They had the same set of shoulder, the same rolling gait – Einar might not know it yet, but he was turning into his father.

That made her think of her *real* parents – how one day they'd just been *gone*. For the first couple of years she'd kept asking Hildigunnur what had happened, but her new foster-mother just got tight-lipped, said that they'd caught ill and had to go. All she'd told Helga was that her father's name was Finn. She'd remembered their faces for a while, but now she found she struggled to picture anyone who wasn't Unnthor in her father's place.

That's time for you. She reached into her bag. Moping wouldn't do anyone any good, but food would. The salty, smoky, meaty smell – 'fee for helping with the guests', Mother had said – was already making her mouth water. The sky stretched out above her, an infinite blue; the sun warmed her skin just right, and for a moment she allowed herself to close her eyes and just enjoy life.

When she opened her eyes again the old man was right *there*, somehow, leaning on the fence post by the field gate. In a blink all the advice Hildigunnur had ever dispensed came flooding back to her: make noise; run – and, if necessary, go for the crotch and the throat. For some reason, though, she didn't feel at all uneasy.

'Ho there!' the old man called out.

'Ho yourself,' Helga called back. 'Where are you going, Greybeard?' She glanced over to Jaki and Einar, just for reassurance, but they must have gone off into the forest somewhere.

'Oh, just walking,' he said. There was a smile in his voice. 'But I am mighty hungry.'

'Should have planned ahead and brought a packed lunch,' Helga shouted back.

'Didn't plan on walking this far,' the old man said.

Something in her softened. 'Come on then. I've a bite to share with you.'

The old man dropped his head respectfully, and Helga got a good look at him as he shuffled towards her, leaning on a thick walking staff. A piece of cloth was strung over his head, doubtless to keep the sun off. His clothes looked grey and faded, and his thick woollen coat dragged on the grass.

'No wonder you're needing feeding, Granddad – you're dressed for winter. You'll cook yourself weak in all those clothes.' She laughed as he drew closer.

'You're not wrong,' he said. Despite his frail appearance, his voice was surprisingly strong. 'I go through some cold places on occasion, and sometimes I forget to dress for summer.'

Helga smiled. 'So: what are you selling?'

The old man's eyes twinkled at her. 'Oh, this and that. Mostly to bored farm wives, and you don't look like one of them.'

'Not yet,' Helga said.

'Not ever,' the old man said. 'You might be a farm wife at some point in your future, but I doubt that you'll ever be bored.'

Without thinking, Helga stood up from her comfortable place and offered the old man a seat. 'What makes you say that?' she said.

'Oh, the set of your jaw, I reckon,' the old man said, leaning on his staff to lower himself down to the tree stump. 'And you've got a spark in your eyes as well.' He looked her up and down once more. 'Am I wrong?' he said.

Helga found herself compelled to look at her shoes. 'I don't know,' she muttered. A flash of annoyance struck her and she looked the old man straight in the eyes. 'And how should I when I've not been there yet?'

The old man grinned, teeth pointing this way and that. 'Good answer!' he said. 'Woe betide the thick-necked farmboy who ever tries to tame you.'

Helga snorted. 'I'd like to see 'em try.' She tore off a chunk of her meat. 'Take this for your prophecies,' she said.

The old man's bony fingers closed delicately on the chunk and he lifted it gently towards his mouth. He bit down and chewed slowly, savouring the taste. 'This is delicious,' he said finally. 'Fit for a king. You are a generous host, Helga Finnsdottir.'

She frowned and blinked. Something strange had just happened, but she couldn't quite figure out what it was. Had she told him her name? 'What did you just say?'

'I said you were a generous host.'

It scrabbled at her mind, but darted out of sight when she reached for it. The sun felt hotter, and she found herself wishing that she had a cloth like the old man's.

'That's – it's nothing, I guess,' she said. 'You're welcome. I live down at—'

'Riverside,' the old man said. 'I know. And I would love to stay and talk, but I've got places to go. Take this as a token of my appreciation,' he added, rising quickly from the stump. Helga blinked. For a moment he'd looked downright sprightly, but the man in front of her was just as old and frail as the one who'd sat down. There was one thing different: in his bony hand was a small black stone, shimmering in the sunlight, suspended from a thin leather thong.

'What's this?' she said.

'Who knows?' the old man said. 'Maybe it is your future.' The tiniest twist of his fingers and the stone spun in his hand. Dark lines formed and disappeared.

'Is it a rune?' Helga said.

The old man smiled. 'It is. You don't know how to read them yet, do you?'

Helga frowned, feeling drowsy and dim at the same time. 'No,' she admitted.

The old man leaned in towards her. She could see his bony hand on her arm, but it felt oddly warm and solid. Then his arms were around her, behind her head, fastening the necklace. It felt light against her skin, but she had no time to think because suddenly the voice was in her ear, whispering,

The Rune of Nauth.

Wants, wishes and needs.

—and the old man seemed to be both in front of her and behind her at the same time. She blinked, shook her head to clear it – and there was nothing.

In the distance, the old man was waving at her from the field gate. 'Goodbye! And thank you for the food!' he shouted.

Helga stared at him as he shuffled away. Suddenly dizzy, she sat down on the stump, but still she couldn't shake the feeling of unease. She squeezed her eyes shut and opened them again, but the gate was just that – a gate. The old man had already disappeared around the bend and Einar and Jaki were back, standing over the log and arguing over measurements . . .

She'd just closed her eyes for a moment. She'd not seen him arrive. She'd not seen him leave.

She must have dreamed it.

'Stupid girl,' she muttered, 'falling asleep in the field. Be thankful Mother didn't find you.' She reached for her bag, but when she pulled out her lunch, she froze. Someone had clearly ripped a chunk off it.

'Bloody mice,' she muttered. 'Mice.' With quick, nervous fingers she ripped off a sliver of meat and shoved it in her mouth. 'This is delicious,' she said. 'Fit for a king.' Something about the words annoyed her immensely. 'Get to work,' she snapped at herself. 'Get to bloody work.'

She stood up and stomped over to the men, but her first words were drowned in the sound of Einar's axe biting into the wood. They both glanced at her, but then turned to focus on their work. Neither of them appeared to have noticed her visitor, and if they had, they clearly weren't in the least interested in talking about him. It felt a lot less important now, anyway. She touched her rune-stone for assurance. A gift from her parents, someone had said, but she couldn't remember who. It probably didn't matter anyway.

Chapter 6

CONTEST

Bjorn rolled his shoulders and looked at the pile of stones by his feet. He reached down, picked one up and weighed it in his hand. Glancing over at the three boulders, each placed by the base of a wooden pillar, and the targeting ranges complete with low barriers to mark distance, he frowned. 'Is this field smaller than it used to be?'

'I think it's your arse that's got bigger,' Karl said, leaning on the gate in a studied show of boredom.

'Save your breath for the challenges, ball-sacks,' Jorunn said. 'You're going down.'

The brothers both laughed. 'And who's going to win? You? The squirt?' Karl hooked his thumb down the path, where Aslak tried in vain to guide his children in a straight line towards the gate.

'Sigmar will also take part,' Jorunn announced.

'*Pff*—'

Karl glared at Bjorn. 'Shut up. He's family.'

'Thanks to you,' Bjorn said. He glanced at Jorunn, but their sister didn't speak. 'And so what? I'll have him at stones any day.' He looked towards the wooden pillars.

'Maybe you will,' Jorunn said, 'but there's more than one event.'

'So why don't we make it interesting?' Karl said, pushing off the fence and closing the distance to his siblings.

'What do you mean?' Bjorn said, eyeing his brother.

'What I said: we need to make this interesting. The one who wins the most events—' Karl reached for the purse tied to his belt.

'—gets to order the others about,' Jorunn finished. 'For a day.'

'About what?' Aslak said behind her. 'What did I miss?'

Karl reluctantly let go of his purse. 'Fine,' he said. 'Just don't run off crying to Mother when I tell you to fetch my food like a common slave.' He walked off towards the throwing range.

'It's almost comforting to see that after all this time he's still exactly the same arsehole,' Aslak said.

Bjorn chortled. 'You're not wrong there. Some things do not change.'

Jorunn watched Karl as he stopped by where the hand-axes were lying, picked one up and hurled it with force at the target. The blade thwacked into the wooden plate, three fingerbreadths off-centre. 'I don't know,' she said. 'I think our loving brother may be getting worse in his old age. Something is seriously bothering him: he was about to try to take us for money.'

Aslak raised one eyebrow. 'Hm. Cocky bastard,' he said.

Bjorn rolled his neck. 'I'm glad we kept money out of it,' he said. 'If – no, *when* – I win, I will take great pleasure in having Grumpy-tits over there call me your Majesty for a whole day.'

Jorunn nodded. 'Good. Although you're not going to win, obviously—'

'Oho! Says who?'

'—you're clearly too old and fat for that—'

Bjorn stared wide-eyed at his sister, then glanced at Aslak. 'Do you hear the mouth on 'er?'

'—but if you defeat Karl in anything you do, we're fine.'

Bjorn leaned over to his younger brother. 'Never listen to a woman's advice,' he whispered loudly. 'Sometimes they don't have your best interests at heart.'

Aslak glanced at Jorunn. 'You're right,' he mock-whispered back, 'it's probably best to let Karl win. I think that will turn out well for us.'

Jorunn cracked a smile and patted Aslak's head. 'You're a smart-arse, little brother,' she said, 'but we'll let you live.' She thought for a second, then added, 'Well, for now.'

The muscles in Helga's arms were taut with tension; the sacks she was carrying were really heavy – but Hildigunnur was walking beside her, carrying twice the amount with no complaint. The line of people walking from Riverside stretched out in front of them, with Volund ahead of her, tagging after Gytha. The little ones had run back to their mother and ahead of the three of them were Agla and Thyri, whispering conspiratorially together. Jaki stood by the cart next to the gate up ahead that marked the entrance to the games field. Einar was standing beside his father, and Sigmar was not far from them. The siblings were already in the field, and as she watched them, Helga saw Karl grab a hand-axe and throw it at a target. Moments later Jorunn patted Aslak's head, but whatever she was saying to her brother got interrupted by a sharp, clear ringing sound: Unnthor, standing up in the middle of the field, was ringing a large metal bell he'd produced from somewhere. 'Get a move on!' he shouted. 'It's time for all of you to get beaten by your betters!'

'And who would that be, then?' Karl shouted back. 'All I can see is an ancient hill-troll with his helmet.'

Helga noticed Runa, a couple of yards ahead of them in the line, grinning.

'Always was a sharp tongue on that boy,' Hildigunnur muttered.

As the families made their way past the gate, Einar ushered them over the logs that had been set out so they could all sit and watch the contestants. Helga placed her sack at her feet, next to her mother's. Hildigunnur had spent the best part of the morning cooking, and the sacks were heavy with roasted meat, fire-baked sweetroot and skins of mead.

'Listen up,' Unnthor's voice boomed. 'Throw, then stones. Targets, then the run. I am the final arbiter, but Jaki has promised to make sure I don't cheat.'

'As if,' Bjorn said, then, 'And who watches him?'

'I do,' Hildigunnur said. 'I watch all of you.'

Bjorn shrugged. 'Fine. Let's get to it!'

The siblings closed in on the throwing triangle like thunderclouds over a sailor's head, followed by Sigmar and Unnthor.

'Time for throw,' Unnthor announced.

'Who goes first?' Karl asked.

'Guests?' Unnthor said, smiling.

'Sure. I'll go.' Sigmar bent down to the pile of stones. Hefting the top one, he weighed it in his hand, moving his elbow experimentally, getting the weight of the stone, spreading his fingers as wide as he could. Then, without warning, he took three quick steps to the point of the triangle and launched the stone.

It flew through the air – and landed just past the midway point.

Sigmar spun away, his neck muscles taut, and barked a quick curse in the language of the Svear.

'What's the matter, East-man?' Bjorn said. 'Not as easy as you thought?'

Sigmar turned back to the group. 'No, it's fine,' he said, tight-lipped. 'It's just been a while since I did anything like this.'

'Me too,' Karl said, stepping up to the pile of stones. 'But the difference between the two of us is' – he picked up a stone, stepped to the throwing line and launched it through the air smoothly. It sailed comfortably past Sigmar's stone and landed with a thud three feet away from the line – 'I don't bark like a little bitch.' His grin was three parts delight and one part challenge.

Sigmar smiled earnestly. 'Well done, *Brother*. It is clear that you are better than me at throwing things away.'

Karl's brow furrowed. 'What's that supposed to mean?' he said, scowling.

'Get outta the way,' Bjorn said, shouldering past him as Sigmar smiled and shrugged. '*My* turn.'

Reaching down, Bjorn palmed the nearest stone and threw it without preamble. 'Shit,' he muttered. The boulder flew a good six feet past the line.

'Troll-baby,' Jorunn mocked.

'Shut up,' Bjorn said. 'Let's see you do better.'

Jorunn smiled as she stepped up to the pile of stones. 'You know I can't match a man for half of his power, Brother dear,' she said. Elbows out, she backed up until she had a good twenty-foot run-up to the throwing line. 'So I have to rely on' – she rose up onto the balls of her feet, dipped, then pushed off hard, running to the line, swinging the stone up, letting it fall in her hands in a furious arc, then at the very last moment controlling the path, inching it upwards and releasing at the exact point when she hit the throwing line – '*speed!*' she screamed after the flying stone.

Helga glanced at Gytha, who was watching her Aunt Jorunn with undisguised awe. The young girl's hands were tightly clenched as she watched the stone fly towards the mid-line – past the mid-line – towards Karl's stone ... and drop to the ground just a few inches away from it.

A collective '*oooh!*' was drawn from the audience. Karl looked like he'd eaten a wasp.

Jorunn turned and smiled at her oldest brother. 'Not quite as far as you. I might need to try next time.'

Unnthor's stone was already airborne. It fell with a thunk a foot short of Karl's. Moments later Aslak launched his stone, which didn't even reach the mid-line.

'Karl wins,' Jaki shouted.

'Look at him,' Hildigunnur muttered by Helga's side.

'What, Mother?'

'He grins – but there is no joy in him, only darkness.' But an instant later the old woman's face had reverted to her normal neutral expression and she stared impassively at the action. Helga wondered if she'd imagined the look and the comment.

'What's next,' Bjorn said, 'stones?'

'No – targets,' Jaki said. 'Hand-axes first: Sigmar, then Bjorn, Aslak, Unnthor, Jorunn and Karl.'

Sigmar stepped up and hefted the hand-axe. He looked critically at the wrapped handle and turned to Jaki. 'Do you have another bit of leather?' he said. Without a word, the old man pulled up his sleeve and unravelled a long leather strap. Sigmar took it without comment and wrapped it with practised movements around the handle, weighing the axe as he went. When he was satisfied, he looked up. The target was a wooden board thirty feet away. A circle had been painted on it with an x in the middle. His arm stretched back, then whipped forward.

The axe flew, spinning in the air, and buried itself in the plank with a dull thwack.

Jaki whistled. 'Gonna be hard to improve on that one,' he said as Einar ran back with the axe. The mark in the plank was about a finger's width away from the centre.

'Not bad, Swede,' Bjorn said. 'Not bad.' He took the proffered axe and frowned. 'Never been much for throwing axes,' he said.

His throw immediately and firmly supported the statement. The axe clattered hard but sideways against the board, falling harmlessly to the ground. Wincing, Aslak threw the axe half-heartedly at the board. It stuck, but far to the side. Unnthor's effort hit the mark a palm's width away from the centre.

'No luck, old man,' Karl said.

'I've never trusted in luck,' Unnthor said. 'The gods guide the axes where they wish. All you can do is throw.' Standing next to him, Jorunn watched intently as Einar retrieved and handed her the axe.

'You're never lucky because you never chance it, old man,' Karl said. Without pause, Jorunn whipped her arm back and launched the weapon. 'Sometimes you have to—'

The axe hit the board with a sharp, short thwack and the brothers fell silent. Jorunn glanced at Sigmar, who looked back at her and did not drop his gaze.

Einar and Jaki approached the target and stared at it for a moment. Then they whispered among themselves.

'Just a hair separates them – but Sigmar is closer,' Jaki shouted.

Karl barked a laugh. Jorunn's lip curled in anger, but her husband didn't show any kind of reaction.

By the logs, Hildigunnur leaned in again. 'And what do you make of that one?' she whispered, eyes on Sigmar.

'He doesn't give much away,' Helga said, 'but . . . his fists were all balled up when Jorunn threw, and now he's relaxed.'

'Which might mean?' Hildigunnur said, adding quickly, 'Remember: don't stare.'

Helga relaxed into it and looked *better*, like her mother had taught her, keeping her face relaxed. She was aware of Hildigunnur only as a sound by her ear. 'He's – he wants to win, quite badly, but doesn't show it. And I think he likes Jorunn, a lot.'

'Why do you say that?' Hildigunnur said. There was a hint of a smile in her voice.

'The way he looks at her, for a start,' Helga said. 'And I think he wants to impress her. Especially with the boys around.'

'Not bad,' the old woman said. 'Not bad at all.'

Helga beamed as Karl stepped up and cried, 'My turn!' He spread his arms and rolled his shoulders. 'Give it here,' he said to Einar as he arrived with the axe, then he glanced at Jorunn. 'This is how it's done, little sister.' The axe-blade caught the sun as he raised it, up and back, far behind his head, limbering up the shoulder before he launched—

—and the haft of the axe bashed into the target. The weapon fell harmlessly to the ground.

'Sigmar wins,' Jaki said emotionlessly.

'That is horseshit!' Karl snapped, red-faced. 'He tampered with the fucking handle!' Spinning, he was in Unnthor's face. 'That's cheating! Where's the fucking honour? Is this what being a chieftain is about, huh?'

'Calm down, Karl,' Bjorn said.

'DON'T YOU TELL ME TO CALM DOWN!' Karl shouted. He rounded on Sigmar. 'Think you're so fucking clever, eh, Swede?'

A blink of an eye, no distance between the men.

Karl pushed Sigmar in the chest, hard. 'Think you're going to fucking cheat? Here, at *Riverside*?' Thick arms pushed in under Karl's armpits and Bjorn and Unnthor lifted him off his feet, locking his arms in place, grunting with the effort. Karl flailed and kicked at his target, connecting just as his father and brother dragged him off.

Sigmar's eyes flashed, but he held back as Karl shouted again, 'Fucking *cheat!*'

'Easy now,' Unnthor said, voice low. 'Easy. There was no

cheating. You won the first one. You're still in the lead. You just have to share it.'

Suspended in midair, Karl flailed for a moment longer, then hung still. 'Fuck you all. Let me down.'

Bjorn made to speak, but a vicious glare from his father shut him up. 'Are you going to be fit for company?' Unnthor asked.

'Yes,' Karl said between clenched teeth.

'Did Sigmar cheat?'

No answer.

Helga caught the slightest adjustment in Unnthor's stance. Pain blossomed on Karl's face as his father's knuckles dug into his ribs.

'—no,' he hissed.

'Good. We're going to put you down now. If you act up, I'll knock you on your arse. Understood?'

'Yes.' The sound was closer to a growl. Karl dropped to the ground and staggered forward, glaring at Sigmar. Although the Swede was shorter and altogether less imposing, he stood his ground.

'Good throw, *Brother*,' he snarled.

Sigmar looked at him. 'Thank you.'

'Spears,' Jaki said, clearly reluctant to hand over weapons to *anyone*. 'Are we going for spears?'

'Yes,' Unnthor said firmly, 'we are.'

Karl didn't speak but stared at the target for a moment, then held out his hand without so much as glancing at Jaki. The spear was short, only two-thirds the length of a man, made for throwing rather than line-fighting. When it landed in his hand

Karl weighed it up, mouth set. Then he took time to look first at his father, then Bjorn, then Sigmar.

Five steps back.

He gritted his teeth, took a couple of fast steps as he twisted his body and then—

The release was silent.

The flight was silent.

The first sound was the splintering of wood as the missile smashed into the target, sending it spinning, and shattered to the ground. Helga watched as Karl turned to Unnthor. Something passed between them, but no one on the logs could hear.

As quickly as it had begun, the spear-throwing was over – Karl had smashed the target to bits.

An eye-blink – and then Bjorn had stepped between them. 'Karl clearly wins this round,' the giant exclaimed. 'Applause!'

The spectators clapped in confusion. Helga glanced at her mother, but the old woman's eyes were elsewhere. Following her line of sight, Helga couldn't help but see that Runa looked particularly delighted.

Jaki hurried to fetch the bow and arrows, and Unnthor won, but only by a hair – much to everyone's surprise, Aslak's arrow was only a knuckle away.

'Right: it's time for stones!' Jaki said, louder than he had to. 'You all know the rules: every stone has to touch the top of the pillar. Quickest to all three wins.'

'Come on, you grouchy old bastard,' Bjorn said, putting a huge arm around Karl and shifting him towards the wooden pillars.

'I'll sit this out,' Jorunn said.

'Don't be so boring, Sister,' Bjorn said. 'Give it a try!'

'Bjorn,' Jorunn replied patiently, 'the ability to think fast, solve complicated problems and make tough decisions is exactly opposite to the ability to lift heavy stones, and I happen to be very good at the former.'

The big blond man stared at her for a moment. 'Are you saying—?'

'—you're big and stupid, and go play with your stones, troll-baby,' Jorunn finished for him.

'If you will,' Bjorn said, bending low in a mockery of a bow, '—your Highness.'

'I won't take part either,' Sigmar said.

'Why not?' Unnthor said.

'Bad back,' Sigmar said. 'Have to be very careful around heavy things.' Karl looked like he just caught some words before they came out of his mouth, but his smirk spoke volumes.

Beside him, Aslak winced. 'Me too. Elbow, in fact.'

Jaki started up, nervously. 'Karl, if you would—'

'Right,' Karl said, 'I finished last' – bending at the knee, he growled – 'so I go *first*.' He grasped the first stone, growled low and hefted it up on the pillar. 'ONE!' he shouted and let go, pushing so the boulder fell clear of the wood. On to the next one. Karl fumbled to find the grip. Arms spread wide, he started straining – and the stone went up, but no further than his thigh. His face went red as he stood, squatting, the boulder on his leg, digging into the muscle. A roar – and up it went. 'TWO!' he screamed, and pushed away with another roar, punching himself across the chest, and stormed towards the third and last one.

He launched himself at it. Throwing his arms around the rock, he squeezed, raised it three inches off the ground – and then dropped it, spinning away and screaming in frustration, fists clenched by his sides, veins pulsing in his neck.

When he was sure Karl had screamed his fill, Jaki spoke carefully. 'Two.'

'My turn?' Bjorn asked calmly.

Jaki glanced at Karl, who was still facing away from the stones. 'Yes.'

Bjorn approached the first stone and lifted it like it weighed nothing. 'One,' he said, then put it gently down again. Moving on to the next, he looked at it for a while, then glanced at his father and grinned. 'Sneaky old bastard,' he said. Bending down all the way to the ground, he squeezed a thick hand under the stone and rotated it just a tad. Then came the hold – and up it went. 'Two,' he said, dropping the stone carelessly on the other side. When he approached the third stone, he slowed down. A big, round thing, it looked as if it took up less space than the second stone, but Bjorn stopped in front of it, and this time, the look he shot his father was not as amused. The big blond man drew a deep breath, smacked his palms together and wrapped his arms around the boulder. Massive muscles strained in his back and shoulders.

The boulder rose: two inches, then four, then six. Bjorn firmly pushed air out through his pursed lips until he got the thing balanced on his thighs, then leaning back into the squat, he adjusted the hold and drew a deeper breath. With the rise of the stone, the heart rose in Helga's throat. A deep roar started somewhere at Bjorn's core as his back slowly straightened. 'THREEEEEEEE!'

he growled as the boulder climbed, torturously slowly, up to the pillar, and just as slowly, the edge of the massive rock edged onto the flat of the wooden stake. The moment it was up, Bjorn let go and leaped back with surprising nimbleness for such a big man. The stone fell to the ground with a thump.

Karl stared at his brother.

Bjorn looked at his father, breathing hard. 'Right, old man. Your turn.'

Unnthor glanced over at Jaki, who nodded.

Without any sort of a rush, the chieftain walked over to the first stone. He bent down slowly and felt around the edges. Moments later the stone was in the air.

'One.'

The second stone soon followed the first.

'Two.'

When Unnthor came to the third stone, he glanced at Bjorn. 'You are very strong, Son. Always have been.' The old man adjusted and tightened his belt. Then he bent down and ran his fingertips along the stone's surface – and pushed.

'What are you doing?' Bjorn demanded. 'You're going the wrong way – you can't carry it to the pillar—'

'You son of a—' Karl muttered.

Unnthor glanced at his sons and grinned. 'But you're neither thoughtful nor deliberate, and both of you would choose the hard way' – satisfied, the old man stood up. Then he planted a boot on the pillar and pushed with all his weight. The wood gave, the pillar toppled and the top touched the stone – 'when the easy way is right in front of you.'

'Hah!' Jorunn's laugh was clear and sharp. 'Father wins!'

'Oh come *ON*,' Bjorn said, 'that's so unfair!'

'Brains wins over brawn, son,' Unnthor said. 'Although I'm mighty impressed that you managed that third one. He was an absolute beast.'

'How—?' Karl began.

'Found it in the field and rolled it up onto the cart,' Unnthor said. '*I'm* not going to lift that bastard.' Behind him, Sigmar smirked.

'Footrace,' Jaki shouted.

'I'm in for this one,' Jorunn said quickly.

'Me too,' Aslak said.

'I'm out,' Unnthor said, glancing at Bjorn. 'Those stones really took it out of me.'

'Bastard,' Bjorn muttered, lining up on the starting line alongside his brothers and sister.

'Sigmar?' Jaki said.

'Not for me,' Sigmar said. 'I caught her once, and a man has to know his luck.'

Helga glanced over at Hildigunnur. 'This won't be ... nice, will it?'

Hildigunnur shook her head.

Moments later, the siblings were lined up on the starting line. Jaki cleared his throat. 'Aaand – *GO*—!'

Karl wasted no time and immediately shouldered Jorunn to the ground.

'HEY!' she shouted, bounding up almost faster than she'd

fallen, but the boys were already a fair bit ahead, with Aslak quickly pulling away from his larger brothers.

'Get out of the way,' Karl snapped at Bjorn.

'Make me,' Bjorn said, huffing along.

Aslak reached the first post and turned sharply, feet sliding on the grass as he fought for balance.

Horrifyingly slowly, Helga saw what was about to happen.

Karl's almost unnoticeable tilt of the head; Jorunn coming up behind them at speed; the big man slowing down just a little too much, just as he was about to turn, his leg pushing out, looking for all the world as if he were sliding, losing his balance . . .

Just when Jorunn was passing, an arm shot out and caught her square across the face, sending her sprawling.

'Oh,' Karl shouted. 'I'm so sorry, Sister!' he called over his shoulder as he continued running. 'Didn't see you!'

Jorunn was slower to get up this time, but when she did, her entire body was taut with anger. Up ahead, Aslak was closing in on the second corner. She spat, a thick glob of blood – and *ran*.

'Come on,' Hildigunnur hissed. Helga glanced over – her mother's fists were clenched and the old woman was seeing nothing but the racetrack.

Legs pumping, knees raised, elbows sharp, Jorunn became a sliver, a blade cutting through air and carving up the field. Within moments she had closed the distance on Karl and Bjorn, sidestepping their lurching frames with no more effort than a bird flitting out of the way of a horse. She caught the second corner before them, stepping nimbly around it. Ahead of her, Aslak glanced over his shoulder and then sprinted for all he was worth – but it was useless. Jorunn caught up with him with six yards to go.

Helga stood with Bragi and Sigrun, who had stopped playing with their bones long enough to watch the finish, as the lithe young woman crossed the line. 'Did Father win?' Bragi asked, looking up at his mother with big blue eyes.

'No, he didn't,' Runa said, her face like curdling milk. 'He couldn't beat his sister, not even with his brothers holding her back.'

'That's a shame,' Bragi said, turning back to his toys and forgetting about the race in an instant.

When Aslak crossed the line, Jorunn gave him a quick hug. 'You're so fast,' the young man huffed.

'You're faster than you were,' she said. Moments later Karl crossed the line. After a moment to catch his breath, he looked up at his sister. 'Jorunn – I'm sorry, I was falling – I didn't see—'

She spat in his face.

A thick glob of blood leaked down Karl's chin.

'Sorry,' Jorunn said, 'I didn't see you there.'

Bjorn stumbled across the finish line and caught Karl in his arms just as the warrior lurched towards Jorunn, spouting profanities. Then Unnthor stepped in between the siblings and caught Karl's eye. The furious raider stopped straining at Bjorn's arms, instead wiping off the gob of spit with the back of his hand.

Jorunn, flanked by Sigmar and Einar, glared at him.

'Jorunn wins!' Jaki exclaimed.

'Right,' Karl said, chest heaving. 'Done.'

'Not quite,' Jaki said. 'There is a new event.'

'What?' Bjorn said.

In response, Hildigunnur rose and pulled out a small satchel from her sack.

'What's that, Gramma?' Bragi asked, dropping the bones.

'This is *my* beating stick,' Hildigunnur said, walking towards the centre of the field. She waited patiently as Jaki and Einar rolled out three tree stumps – two seats and a table. Then she sat down, pulled out a square game board and placed it on the table.

'Oh – what?' Bjorn groaned. 'You're going to make us *play*?'

'Your mother has decided,' Unnthor said, 'somewhat belatedly, that her children should not grow up to be fools. The last trial is to play her. Anyone who defeats her gets to count the win double.'

'I'll go first,' Bjorn said. 'How hard can it be?' Fifteen moves later, he rose. 'I always suspected,' he said loudly, stepping away from the table, 'that she was a witch.'

Hildigunnur smiled and reset the board for the next game.

Karl was next. He sat down with a scowl, glaring at the pieces as if he could scare them into place.

A while later, Bjorn glanced over Jorunn's shoulder. 'He hasn't started screaming,' he noted, 'so he must be doing—'

'WHAT THE—?' Karl yelled. 'HOW THE—?' The rest of the sentence was drowned in colliding vowels.

'—reasonably well,' Jorunn finished for him.

Moments later Karl stood up from the table. 'This is a stupid game,' he growled. 'And you probably—'

'—want to go away and think about it for a while before you say anything else,' Unnthor said, inching closer to his wife's shoulder.

Seething with anger, Karl snorted and walked off.

'Aslak,' Hildigunnur said. 'Your turn.'

The slim man sat down opposite her. 'You know I can't beat you, Mother,' he said.

The old woman smiled. 'I know.'

'So I do not wish to play.'

She looked him up and down. 'Why not?'

'Because I can spend our time better doing something less heroic and more clever,' Aslak said. Hildigunnur smiled, and Aslak rose from the table.

Jorunn sat down before being summoned. 'Mother,' she said.

'Daughter,' Hildigunnur replied.

The first moves on both sides were dispatched quickly, then Hildigunnur slowed down. 'You've been playing,' she said.

Jorunn glanced at Sigmar. 'We have a set at home,' she said.

Hildigunnur looked at the Swede with renewed interest. 'I didn't know that,' she said. 'Do you like it?' She made her move.

'It's an interesting game,' Jorunn said, moving immediately.

Later, with all the family gathered around them, Jorunn reached out and tipped her king to the side. 'I am defeated,' she said.

'You are,' Hildigunnur said, looking her daughter up and down. 'This time, I suppose.'

The look she gave her daughter was one Helga had not seen before.

Chapter 7

EDGE

It was well past midday when they finally started the walk back to Riverside. With sun warming her skin, food in her belly and the scent of summer in the air, Helga allowed her feet to guide her as she took in the familiar sights – a horizon of fields to the right, sparse trees massing gradually into forest on the left. She closed her eyes and smiled. *Just a moment*, she thought. *Just a moment of peace—*

'That went better than we thought, didn't it?'

Einar's voice by her ear made her jump. 'What?'

'The games – no blood, no broken teeth or bones, no deaths. The old folks won in the end. Once they got something to gnaw on and a little mead in their bellies, the brothers calmed down – storm's blown over. We're safe.'

Helga thought back on what she'd seen in the field: those clenched fists, hateful looks, pursed lips. 'I wouldn't be so sure,' she said. Her stomach felt suddenly tense, like she'd swallowed a rock. 'I'd still step carefully and keep my mouth shut for the next little while.'

'Why?' Einar said.

'I don't know,' Helga said. 'I just . . . I feel like there's something about to happen.'

'And what do you base this on?' he scoffed. 'Woman's knowledge?'

Helga glared. 'Yes. Anything wrong with that?' Her heart thumped and her hand went to touch the rune-stone amulet.

'Um . . . but there's no—'

'Proof? Would you like me to tell Hildigunnur that you think intuition is stupid and useless without proof?'

Einar's alarmed face was almost enough to calm her down. *Almost.* 'You know what, Einar Jakason? You go ahead: stomp around, swing your elbows and say whatever you want to Karl and Bjorn – but don't expect my sympathy when the knives come out.'

There was a silence as the words hung dark and dangerous in the air between them.

'What do you mean, *knives*?' Einar said quietly.

Helga prised her fingers away from the rune-stone around her neck. The heavy feeling was gone, but there was no relief in it. 'I – don't know,' she said. 'I just . . . said it.'

Einar looked her over as if seeing her for the first time. 'There's something about you,' he said. 'Something different.'

'Flattery will get you nothing but trouble,' Helga replied, her voice flat.

He looked back at his father, who was bringing up the rear.

He looks scared, Helga thought.

'I should go and help,' he said.

'See you later.' A chill crept up on her, and somewhere in the back of her head she felt like she could hear a *whisper* of something; she could almost catch the glimpse of a shadow, but it remained elusive.

Jorunn, further up the line, leaned in towards Sigmar. 'So what do you make of my family, Husband?' she asked.

'Much like you said,' Sigmar replied after glancing over her shoulder to confirm that they were out of earshot. 'Karl's still a bastard, Bjorn's an oaf.'

'And Aslak?'

'What about him?'

Jorunn smiled. 'He's small and quiet, but don't underestimate him.'

'I won't. Will he get in our way?'

'No,' Jorunn said, 'not if we tread carefully.'

'And just to be certain – you're absolutely sure?'

'I am.' Jorunn looked at him. 'My father can protest all he likes, but there is treasure hidden somewhere on the farm.'

'Keep walking,' Sigmar murmured, 'and listening, and watching. We'll get our chance – and we'll take it.' He smiled and inclined his head in greeting as Helga walked past them, but the girl didn't seem to notice.

Nothing makes sense, Helga thought. Even though the feeling she'd had when talking to Einar was gone, the memory of how it had felt when the inside of her head was like the air before a thunderstorm still lingered. She glanced at Aslak, busy corralling his children. In their merry confusion, the three of them looked happy.

A burst of deep, rough laughter from Bjorn, striding ahead with Hildigunnur, broke her trance. Helga caught a fleeting glimpse of the cheeky grin on her mother's face. *Finally, an appreciative audience for her rude jokes.* The thought made her smile, and the sensations of summer caught up with her. Her mood lifted again. It was nothing, just a remnant of a bad dream. She'd make up with Einar later. Like before, now that she was standing close to Bjorn, the big man's mass just drew her in. He was deep in conversation with Hildigunnur, and she was close enough now to make out the words.

'I've tried leaving her with him, but that doesn't work either,' he said. 'That bull, he's having none of it.'

'Maybe he likes his grass? Have you thought of covering her tail in it and having him eat his way in?' Hildigunnur said.

What are they—? Then Helga went beetroot-red as her mind supplied her with images. She stared hard at her feet. The path had turned into road and was now curving past the trees and into the clearing. Riverside sat in front of them, sparkling in the reflected light from the fast-running water.

Bjorn chuckled again. 'Mother, you're *dreadful*! He'll figure it out at some point . . . he's done it before.'

Hildigunnur acknowledged Helga with a nod as she walked alongside them. 'If all else fails, send him my way. I'll have him spend some time with Unnthor.'

'*MOTHER!*' Bjorn and Helga cried in unison, making Hildigunnur positively cackle with mirth.

'I love you, my children, but I'm pretty sure you'd all like to believe you were found in the woods. And speaking of – can one of you fetch me some firewood?' She opened the gate and stepped into the farmyard. Helga had heard stories of queens at court, but could imagine none more regal than Hildigunnur.

'That'd be me, then – Twiglet here can hardly lift herself, let alone a bit of kindling,' Bjorn said, winking at Helga.

'Oh, she's stronger than she looks,' Hildigunnur said. 'But you go, my little troll-baby,' she added, standing up on her tiptoes and kissing the giant's cheek.

Bjorn pushed her off, grinning. 'So what does that make you, Mother?'

'Able to live with your father and raise the lot of you,' Hildigunnur shot back. 'Axe is in the tool-shed. Go north, up the hill – there's a side path to the bit there your father's trying to clear. You'll find it. Drop it with the new wood when you're done, but don't chop down more than you can carry.'

'I never do, Mother.' Bjorn grinned, and strode away.

'Come on, lazy-bones,' Hildigunnur said. 'We need to get going on the preparations for tomorrow night.'

Helga trailed after her. Being within the fence, in the farmyard, felt safe. *Contained.*

The wolfhound barked once in greeting at Bjorn as he walked past, and the big man stopped and knelt down to scratch the dog behind the ears, then walked away from the thumping tail and towards Jaki's tool-shed. When he emerged a few moments later he was carrying an axe with a thick haft, a real woodcutter's tool.

'Probably broken a few bones, this one,' he muttered, glancing at the oft-sharpened blade. The dog gazed pleadingly at him as he walked back towards the fence. 'A clearing?' He looked at the solid wall of trees hugging the foot of the hill. 'Why doesn't the old goat just take these? Well, best do what Mother says,' he continued, marching past the trees and towards the path, as she'd ordered. The air was still in the lee of the trees and a smile spread across his face as he climbed the hill.

He found the side path without much trouble – then he heard a cry, quickly muted.

Axe at the ready, Bjorn burst into the clearing – only to see a flash of white skin – legs and arms, and a broad back – and Runa on the ground, pulling at Karl's hair, pushing at him, urging him on.

'Behind you!' she hissed in her lover's ear, and he stopped mid-thrust and looked over his shoulder at the giant with the axe.

It took him a moment to understand the situation.

'Pretend you didn't—' Karl began, but Bjorn had already turned away.

With a mighty swing he buried the axe in the nearest tree. Without looking at the two of them, he spoke. 'Mother needs firewood.' Then he walked away.

The moment he left, Runa's hand was on the nape of Karl's neck, stroking his skin. 'Come on,' she whispered, pulling him closer, 'don't stop.'

Karl pushed her off and rose to his knees, pulling his trousers up over his deflating cock. 'I'm done,' he said.

'Well, I'm not,' Runa said, flashing a seductive smile as she rose to reach for his thigh.

Karl pushed her hand away and stood up. 'I said I'm done.'

Anger flashed in her eyes as she scrabbled to her feet, reflexively straightening out her dress and shaking the grass and twigs from her hair. 'But I thought—'

'Well, you shouldn't have. I just needed to fuck something.'

Tears welled up in her eyes and her jaw clenched in fury. She bit her lip, then took to her heels and ran away from the farm, heading deeper into the forest.

Karl squeezed his eyes shut and sighed.

He opened them again and, stepping over to where the axe was buried in the tree, muttered, 'Right. Firewood.' He pulled on the handle, but the blade didn't budge. Cursing, Karl yanked the axe back and forth, again and again, until he was finally moving the blade, just a fingernail's width at a time.

Helga always felt that working in the longhouse with her mother was a privilege. Everything became nicely rhythmic and quiet and her mind wandered as she wielded the knife automatically, chopping carrots.

'Be kind to your old mother and fetch me some more wood,' Hildigunnur asked. 'We need a little more heat under the pot.'

The sunlight hit Helga in the face as she stepped out and she had to squeeze her eyes shut for a while to get used to it. She could faintly hear the children, splashing down by the river, and had no trouble at all imagining Gytha's bored face as she sat there looking after them.

Her feet carried her around the house to the shadowy end, and the shelter where the wood was stacked. She glanced at the few cords of green wood. *Glad someone else has been sent out to get more.* She gathered up an armful of seasoned firewood and carried it back carefully, checking the ground even though she was pretty sure she could walk that route blindfolded. She dumped her load in the wood-basket. 'Done.'

'Thank you,' Hildigunnur said. 'Did Bjorn get a lot?'

'Didn't look like it,' Helga said. 'I don't think he's been back. The axe is still out.'

'Hm.' She grabbed three logs and threw them on the fire, and the hungry flames immediately grasped for the wood.

Behind them, the door opened and Bjorn ducked in.

Hildigunnur turned to him. 'Where is my lumber, you big oaf?'

'Karl said he'd do it,' Bjorn replied.

Helga glanced at her mother. *She's less than pleased by this*, she thought. And why was Karl in the woods in the first place? She tried to remember when she'd last seen the eldest brother.

'Well, grab another axe and go and help him,' Hildigunnur ordered. 'You're no use to us here.'

Bjorn turned without a word and left.

When the door closed, Hildigunnur sighed. 'It's hard to keep track of all the animals,' she muttered.

Helga wasn't sure she was talking about the livestock.

The forest echoed with the sounds of metal biting wood. Bjorn strode up the hill, axe on his back and found the clearing. His elder brother stood by a big pine, covered in sweat and grinning maniacally as he really laid into it. Two trees, each three times the size of a man, were already lying on the ground. Karl looked round, spotted Bjorn and attacked the tree with renewed vigour.

'Greetings, Brother,' he growled across the clearing, in between fierce axe-blows. Bjorn said nothing but walked over to the felled trees and began methodically chopping branches off. 'Have you come to tell me how bad I am? What an honourless bastard I can be?'

The big man's knuckles turned white around the axe-handle as he turned to face his brother.

'Yes, I have,' he said, cold anger in his voice. 'You're an arse – you always have been, but you usually only do things to hurt yourself. Why would you split up Aslak's family?'

'She wanted it—'

'And even so, you would have had to want it too. You are selfish, and you break things. It's always been that way. Now it needs to stop.'

The two brothers stood for a moment in silence, face to face, in the glade.

'I've killed men, Bjorn,' Karl said softly, 'more than I can count. Small men. Young men.' He rolled his shoulders and shifted his grip on the axe, eyes still trained on the giant, looking him up and down, measuring him. 'Big men.'

Bjorn stared at his brother, lip curled in distaste – then he made a decision, turned away and set to clearing the rest of the branches.

Karl looked at the back of his brother's head. 'However you

want it to be, my baby brother,' he muttered, before sinking the blade of his axe back into the huge pine tree.

The sun was halfway down to the ground by the time they hefted the first of the trees, now hewn in half, onto their shoulders. Not a word had passed between them since they'd faced off, but the brothers had worked together often enough to need little in the way of communication. Moving briskly, they made their way between the clearing and the farmyard, chopped the trunk into logs and piled them in a neat stack by the wood shack, next to last year's wood.

Karl moved towards the longhouse and Bjorn walked towards the smithy. They didn't look at each other.

Breki rose to his feet, tail thumping wildly at the sight of his master.

'Ssh, boy.' Bjorn's voice buzzed low. 'Ssh.' He scratched the dog behind the ears, finding that particular place that always turned him to mush. He gave him another scratch for good measure, starting when he realised that he was being watched: Volund was standing by the corner of the smithy, staring silently at him.

'What do you want, boy?'

His son remained silent, and Bjorn sighed. 'Go to the clearing up towards the new barn, Son. Fetch the axes, and as many branches as you can carry. Go on – move!'

Spurred by his father's loud voice, Volund stumbled into action.

Bjorn watched the boy half-run, half-amble away, drew a deep breath and sighed again. 'Should've drowned you when you were a babe,' he muttered. Looking down at the dog, he pursed his lips. 'If only he were more like you, eh?'

The wolfhound gazed up at him adoringly, tongue lolling, panting happily.

Helga picked her way down the hill towards the new barn. The little band of trees that she had apparently called 'her forest' when she was a child stretched just around the hill, that was all, but there was a delicious *sound* to it, she thought. Sometimes it was quiet, sometimes all rustling and bustling with life. This was one of the places where she felt most at peace. She'd jumped at the chance to get away, to sneak a little time to herself, when Hildigunnur had mentioned that she needed some tools from the box up by the new barn – she must have left her bone-handled knife up there, she'd said, and she needed it, because it was the best blade on the farm. Bjorn had offered to go, too, but Hildigunnur had told him to sit tight and sent Helga. She had a lot of things to think about: did the siblings like or hate each other? Karl snapped at everyone and everything, but was his bark worse than his bite? And was there more to Sigmar than met the eye? Despite his less-than-imposing frame he hadn't moved an inch when Karl went for him at the games.

She was so deep in thought that when she turned a corner she almost knocked Volund over.

'Oh – hello!'

Volund looked at her, dully at first, then there was a spark of recognition followed by the tiniest of smiles. 'Hello,' he mumbled.

'Where are you going, then?'

The smile vanished. 'Gotta go get, uh, axes,' the boy said, looking down. At his side his fingers started twitching, forming and re-forming fists. 'Clearing – um . . . don't know—'

Helga placed her hand gently on Volund's shoulder. 'It's all right.'

The boy's lower lip quivered. 'Don't know,' he repeated plaintively.

'I know where you need to go,' Helga said.

Volund looked up at her, shyly scanning her face. 'You . . . do?'

The smile came easy to her. 'I do. Follow me!' She pushed past the boy and ducked down the side path, and moments later, she emerged into the clearing, Volund hot on her heels.

'There!' Volund shouted behind her and ran towards the discarded axes, beaming as he scooped them up. 'I found them!'

'Yes, you did,' Helga said, watching the blades resting a hand's width away from his grinning face. 'You're right. Now, let's be careful, shall we?'

Volund nodded, gazing at Helga. 'You *saved* me,' he said.

After gently rearranging the axes in the boy's arms to decrease the likelihood of severed limbs, Helga led him like an ox to a large pile of branches. 'What do you mean?'

'I didn't know where to go, and Father gets angry when I don't know where to go.' Volund blinked. His shoulders tensed, his brow furrowed and suddenly the boy looked more like a man. 'You're stupid, boy,' he growled, sounding *exactly* like Bjorn. 'I'd break your head open if I thought there was anything there that could escape.' His grip on the axes tightened. 'Get out. GET OUT!' Then he looked at Helga and something went slack in him. His usual innocent cow-face was back. 'And then Mother will say, "Please, Bjorn – leave him! Leave him be, he's just a babe!" and then Father will say, "He's nothing but a lump and it would be better if he didn't exist." But I found the axes and now it's all right.'

Almost outside her body, Helga looked down on her arms. Despite the lingering evening heat, the hairs stood on end. She tried to imagine Bjorn drunk, hemmed in by walls, furious at his idiot son, with Thyri hovering behind him like a worried mother duck – and Volund, unable to grasp what was happening, unable to do anything, just . . . *there.*

'You're right,' she said, her voice catching in her throat, 'everything is all right. And everything will be all right from now on.' She put as much conviction into the last sentence as she could, though she still didn't quite believe herself.

The rune-stone felt heavy at her breast.

Thyri and Agla had taken up stations at the workbenches near Hildigunnur, who was directing the work with her usual quick gestures and quiet commands. Jorunn was sitting in the corner, talking to her father. Sigmar, Karl and Bjorn were nowhere to be seen.

'Just go and sit quietly over in your spot,' Helga whispered to Volund. 'I'll bring you some things.' The boy looked at her, eyes wide, and nodded. She watched him shuffle over to the children's play area, large and ungainly, nothing but a bull calf. It took her no time at all to find the bones the kids had been playing with last night, and when she brought them over to Volund, he touched them reverently before looking around for confirmation that he was indeed alone with the toy hoard and wouldn't have to share.

He immediately sank into some strange, incomprehensible game of his own devising.

'. . . but that is no excuse,' Agla said from the workbench, voice raised. Curious, Helga drifted closer.

'I don't know,' Thyri said. 'There are different situations.'

'I don't care. If you've promised yourself to a woman, you stay promised to her.' The knife in her hand hit the carving board with a series of sharp noises, like a woodpecker in a tree.

'You're absolutely right,' Hildigunnur said in a soothing voice. 'Men shouldn't go sniffing where they have no business. But even the best behaved sheep will stray if the gate is open and the dog is sleeping, won't they?'

Helga watched Agla's face as Hildigunnur's imagery battled with her emotions. 'Still no excuse,' she muttered. 'But I see your point.'

'Bah – they're good for nothing,' Thyri said with forced cheer.

Helga watched as her mother pounced on the opportunity. 'I'd say they're good for one thing, at least,' she added, drawing chuckles from the women. *And then*, Helga thought, waiting – yes, there it was: the indrawn breath, the serious voice. 'All women should know' – Agla and Thyri leaned in – 'that men are like bridges.' Confusion on their faces; Hildigunnur had them in the palm of their hand.

'Lay 'em right the first time and you can walk over 'em for the rest of your life.'

The gales of laughter bounced around the longhouse. Even Helga found herself smirking through reddened cheeks.

'Will you hens keep it down! We're trying to have a conversation in the same valley,' Unnthor shouted from the far end.

'Of course – anything you say, *Husband*,' Hildigunnur said sweetly, batting her eyelashes across the room to another burst of laughter. When she turned around to continue work, Agla and Thyri did so as well, only now they had real smiles on their faces. When both women were engaged in their work, the old woman in the middle looked over her shoulder at Helga, caught her eye and gave her a look that said, *That's how you do it.*

Helga smiled back. *I saw. I understand.*

Behind her she could hear the door opening. Gytha stepped in, scanning the room before walking over to her bed.

Without turning, Agla asked, 'Who's watching the children?'

'Runa,' Gytha replied. 'And I figured why not? They're her kids.'

'So young, yet so wise,' Hildigunnur said, smiling.

'Yes,' Agla said, 'there's nothing that one can't puzzle out.' Hildigunnur rewarded her with a smile, and she grinned.

'Helga – come over here,' Unnthor rumbled. 'Don't spend your time in the hen-house.'

'What does that make you, Husband?' Hildigunnur shouted across the room, and giggles again turned to laughter as Agla and Thyri exchanged grins. Helga drifted across and perched on a bench a safe distance from Jorunn. The slim woman smiled at her, but it didn't reach the eyes.

'Settle one thing for us, child,' Unnthor said. 'Why does your mother always win at Tafl? Jorunn says it is because she thinks ahead. I say it is because she is a witch.'

'Both,' Helga said without thinking.

'I heard that!' The mock outrage in Hildigunnur's voice cut through the hall.

Jorunn smirked. 'So what does that make us?'

'Lucky?' Helga said. 'We're still alive.'

Jorunn's smirk grew to a smile as she moved closer to Helga. 'She's either a wise head or a smart-arse, this one,' she said. 'Either way, I like her.'

Unnthor gave Helga a smile of his own. 'You're one of mine, I reckon,' he said. 'Even though we did get you for free, sort of.'

'And of course, if you go after our inheritance we'll kill you,' Jorunn said.

A bubble of nervous laughter burst out of Helga. 'Of course,' she said.

'Leave the child alone, Daughter! There'll be no inheritance for another forty years. My dear witch-wife will keep me alive for some time yet. I remember one time when—'

Helga's focus was broken by a light touch on her arm: Gytha stood by her side, looking flustered.

'Can we . . . ?' she mumbled, glancing at the door.

Helga rose. Out of the corner of her eye she caught Jorunn looking at her father with a fixed grin. 'Come on. Outside,' she said.

The sky was a dark blue dotted with the dull white of clouds drifting overhead, and Helga shivered. Night-time had a way of bringing out the cold, and sitting in the warmth and listening to Unnthor ramble on suddenly felt a lot more appealing. She turned to Gytha and was about to snap at her when she remembered what Hildigunnur had just taught her about being gentle and patient. Instead, she asked softly, 'What's the matter?'

'It's Runa,' Gytha said. 'She was acting really strangely – down by the river.'

'Isn't that just what she always does? She's spiky, that one.'

'Well, yes, but it wasn't like that,' Gytha said. 'She was almost – well, *quiet* – but not in a good way.'

'Oh?' Helga was fighting to keep calm. *Knives. Knives in the dark* ... The sensation was like intense hunger scraping at her insides. She managed to keep her voice level. 'Tell me more.'

Gytha looked at her feet. 'I don't know that there is more to tell. It was just ... She came to us from upriver, kind of just stomping through the grass, then when she saw me she seemed to ... well, reel something in within herself – and then she sort of nodded, as if I should just go, you know? She *really* meant it, and I felt ... well ...'

'Runa doesn't strike me as the sort of person who holds too closely on to something that's angered her,' Helga pointed out, and Gytha snorted.

'Somewhere up north there's a lair with no she-bear in it,' she said.

Helga smiled, but she couldn't shake that growing feeling of unease. 'I'm sure if there's something bothering her we'll find out soon enough.'

'So do you think we should talk to her?'

'Us?' Helga thought about it for a few moments, wondering if she really should go and find out what was up, but the thought of speaking to Aslak's wife didn't appeal, even when she wasn't furious. She shook her head decisively. 'No . . . no, it's probably nothing. At Riverside, if something needs sorting, my mother will get to it. But you did the right thing, telling me. Come on, let's go back inside.' She opened the door and all but pushed Gytha in.

Above, darkness bled into the summer sky.

It hadn't taken Einar long to set up the big table. Einar'd told her Jaki had made two or three before he got it right, but this one was perfect: a really clever build that was just as easy to dismantle as to slot back together. When it was just the five of them it spent most of its time tucked away along one side of the longhouse, but now her parents' table was once again a place of laughter and nourishment, laden with platters and bowls heaped full of food from farm, forest and river.

'Eat, children,' Hildigunnur said, and barely a moment later, Bjorn's knife point was buried in a nice fatty joint of mutton half submerged in rich broth.

'Had my eye on this one since we sat down,' he crowed triumphantly.

'Lamb's nice too,' Karl said. Helga looked up and found him staring at her. 'Young and tender.'

'Better than old goat,' Jorunn said pointedly, and Karl glared at her as laughter bounced around the table. Sigmar, sitting next to his wife, was quietly and efficiently stacking his plate with as many vegetables as meat.

Gytha stared at the Swedish man with undisguised disgust. 'Why are you eating so much crap?' she said.

'What do you mean by that?' He smiled at his niece. 'There is no crap on my plate.'

She pointed. 'Roots? Leaves? What are you – a rabbit?'

Agla reached over, scowling, and grabbed her daughter's arm, but Sigmar flashed her a grin before putting on a serious face. 'Yes – on my father's side. Well, I assume so, at least.'

'Why?' Gytha said.

Out of the corner of her eye, Helga could see Hildigunnur smirk.

'Because whenever I was just about to fall asleep as a boy, my mother would call my father and tell him to come and do her like a rabbit,' Sigmar said, smiling sweetly.

A moment, and then—

'Oho!' Bjorn said, roaring with laughter as Gytha turned crimson. Jorunn elbowed her husband, but the grin on her face suggested she might not be utterly outraged.

Helga glanced down towards the end of the table where the youngest of the brothers was sitting, head bowed and hands folded in his lap. Next to him, Runa was looking like a thundercloud, lips pursed, brow furrowed. She muttered something to Aslak, who looked at his hands and nodded.

The sound of Unnthor's mug slamming down on the table silenced them all – the father of the house still had that ability. He frowned, drew the noise around him into himself, and looked *commanding*. 'You children! You are all awful and horrible—'

'—which clearly means you must be ours,' Hildigunnur finished, her eyes sparkling.

Unnthor turned to his oldest son. 'And now we're all here together. It won't happen again for too long a time. Tell the family how you're living,' he said. 'Give us your news.'

For once the dark-haired man looked less than confident. 'We – we live well,' he started, and Agla, beside him, beamed. 'We have a big farm just inland from the sands.'

'Always thought you'd end up a soft Southerner,' Bjorn said, grinning.

'Shut up,' Karl snapped back. 'We employ four workmen, two of whom have wives.' Helga was moving around the table, filling up bowls where needed, and she thought she saw a glance passing between Bjorn and Thyri, but it was gone again in the blink of her eye. Beside them, Volund slurped at his food, blissfully ignorant.

'And you bought this after raiding?' Jorunn asked.

'Yes,' Karl said, 'we chose a beautiful farmstead. It's shielded from the wind, the soil is fertile and in the distance you can hear the ocean. We have twenty-four head of cattle and forty head of sheep, and Gytha is about to come of age to be married.' Helga looked at the oldest son of Unnthor. For the first time she felt a shred of pity for the man. He looked uncomfortable – no, more than that, he looked *sad*, like he was reeling off things he knew he should be happy about but somehow wasn't.

'And does anything happen in this magical place?' Hildigunnur said.

'No,' Gytha interrupted. 'Well, I say that. There's a lot of cowshit. But apart from that, not much.'

Hildigunnur smirked, and Agla rolled her eyes. 'We still haven't found a king to marry this one off to,' she said to grins around the table. 'Or maybe Freyr himself?'

Gytha sniffed and turned her nose up. 'Too old for me,' she said, to general murmurs of approval from the women.

'And are you adjusting well to the farming life?' Unnthor rumbled. 'Because it's different, isn't it?'

'Yes,' Karl said, glaring again, 'of course it is different.'

'Lot of hard work,' Unnthor said.

'Yes.'

'Up at dawn, sleep when you're dead.'

'Yes,' he managed through gritted teeth.

'If you want something from your farm you have to *earn*—'

Karl rose with such force that it almost tipped over the bench his family sat on. 'I KNOW, FATHER!' he roared. 'I was RAISED on a farm! Here! *Remember*? Or were you too busy being Big Man of the Valley?' He slammed the table for emphasis.

Aslak's arm was outstretched in front of his cowering children. On the other side, Volund keened low into his bowl of soup, thick muscles rigid with tension. Thyri shot a savage glance at Bjorn, then went to mutter soothingly in her son's ear.

Karl sneered at his family and the world. 'We're doing *fine* – and we will *continue* to do fine, without *anyone's* help!' He looked around the room, wild-eyed, daring anyone to meet his gaze. Agla moved on reflex to right an upturned cup, but a quick glare from her husband stopped her in her tracks.

At the top of the table, the old man glanced at his wife – *Do you want to take this one?* – who pursed her lips and tilted her head. *No, go ahead. You deal with it.* They looked calmly at Karl.

Laying both slab-like hands on the table, Unnthor smiled. 'Good. I am sure you'll do us proud. Bjorn?'

For a moment Karl looked like he was going to walk away, but he was pinned in behind the table, with his back up against the wall. Deciding against clambering across his whole and extended family, he sat down again, angrily shaking off Agla's proffered hand on his shoulder.

Across the table, Bjorn cleared his throat as Volund's keening faded. 'Well,' he said, 'we're not doing as well as Karl—' His head snapped up and he scanned his brother's face for signs of mockery, but found nothing so continued, '—but we're doing fine, more or less. Got a small farm that feeds us, we are well thought of in our valley and surroundings, and we can help our neighbours.'

'Sounds good,' Hildigunnur said.

'What about your idiot son?' Karl snapped.

For the space of half a breath, Helga's heart leaped into her mouth and stopped there.

The silence filled the longhouse.

Then Bjorn very calmly put one of his big hands over both of his wife's and looked Karl straight in the eyes. 'My idiot son,' he said, voice like a moving iceberg, 'is kind and gentle, doesn't hurt anyone, rarely breaks anything and is going to be *very* strong indeed. So he'll be quite handy on the farm, and people will like him. Which makes him completely your opposite, *Brother dear*. What do you have to say to that?' The words were delivered calmly, but as he stared across the table at his brother anyone could see that Bjorn was absolutely spoiling for a fight, and this time Karl would not catch him unaware.

Einar nudged Helga a safe distance away from the table and led her with a look to glance at Bjorn's feet. They had slowly slid under the bench and he was ready to launch himself forward at the smallest provocation.

Karl opened his mouth to speak.

'Be *quiet*.' Hildigunnur's voice hit them like the sound of a snapping branch. The spell was broken. There was no smile to the old woman now, no twinkle in the eye. She was hewn from the land and the mountain, and like all mothers who had gone before her she would not be denied. 'I will not have my sons going at each other like their own half-mad farmyard mongrels. Karl, you're picking fights. I know you love them, but you do not hurt your family with words or actions beneath my roof. And Bjorn – you will leave your brother alone and ignore anything he says. Understood?'

Her sons looked down at the table. 'Yes, Mother,' they mumbled.

'I can't hear you. And *look at me* when you're speaking to me,' she barked.

Two heads shot up; two sets of eyes fixed on Hildigunnur. 'Yes, Mother,' they chorused, louder this time.

She nodded, satisfied for the moment, and leaned back in her chair.

'So things are well with you then,' Unnthor rumbled, and Bjorn grunted his assent, taking care not to look in Karl's direction. 'Good. Jorunn?'

The sister smiled sweetly at Unnthor. 'Yes, Father of mine?' she said, cheerful obedience dripping from every word.

The brothers glared at her.

'Goes for you too, smartarse,' Hildigunnur snapped, but without any real conviction.

'Tell us about life out east,' Unnthor said. 'We've heard some stories, but nothing definite.'

'Oh? What have you heard?' Sigmar said, smiling. *It doesn't reach his eyes either*, Helga thought, and made a note to keep an eye on the Swede when he wasn't looking.

'This and that,' Hildigunnur said. 'Apparently old King Eirik was on the move.'

'Hm,' Jorunn said. 'Two years ago?'

'Sounds about right,' Hildigunnur said.

'Wasn't much, really,' Sigmar said. 'A bit of family trouble with a cousin. They sorted it out amongst themselves eventually. Funny story.'

'We heard stories of armies massing,' Unnthor said.

'Isn't that what armies do?' Jorunn said. 'They mass, they clash and they go home when they find out war's boring.'

Hildigunnur looked at her daughter in the same way she'd evaluate a particularly tricky mare. 'I suppose so,' she said, 'but then, important news from the outside world rarely reaches us here.'

Jorunn returned the look. 'I don't know that information has been able to keep away from you for long, Mother dear.'

'I know what I know,' Hildigunnur said, 'but not much more than that.'

'I think we've told you everything of note,' Jorunn said. 'The east is dull, really. Apparently most of the news comes out of the south these days. Down by the borders of the Danes. Lots of trade coming from there.'

'Interesting,' Hildigunnur said.

It was only her imagination, but Helga felt she could hear the Tafl set being put away. *What had they been playing for?* She'd heard the rhythms and notes of Hildigunnur's voice well enough – she'd given Jorunn any number of chances to reveal information, but she'd gained nothing. *Or maybe Jorunn's evasion was what she was hunting for?* The battle of wits was over – but she couldn't tell who'd won.

'Tell us of Uppsala,' Unnthor said.

'We go regularly, to attend the court,' Jorunn said. Gytha's eyes widened as she went on, 'We negotiate trade for the south and the bogs.'

Gytha couldn't stop herself. Her voice awed, she said, 'You go to *King Eirik's* court?'

'Yes,' Jorunn said offhandedly, 'it's a pain, really. You have to put on all manner of expensive clothes and—'

'Would you take me? Could I come with you once? Just once?'

'I can't see why not. I'll ask—'

'No.' Karl's voice was firm. For a moment, all was silent as the guests around the table registered the word, then four voices spoke at once.

'Karl – I think—'

'Why not? There's no harm—'

'Are you sure?'

'Come on, Brother, let the gi—'

Gytha's cry cut through all of them. 'I HATE YOU!'

Beside Runa, Sigrun and Bragi started crying in unison, thin, shrill voices rising to the rafters. Karl's fists smashed down on the table yet again and he rose in his seat and faced his scowling daughter. 'You will SHUT your MOUTH and do what you're TOLD,' he roared back, spittle flying. 'I've had enough of all of you, yapping at me, biting my heels. You're going back with me and your mother and you're going to get married. You're not going to fucking Uppsala with a couple of fucking rag-traders.'

A moment's silence, then—

'*Rag-traders?*' Helga watched as Sigmar rose, still calm, his movements measured. She also noted the empty place by his plate where the knife had been.

Karl glared at him. 'You're soft and weak and you do fuck-all but ponce about – all this so-called "trading" is just yap-yap-yapping.'

Sigmar smiled. 'Whereas what I *should* be doing is, what, exactly? Go "raiding"?' Helga could hear the quote marks around the word. 'Kill a couple of unarmed villagers over in Saxony?' He locked eyes with Karl. 'Come home and buy a big farm? Try all the shortcuts I can find to become a man of note?' The grin was wolfish now. *Come on then*, it said. 'Borrow too much and run crying to my father?'

Agla just had time to pull a face of confusion before Karl was up and over the table, kicking bowls aside as he launched himself at Sigmar, roaring at the top of his voice.

'Bjorn!' Thyri shouted, but the big man only put his arms out to shield his family and stepped back.

Expecting the move, Sigmar had stepped nimbly backwards, pushing Jorunn out of the way as he went and gaining open space on the floor. Poised like a cat, the point of the purloined knife glinting in the firelight, he looked across at Karl.

Somewhere on the way across the dining table the raider's survival instincts had kicked in. His murderous gaze was still trained on Sigmar, but instead of rushing in, he started circling. 'I will snap you in half, Swede,' he growled.

'You'll have to catch me,' Sigmar replied, 'and if you do, I'll open your veins. The fact of the matter is, Karl,' he continued calmly, stepping out of reach of a testing side-swipe, 'that you don't *know*. You have no idea what I've been up to since we met last, and that is a long time ago.' As a bench scraped behind him, Karl growled and stepped closer. Sigmar swiped at him, the point of the blade carving an arc at throat-height. 'And to add to that, I have six men of my own, just a way down the road. Do you?'

'You're bluffing,' Karl growled.

'Maybe,' Sigmar shot back. His smile invited questions.

'Right,' Unnthor said. 'Either you two both sit down and shut up, or there'll be two widows at the table.' In the flickering fire-light, the chieftain looked even larger. The axe he held was nearly half his length.

'Back off, Father,' Karl said, 'this is between me a—'

'SIT. DOWN.'

Sigmar stepped back, both hands in front of him, palms up.

The knife had disappeared – not on the floor, Helga noted, so back into the folds of his tunic.

Sneering, Karl took three quick steps towards the Swede—

—but Unnthor was a blur of motion, the axe spinning in his hands. The handle smacked into Karl's kneecap, scraped down his shin to his ankles and then, moving almost like a harvester, Unnthor swept his eldest son's legs from under him and Karl hit the ground with a great thud.

Unnthor was already there, kneeling by him, big hand on the back of his neck. 'Don't move,' he said, almost gently. Karl squirmed, and the chieftain grabbed a handful of his hair, and yanking his head up, growled, 'I said, *don't move.*' He pushed Karl's face down to the floor. 'You were ready to spill blood in my house. In *my house.*'

'He had it coming,' Karl muttered. 'Runs his mouth like—'

A quick push; they all heard his forehead meet the planks.

When Unnthor spoke again, there was a weight to his words. 'You may have come back from the raids with great wealth, Son, but you've lost your head. I've seen it before, but I had hoped you'd be tough enough to keep your senses. Now I'm going to pull you up to your feet and you're going to go out for a walk. Take the dog. Go and drink some water. In fact, go and dunk your head in the river.'

Karl mumbled his assent and the big chieftain rose to his feet. It was only because she'd watched her father work for a decade now that Helga saw the little wobble as he pushed off his knees. She was pretty sure she was the only one who'd noticed – well, no, *nearly* the only one. For an eyeblink, Hildigunnur's face was a mix of anger and worry.

The door slammed as Karl disappeared out into the night.

An awkward silence followed. The guests weren't quite able to bring themselves to look at Agla, who sat very still, claw-like hands gripping the edge of the table. Gytha looked uncharacteristically subdued by the whole thing, as if she couldn't quite believe what she had seen.

'Should someone go after—?' Aslak began.

'None of our business,' Runa growled. 'He can look after himself. I'm sure he'll be *fine*.'

'Don't you dare chew on this, you hedge-bitch!' Agla snapped.

'Oh?' Runa hissed. 'Stop me.'

In a graceful, fluid motion Agla spun off the bench and headed towards Runa, her fists up. It took her three steps before she realised that she was in fact suspended in midair, hoisted by Bjorn.

'Calm yourself, Connected-wife,' he said in a deep, soothing voice.

'Let my mother go!' Gytha shrieked, grabbing the nearest pointy thing she could find.

The slap rang out, cutting through the commotion, and Gytha spun back down onto the bench, clutching her cheek. Hildigunnur was up and past the girl, seizing Agla by the hair and tossing her back towards the seat next to her daughter. Within a blink was facing Runa. Her hand shot out like a striking cat as she grabbed the short woman by the neck of her shirt and marched her outside. Wrong-footed, Runa stumbled for several paces until she finally managed to catch her balance halfway across the room.

The door slammed shut on the two of them. The only sound

was Agla sobbing in her seat, with Gytha and Thyri hovering awkwardly by.

Einar glanced at Helga. 'When I said it was going to be interesting? This is more like it,' he whispered.

Chapter 8

CLEAN-UP

Sunlight seeped into the longhouse from the open air-slits. The smell of blooming flowers and grass drifted in from outside, and in the distance they could hear Jaki shouting something. Einar worked to dislodge the leg of the table he'd just effortlessly tipped over onto the side.

'So what did you expect?' he said over his shoulder.

'I don't know,' Helga said, piling knives onto a cloth. Standing at Hildigunnur's spot felt strange, wrong. 'I thought maybe they'd be happier to see each other.'

Einar looked at her then, a note of pity in his eyes. 'Not all family bonds are strong,' he said. 'How were they this morning?'

'Quiet,' she said. 'Karl came in after Bjorn and his lot had left the longhouse to go to their beds and almost everyone else was asleep. Unnthor waited up for him, and I heard them talk a bit – well, just a couple of words, really – but they weren't angry, I don't think. I don't know what Mother said to Runa, but she's not been around.'

'That's something, I suppose,' Einar said, grunting with satisfaction as the leg gave way and came loose in his hand.

'None of them spoke to Karl this morning. He didn't even look at Sigmar. They all found reasons to be somewhere else . . .'

'Bjorn did the same,' Einar said. 'I saw him leaving early – when I asked, he just muttered something about showing his family all the best trails or some such rubbish. He didn't even look me in the eye.'

Helga finished the parcels to go and wash in the stream. 'I just don't understand,' she repeated, still upset. 'I mean, why are they even here if they're not happy to meet up?' She grabbed as much as she could carry and headed towards the door. 'Why would they want to come back here when they obviously hate each other so much?' she mused.

Sigmar perched on a boulder, looking down upon the hills and the patches of forest, the longhouse that was no bigger than his hand from up here, the path they'd come up, and the face of his wife.

'Well?'

'I talked to Father a *lot* yesterday,' Jorunn said. 'I flattered, I teased and I questioned. I got him half drunk, I made him sad and I made him happy.'

'Like a good daughter should,' Sigmar said.

'Like a good daughter should,' Jorunn agreed. 'But the old bear gave *nothing* away. The farm is going well, he said. They have what they need – I offered him coin, like you said, but he refused, and he *still* didn't even *hint* that he was sitting on a pot of gold.' She looked Sigmar dead in the eye. 'But it's here, my love: I know it is. And I have an idea about how we could get them to give it to us freely.'

He smiled. 'I believe you – in fact, I can almost smell it. And the way Karl is behaving—'

'How did you know?'

'Know what?'

'That he was so badly in debt.'

The Swede smiled. 'A bladesmith from down south tried to use some of it as a trading chip.'

'Why didn't you tell me?' Jorunn said.

'Because you'd have made me use it,' Sigmar said.

Jorunn paused at this. '. . . I suppose,' she conceded. Then she smiled. 'You're soft, Husband,' she said.

Sigmar slid off the rock and walked towards her. 'In all this fresh air? With all this . . . *nature*?' He pulled her close. 'I think you will find I am not.'

Jorunn reached behind him, and in a flash her husband was on his knees, whimpering through gritted teeth, his hand bent at a very uncomfortable angle. 'Good,' she hissed. 'Don't think with your dick – don't forget why we're here – and *don't* let my brothers goad you into stupid man games.'

Even on his knees, Sigmar could still manage a grin. 'You are truly the daughter of Riverside,' he said.

'And don't you forget it,' Jorunn said, mirroring his smile as she leaned down to kiss him, hard.

Gytha's mother had not said a single word once they were past the gate. They'd got out of bed at sun-up, inched past her snoring father and dressed in silence. Her mother had grabbed two hand-baskets as she went out. In the yard they'd found Hildigunnur, busy splitting logs into sticks for kindling. Gytha had watched her mother exchange not much more than ten words with the old woman, who pointed down the road and gestured some. Agla just glared at her and gestured with her head that she should move, and so she did, following her for what felt like nearly half the morning already, until her mother suddenly turned sharply to the left and led the way off the path and into a copse full of strongly scented berry bushes.

Now Gytha watched as her mother got down on her knees and reached into the bush for a ripe cluster of blackberries hidden behind the already stripped branches. Suddenly she yelped and yanked her hand back, shoving her finger in her mouth and sucking furiously.

The question tumbled out before she could stop it. 'Mum . . . is it true?'

'What?' Agla snapped, staring down at the ground.

'Is Father—? Do we—?'

'I don't know,' Agla said. 'I don't bloody know.' She turned around and stared at Gytha, unblinking, as she rose from her crouch. 'I hope it isn't.'

Gytha smiled weakly. 'It's probably all lies.'

Agla held her gaze for a moment that felt like it would last for months. 'What do you know?'

'Nothing! Nothing,' Gytha said. 'Probably less than you do.'

Standing right in front of her, Agla took a deep breath to centre herself, then another, and another. 'Good,' she said, finally. 'And if you do find something out, you come and tell me, right?'

'Of course, Mum,' Gytha said. 'I wouldn't let you suffer just because Father's been unreasonable.'

Agla eyed her suspiciously, but moments later she was back on her knees in front of the bush. 'Help me with this, then,' she snapped. 'Here, hold this branch out of the way . . .'

Behind her Gytha rolled her eyes as she got down on her knees. 'It'll take us *for ever* to walk back,' she whined. 'Why didn't we take the horses?'

'They're *his* horses,' came the terse reply. 'He doesn't have to lend them.'

'Why didn't you ask him last night? About everything?'

'They're his answers. He can keep 'em if he wants.'

'But why didn't you—?'

Agla turned towards her daughter, and to her shock, Gytha was facing a broken woman. 'Because I'm his wife,' she whispered. 'I'm his. He *owns* me – he owns *you*. And if he decides I'm more trouble than I'm worth – what then? He can throw me out and I'll have nothing. The only way I get to keep anything to my name is when he dies, and he's not doing that anytime soon.'

She breathed deep and tried a smile. 'So I live, and he lives, and we go back to where we live and we don't come back to this stupid farm for another decade, if ever.' She took a step towards her daughter and placed a hand on her shoulder. 'You'll find a good man to marry, I'll make sure of it. Someone you like. And just like that, you'll be gone, and none of this will be yours to worry about. I'll keep your father under control. I've managed so far.'

Gytha's lip trembled. 'I just wanted to see Uppsala, Mum – just once.'

She smiled again, more brightly this time. 'You have to learn that it's not just the question, but *when* you ask it. We'll see what we can do,' she said, winking at her daughter. 'Now shut up, dearest Daughter, and get to picking blackberries. It helps to pass the time.'

Gytha smiled at her mother and they started again, plucking the sweet, juicy morsels from between the vicious thorns.

Unnthor wiped the sweat from his brow and leaned on his hoe. He had dug out a square patch twice the size of the farmyard, but the rest of the land stretched away to all sides, untamed and overgrown. The ground that dipped just past the new barn was covered by a dense line of trees.

'Father,' Aslak called, coming up the hill from the direction of the longhouse.

He raised a meaty arm in greeting.

His youngest son was slim but he carried a big spade over his shoulder. As soon as he arrived, he set to digging, turning the earth over and letting it fall, ready for his father's hoe to remove the rocks. They fell into a silent rhythm, working companionably together.

After a long while, Unnthor spoke. 'You didn't get to speak last night, Son. The idiots saw to that.'

'It's fine,' Aslak said.

'Good. We need at least one calm head in the family.'

'Mother's pretty calm.'

'Besides your mother. We won't be around to mop up their messes for ever, you know.'

Aslak smiled. 'You'll be here long after we're gone,' he said.

'Well then,' Unnthor said with more than a hint of a smile, 'tell me of your farm.'

He sighed. 'What is there to tell? We scrape by, and Runa's sick of it. She wants me to be stronger, meaner. More ambitious.' He slumped. 'I am a constant disappointment to her.'

'The truth is, anyone but the gods would be, Son,' Unnthor rumbled. 'She's a hard taskmaster and no mistake. But the children love her.'

At this, Aslak's face lit up and he said enthusiastically, 'She is, she's *great* with them, and they're great with – with *everything*. My family – I have a family, Father: a *family*. And that's the most important thing.'

'Family is important,' Unnthor agreed, hoe smashing into the ground.

Aslak followed up with a vicious stab of the shovel. 'That's the only thing, I think, that might turn me into the man she wants. If someone were to threaten my family.'

Grunting with the effort, he succeeded in pulling the shovel out of the ground, only to find that Unnthor was looking at him strangely, hoe on the ground, held firmly in his grip.

'You would too, wouldn't you?' the old man said, looking his youngest son up and down.

Aslak stopped and looked his father in the eye. 'Yes,' he said without flinching. 'Yes, I would.'

After a long moment, Unnthor grinned. 'Good,' he said. 'It's a poor excuse for a man who doesn't take care of his family. Let's go back to your troubles at the farm, though. What needs to be better?'

'*Hm*,' Aslak said, leaning on the spade and thinking. 'A ram with some life in him. Two dogs to train to keep the sheep off the vegetables. A better horse, while I'm dreaming.'

'I couldn't agree more,' Unnthor said. 'Your old nag was half-dead last year. Is that all, Son?'

Aslak shrugged. 'I can put in a shift – you don't survive at Riverside if you can't, do you?' He laughed. 'But starting your own from scratch is harder.'

'I know,' Unnthor said. 'I had a hand, so I think it only fair that you have a hand too.'

Aslak looked at him, blinking. 'What do you mean?'

'We'll make sure your ram comes this summer, along with two dogs and a horse. If I'm lucky, I'll try to get you a couple of ewes as well.'

The young man stared at his father. 'Wh—? Wh—? What? But Father, that's going to cost a *fortune*!'

Unnthor just grinned. 'There will be a way. The gods will smile upon you. Now, close your mouth and get to work!'

Speechless, Aslak grabbed his shovel and attacked the earth, wondering at what point he would wake up.

By the stream, Helga set to work on the last of the bowls. Einar had disappeared, gone off to tend to the horses, maybe, leaving her alone with her thoughts and the song of running water. She thought of the cold, dark hatred in Karl's eyes as he looked at his siblings, the tooth-gnashing anger of the man, and shuddered despite the summer sun. He was a nasty piece of work, and she couldn't help but imagine what his father must have been like when he was out raiding. The uneasy sensation that had filled her for the last day or so felt like a great load sitting on her. She absentmindedly reached up by her collarbone and caught the leather thong between her thumb and forefinger, rubbing it slowly as her fingers travelled down to the rune-stone that hung suspended by her heart. It felt smooth, strangely soft – and oddly warm.

She glanced up from the river just as Bjorn emerged from the longhouse. The big man took two long steps away from the door, but then he turned to face it, and Helga couldn't quite see who he was talking to or make out the words, but there was something strange about his stance. Although he was frozen in the middle of walking away, his eyes were downcast and he seemed to be listening intently. There was nothing of the usual liveliness about him.

Finally, he nodded and walked off towards the woods. Helga watched him leave, the frown deepening on her forehead. The rune-stone felt heavy against her breastbone. 'Right, girl: those bowls won't wash themselves,' she muttered in a more than passable imitation of Hildigunnur's voice as she set to scrubbing. But she couldn't quite stop herself from glancing up occasionally to see if Bjorn's conversation partner would leave after him. Who had he been talking to? Why had he looked so like someone being told off? She finished drying the bowls and wrapped them up in Hildigunnur's cloth to keep them clean. She'd have to go and see for herself.

She hustled towards the door, struggling a bit with the makeshift bag, opened it carefully and peeked in.

Empty. Empty as it could be—

—except for Karl, who was sitting in his father's big chair, whittling away at a lump of wood.

'Oh – were you—?'

He looked up at her. 'Was I what? Sneaking about?'

Helga felt the colour rush to her cheeks. 'Nothing,' she muttered, making her way to Hildigunnur's end. She heaved the bag up onto the workbench, harder than she had intended, and winced as the bowls clacked together.

'Let me help you.' She froze. In the cool dark of the longhouse, she could feel the heat of him behind her, really, *really* close. His arm brushed her side as he reached past her. It was warm and solid. 'I still know where everything goes, I hope. They don't like to change things.' Karl gently eased her grip on the knot holding the bag together and reached for a bowl.

The words didn't come, but she felt her skin contract and pull away from him, twisting her body as it tugged at the muscles to avoid touching him as he reached down to put the bowl away.

'. . . it's fine,' she stuttered finally.

Kneeling by her side, he looked up at her, a mischievous glint in his eye. The pendant around his neck drew her gaze as the silver caught the light. 'Fine is the right word for it,' he said. He rose, not five inches away from her, and looked at her. Her breath caught in her throat as he leaned in, slowly. She turned her head, but not quick enough to miss the hungry look. Not quick enough to miss that his hand was moving up towards her.

'Helga!' Hildigunnur's voice came from the main door. 'Are you in there, girl?' Karl just smirked as he moved away, making sure she saw him licking her lips, tasting the smell of her fear in the air. He ducked towards the smaller door and disappeared just as Hildigunnur came in through the main door. 'There you are! You're taking for ever!'

Helga started quickly stacking the bowls. 'I'm sorry,' she managed before a wave of nausea, discomfort and fear washed through her, followed by a bigger wave of anger. *How dare he? In his father's house? In my house?* She bit back the fury and blinked.

'Don't worry, we have the day,' her mother said from across the hall. 'They're all out anyway.'

A couple of tears escaped, but the lump in her throat didn't go. She swallowed, once, twice – now, *breathe* – and it was gone. 'Yes,' she said. 'All of them.'

'Seeing them last night made me think,' Hildigunnur said, 'family is important, isn't it?'

'Yes,' Helga said, working hard to distract herself with the mugs.

'And it is important to have peace in a family,' Hildigunnur continued.

'Yes,' Helga said. *Keep talking, please. Just a little longer.* She clenched her fist and tried to let the sting of nails digging into palms clear her head. 'Where did Agla go?' she managed.

'She needed to walk off some feelings, I reckon. I pointed her and Gytha to the berries.'

Helga folded up the cloth. 'Good,' she said. 'They should be all right now.'

'Don't really care,' Hildigunnur said. 'I just couldn't stand her face.' Despite herself, Helga chuckled. 'It looked like a hoof,' her mother added. 'Off the back foot, too.'

'And Thyri?'

'Bjorn took his folks out for a walk, I gather,' Hildigunnur said, which made Helga frown. So the big man had somehow avoided her as well? So what had the brothers been talking about? And why had Bjorn looked so downcast? He'd been willing to go toe to toe with Karl only last night.

'Are you about done over there?'

'Yes, I am,' Helga said, strapping on a smile and turning to face her mother.

Up by the new barn Unnthor whittled away at the arrows with quick, sure strokes. The spot he'd chosen was sun-kissed and shielded from the wind. The tree stump he'd placed by the wall for just such an occasion was well worn and the old man relaxed into his seat. By his left leg sat a pile of straight arrows, already finished; by his feet was a growing pile of wood shavings.

When Karl rounded the corner he had to squint against the brightness. 'Well met,' he said.

'Well met,' Unnthor said, putting down the arrow and laying the whittling knife on his lap.

'I would like to ask your forgiveness,' Karl said, looking down at his feet.

For a while, Unnthor didn't speak. Then, 'What do you want, Karl?'

'I reckon Aslak and Bjorn will talk to Mother, if they haven't already. My darling sister will come to you, because she always has, and I thought I should do the same. I only want what I deserve,' Karl said.

Unnthor snorted. 'Oh, I reckon you're guaranteed to get that.'

If he noticed the edge in his father's words, he did not give any signs of it. 'That's good to hear. Excellent. Tell me again, Father: the treasure—'

'There is no treasure.'

'The stories say there is.'

'The stories lie.'

'Havard Greybeard said there was.'

Unnthor looked at Karl. When he spoke, his voice was ice-cold. 'Where did you hear that name?'

It was just a little contraction of the lower lip, but on Karl's face it was the grin of a wolf. 'Do you remember him?'

'Of course I do,' Unnthor snapped.

'He says he sailed with you for years.'

'Yes.'

'He says you had a sea-chest.'

'I did.'

'And he says you sat on it harder and harder the longer you stayed on the boat, and that you'd let no one near it.'

'That's a lie,' Unnthor said.

Karl just looked at him, one eyebrow creeping up to complete the grin. 'See, *Father*, I don't think it is. I think there *is* a treasure buried somewhere here, and I think you'll give me what I am entitled to. I go home, buy off the debts, you don't get ill-spoken-of in your precious valley and your darling granddaughter doesn't get married to the next passing black-skin merchant with a sack of gold and a taste for flesh.'

Unnthor rose. 'Are you threatening me?' he growled, but Karl stood his ground.

'Not at all. Just give me what's mine and I'll be away.'

The old man looked at Karl, and his shoulders sank. 'I can't believe you would use your own daughter for such a bargain.' He sighed.

'If you'd been a proper father I wouldn't have had to.'

'Fine, fine,' Unnthor muttered, 'but you'll have to wait until tomorrow. We'll see off the rest of the family and settle matters before you leave.'

'Thank you, Father. You are truly a wise man,' Karl said. With the merest hint of a wink, he turned and walked off.

Unnthor watched him go. Then he looked at the knife in his hands and very carefully resumed whittling.

The sun was nearing the horizon when the first of the guests returned. Helga heard the dogs barking and peeked around the corner of the longhouse, where Hildigunnur had set her to splitting firewood while she went to see to the butchering for the night's feast.

Einar was opening the gate for Agla and Gytha, and Helga noticed that side by side and from a distance, mother and daughter looked almost identical – just as Hildigunnur and Jorunn did. Helga thought about her own height, how she was little more than elbows and knees, and how she looked nothing like anyone on the farm. 'Doesn't matter,' she muttered. 'There's more to kin than blood.' She ducked back behind the woodshed and wished she believed it.

Hildigunnur's voice carried around the corner and she knew her mother would be out in the farmyard, the setting sun at her back, beaming at Agla.

'Oh, you are precious, you are. That's more than we manage to pick in a season!'

Helga could hear the smile in Gytha's voice as she announced, 'Five baskets!'

'We were good and ready to be of some use after eating you out of house and home,' Agla replied.

'I can see,' Hildigunnur said. 'We'll have to get this stewing as soon as we can – it'll be good for afters. If you're still up for picking, I could use you to help me get some herbs in. Come!'

Helga heard the slamming of the main door and grabbed the next bit of firewood, but she paused. Something was nagging at her; something from *before*.

Her mother had been out the back when the dogs barked.

In her mind, she traced the journey – through the side door, through the open space inside, out the main door – and reversed it.

Karl had been in there when she got to him, but it could have been *anyone*. Anyone could have been indoors, talking to Bjorn, telling him what to do and where to go, before sneaking out the side door, shielded from the brook. Karl could have entered moments later, none the wiser. Or maybe he was? He'd said something about skulking, hadn't he . . . ?

Helga thwacked the axe into the log and split it neatly. *Who was it?* Who'd made the big man bow his head?

'What did that firewood ever do to you?' Einar's voice startled her, and instinctively, Helga pulled the axe free and to elbow-height, on the defensive. 'Whoa—! Easy,' he added, concern etched on his face. 'It's only me. What's going on?' Behind him she could hear Hildigunnur and Agla prattling as they headed off towards the herb garden.

'I don't know, Einar.' She looked at him then, her sworn brother for as much of her life as she could remember. 'But promise me one thing.'

'Anything,' he said, blue eyes trained on her, easy smile on his face. 'What do you need?'

'I need you to be careful.'

Einar shrugged. '*Pff*. Don't worry, Helga, they're all old and stupid. I have to go now, though. Apparently we're bringing up four barrels of mead for tonight.' He winked at her. 'It should be a proper feast, and no mistake.'

The rhythmic *tak-tak-tak* of Thyri's knife on the wooden board set the tempo for Jorunn's steady strokes as she started slicing finger-length peels off the turnip in her hand.

'I just feel sorry for your brother,' Thyri said over her shoulder to Jorunn, breaking the silence.

She pursed her lips. 'He could change his situation, but he doesn't. And in the end we all build our own house.'

'Still, is there something we could do? Maybe talk—'

'I don't know,' Jorunn interrupted, without looking up, 'I don't know that talking is the right thing to do. I want no part of any of it.'

The *tak-tak* grew quicker. 'Still not right,' Thyri mumbled.

'Lots of things aren't,' Jorunn said firmly.

For a couple of breaths there was no sound in the longhouse other than that of work being done. Hildigunnur's big cauldron taunted them with its open mouth, and it didn't matter how many vegetables they threw in, the damned thing still stayed more than half-empty.

The door creaked and Runa came in.

Thyri looked up, eyed her, then went back to chopping, not saying a word. Jorunn too remained focused on her task.

'And hello to you too,' Runa said. 'Warm family greeting, as usual.'

'About as warm as your bed, I reckon,' Jorunn said.

'Sorry,' Runa said, 'what did you say?'

'You heard her,' Thyri said.

'I did,' Runa said slowly. 'I just didn't understand her.' There was silence in the longhouse. 'See, her accent has gone all funny from too much Swedish cock in her mouth.'

Jorunn's knife stopped moving, but she still didn't look up.

'Oho! And your husband is happy, is he?' Thyri said.

Runa snorted. 'He hasn't said otherwise.'

Jorunn's knife started moving again, flicking the peels onto the board, tossing the slices into the cauldron. 'You mistreat my brother,' she said, quietly. Runa glared at her, but didn't respond. 'I don't care what you do in your bed, but when he is near us, he is happy. When he is near you, he looks like a beaten dog.'

'And yours is a pansy. You can go sit on a pinecone, bitch,' Runa snapped. 'Your brother is supposed to be a grown man.'

'And he is,' Jorunn said, 'but he is also both kind and gentle.' She looked up and straight into Runa's eyes. Without wavering, she placed the point of the knife at the middle of the root and slid it in. 'I am neither.'

Runa's eyes narrowed and her lips pursed. 'Are you threatening me?'

Jorunn rose, dropped the knife and squared up to the shorter woman. 'He is my brother. He's *family*. And our father has taught us that whoever threatens the family—'

'Jorunn,' Thyri muttered.

The main door closed and Hildigunnur's voice rang out. 'I'm glad you ladies have found each other – now get to work instead of all of this chatter!'

With a slight tilt of her head to Thyri in thanks for the warning, Jorunn sat down and reached for her knife. 'Glad we had this talk, *Sister*,' she murmured. Her knife started moving again, slicing the turnip, but her eyes never left those of her brother's wife.

Chapter 9

FEAST

Sigmar's face was flushed in the warm light reflecting from Unnthor's burnished shields. 'What I want to say,' he slurred, 'what I want to say, is that sometimes – sometimes kings can be pitiful little things.'

'Hah!' Karl said, throwing his arm around the Swede and banging his free hand on the table. 'What happened? Did the other one drop? First time you've made any sort of sense since we got here.'

'He's not wrong,' Jorunn said. 'We sometimes get requests from the court that you wouldn't believe.'

Helga watched as conversation sloshed back and forth and siblings leaned over the table, grabbed each other by the arm and interrupted loudly. It had become background noise a while ago as she and Einar cleared plates and filled mugs, then settled back in their corner to observe from afar. Unnthor had slaughtered a pig especially, and they'd prepared plenty of the freshest vegetables. From his saddlebag, Karl had produced a bulging skin of rich red wine from the south, and Bjorn had carried in two in each hand. Aslak had offered two wine skins, under the glare of his wife, but Sigmar and Jorunn had gone one better, producing three skins full to the brim of Swedish honey-mead, which the family was getting through quickly and increasingly rowdily.

'Saw Gytha talking to you again this afternoon,' Helga said to Einar.

The boy looked up at her from his bowl of stew and shrugged. 'So?'

'Come on now,' Helga said, 'she's pretty and she's throwing herself at you. Why do you keep turning her down?'

It was gone in the blink of an eye, but she caught it: he'd glanced at the table, where Jorunn was busy telling a story that had her brothers chortling, all yesterday's animosity forgotten. Her beautiful face beamed with life and joy.

'Dunno,' Einar muttered. 'She's young . . .'

Helga thought back and almost wanted to slap herself. *Of course.* The flirting and the chasing all those years ago; the way Einar had been getting more and more tense all through the long build-up to the visit . . . 'I suppose,' Helga said, and left it at that. The warmth of the longhouse was getting to her. 'How are they for mead?'

'Good enough, I'd say,' Einar said without even looking. 'They're getting louder, at any rate.'

''s just not right,' Agla said, her voice cutting through the din. 'She's so young.'

'I agree,' Runa slurred next to her, 'but she'll be married soon enough.'

Helga glanced at the shape of Gytha, twisting in her bunk to try to get away from the sounds.

'And happy,' Jorunn added. 'Or just happy.'

'Does she keep you happy, Sigmar?' Runa said.

'I can't complain—' Sigmar said.

'—or I'll beat you senseless,' Jorunn added.

Bjorn laughed first and loudest, but the rest of them followed. At the far end of the table Unnthor started up a song, and Karl joined in enthusiastically.

'Husband,' Hildigunnur shouted, 'stop your howling! We're parched! It's time to bring out the barrel!'

Unnthor rose unsteadily to roars of approval. 'This – you ungrateful little whelps – is a barrel of the best—'

'—and strongest,' Hildigunnur added.

'—and strongest mead I've ever brewed,' Unnthor said. 'What you don't drink tonight will be used for me to dip my arrow in and hunt bears!'

'Give us the mead so we can dip our arrows ourselves!' Bjorn roared to more laughter.

Helga glanced at Einar. 'I'm going to crawl into a bunk like the little ones and hope they all fall asleep soon,' she said.

'They will,' Einar said. 'I'll watch over them.'

As she stood up from her corner, she found her mother's eyes across the room. Helga glanced at her bunk and Hildigunnur nodded, smiling.

She wrapped herself up in her blanket, and moments later the voices became like the wind in the trees and the waves of the sea, dancing this way and that, rising and falling, rising, and falling . . .

Sleep took her.

Chapter 10

BLOOD

Helga's eyelids twitched and she shook her head, turning over to get away from the noise in her dreams. Something was bleating, an animal in pain, maybe? It stopped, but then it started again, twice as loud, and close – too close. She frowned. It wasn't an animal, it was screaming. A woman. A woman screaming, very close, her voice raw with horror. The warm comfort of sleep washed off and she sat bolt-upright. There was a moment of silence – had she dreamed it? – then more noise, a twisted, crazed sound that rose and rose into the air.

'Mum!' Gytha's voice sounded terrified. There was a breath, then another anguished wail. 'Mum – *stop!*' Gytha shouted, 'what's *wrong?*'

A moment later, Gytha was screaming too.

Helga took a deep breath. There was a sour smell on the air: stale mead, sweat – *vomit?* But something else as well. And there were voices coming from all over, and now Unnthor was shouting for calm and Hildigunnur was shouting at someone to bring water.

Her eyes were adjusting to the early morning sunlight leaking in through the shutters, but Helga was still struggling to make out the shapes inside. Jorunn was screaming for Bjorn now, and somewhere over her shoulder the door smashed open and the big man bellowed something in reply. Helga swung her legs over the edge of her bunk and stumbled to her feet, self-consciously stroking the wrinkles out of her shift and feeling ridiculous as she did so; whatever was going on meant no one was going to notice her this morning.

Her eyes were still befuddled with sleep, so the picture in front of her made little sense.

Agla was bent double over something; Hildigunnur had wedged herself in beside her and was trying to push the woman away. Sigmar was levering Gytha to the side, then pushing her towards Jorunn, who was grabbing the girl and awkwardly embracing her, pressing her head to her shoulder. As her vision sharpened, Helga realised Gytha was shaking violently.

What in the name of the gods—?

As Helga watched, her mother jabbed her fingers into the crook of Agla's elbow, breaking the grip and shouldering the woman away from whatever she had been clutching.

She was leaning over Karl's bed.

Slowly, ever so slowly, a path opened to the wooden frame and the room suddenly dropped into unnatural quiet after the storm of voices, until the sound of children crying fell like ripples into the silence.

Helga's feet took her towards the edge.

Be careful when the knives come out . . .

Around her, the adults of Riverside started shouting at each other, incomprehensible noises in her head, and probably in theirs as well.

Darkness in their hearts.

She saw the shape before she saw the face, but first there was the smell.

Blood.

Iron, salt, life – everything that flowed in a human.

Karl's face was pale and tilted to the side. A thin line of spittle had leaked into his coarse dark beard. His hands lay by his sides, and he looked exactly like someone sleeping off a particularly heavy night of drink.

The entire lower half of the bed and the blanket covering him, however, were soaked in blood.

Without even thinking about what she was doing, Helga reached slowly for the corner of the blanket and pulled. The thickening tendrils of blood came away with a wet, sucking sound. Karl was still wearing his trousers, but they were as dark red as the blanket. Two big black spots on the inside of his thighs drew her eye. Here, the fabric had almost disappeared under a solid, shiny coating of blood.

Helga felt the heat by her shoulder even before she sensed the presence of her mother. 'Pull,' she said, her teeth clenched in fury.

Fingers suddenly trembling, Helga reached out and placed her hands on Karl's thighs, feeling the sticky residue on her palms, then gently, she pulled on the material and the fabric came away to reveal a neat cut, maybe the length of a thumb, placed just by the big vein in the groin, with a matching one on the other side.

'Both sides,' Helga muttered, and Hildigunnur's hand on her

shoulder squeezed so hard that Helga thought she could feel the bones in her shoulder breaking.

'My son,' her mother said, loud enough for everyone to hear, 'has been murdered in his sleep.'

The beautiful blue sky was warmed by the rising sun, and stood in stark contrast to the family of Unnthor and Hildigunnur, gathered in a circle in the farmyard.

Aslak had his arm around Runa, who stood stiff as a board, her eyes closed, her jaw working furiously. Bragi and Sigrun hung off the skirt of her dress, their faces buried in the folds of the material. They might have been too young to understand what had happened, but they were old enough to have picked up the uneasy atmosphere of grief and fury.

Sigmar and Jorunn, side by side, were grim-faced and straight-backed.

Bjorn, towering over Thyri, had a hand on Volund's shoulder as he blinked sleepily in front of them.

Agla hung off Hildigunnur's shoulder. She was wrapped in a blanket and her eyes were unfocused, as if she were looking at something not of this world. Gytha, standing next to her, was half-heartedly trying to comfort her mother.

Helga thought Gytha looked like she needed a fair bit of comfort herself.

She dared a glance at her father, flanked by Einar and Jaki. Unnthor Reginsson looked like thunder. His massive chest heaved with each deep breath, his jaw was solid, to keep his lips from moving, and his big hands clenched and unclenched like beating hearts. He shook with a pure fury that looked barely under control.

'I will keep this very simple,' he said, his voice a grating, growling stone-slide. 'Einar will tie down your horses. Jaki will watch the gate. And I will hunt down and kill *anyone* who leaves before I say they can. Is that understood?' Nods all around, some sharp, others hesitant, all respectfully terrified. No one who looked at the man standing before them could have doubted that this was no idle threat.

But no one spoke.

Unnthor stood, furiously quiet, and waited.

Even Bjorn had trouble meeting his gaze, but still no one spoke.

A deep breath, and then—

'So what happens now?' Jorunn asked.

Helga's heart bounced in her chest, but if there was one person in that circle who could risk speaking without Unnthor taking their head off, it was his beloved daughter.

'Whoever killed Karl steps forward and we negotiate the blood-price to be paid to Agla and Gytha,' Unnthor said.

'What if no one steps forward?' Bjorn said.

Unnthor glared at each one of them in turn. 'I'll find you,' he said, 'and when I do, the price will be a lot higher.'

No one spoke, and even in the sun, Helga shivered.

'Jaki,' Hildigunnur snapped suddenly, 'set these people to work. Everywhere. Right now. Helga—' A quick nudge towards the house, with no more words attached.

With that, Hildigunnur took Agla in one hand and Gytha in the other and led them down towards the river, muttering in Agla's ear all the way, like she would soothe a skittish horse.

'Wood to fetch, roots to grub, logs to chop.' Jaki listed the chores. 'Get to it. After midday, we dig.'

Letting her feet guide her, Helga walked towards the longhouse. The main doors looked a lot less inviting than they had only last night.

The smell had had time to spread, and the scent of Karl's blood was filling her nostrils. She was in no great hurry to get to the corpse itself, so instead she allowed herself to just drift towards his bed, past the bunks where Aslak and his family had bedded down. She noted that there were two small blankets for the children and two for the adults. The indentations suggested that the youngest of Unnthor's sons hadn't been sleeping very close to his wife.

Jorunn and Sigmar's sleeping bunk was largely untroubled on one side, but well compressed on the other. Despite their tough exteriors, they appeared to enjoy each other's company very much. Helga thought of Einar and felt a twinge in her heart. It must be awful to desire someone and know that someone else is close to them at all times, and closest in the night.

And then, before she could decide on something else to do, her nose told her that she was standing by Karl's bed.

She'd slept in a bed exactly like it for as long as she could remember. It was nothing but a long box, really, with raised edges, well sanded, filled with straw and topped with a thick woven blanket. Karl looked oddly out of place in it, all stiff and pale, as if he'd sunk into himself. The rage that had filled him was gone like hot air. In his own house he'd probably had a bigger bed, big enough for Agla to share. Helga felt her stomach turn as her thoughts went unbidden to what that might be like, so she pushed them away and instead busied herself by looking more closely at his head and neck.

Plenty of scars and marks, but nothing fresh. Karl had clearly put his face in harm's way more than once in his life, but his dead body held no fresh bruises that had been stopped in mid-bloom.

'No one clouted you around the head, and no one held you by the throat,' she muttered. 'So why did you let them cut you?'

She bent down and studied his mouth. A part of her expected Karl's eyes to flutter open at any moment and, with a grin, start dragging her down into his bed-grave with him. She pushed those thoughts away too, telling herself, 'Shush, girl. He's dead as a fence post, and only half as charming. And there's nothing' – she pulled apart the dead man's lips and looked for residue – 'in here but stink. Mead, oh, quite a lot of it, too. So that takes care of the "why". But what about the "who"? Who would have approached the sleeping wolf?' she said out loud.

She heard the main door open and close behind her. 'Is he still dead?' Einar's voice carried across the longhouse.

'I'm afraid so,' Helga said. 'A lot of blood.'

'And that's not supposed to be on the outside,' Einar said thoughtfully. Helga's spirits lifted ever so slightly. Everything was always a little better with Einar around.

'Your wisdom runs deep, as usual. He is as dead as they come.'

Einar stood beside her, looking down. 'How was he killed?'

'As far as I can gather,' Helga said, 'whoever did it must have waited until he was passed out from drink—'

'They did put away a lot last night,' Einar said, 'and him more than most.'

Helga reached over the dead body. 'Then they snuck in, pulled the blanket aside and cut open his leg veins. Even if he had woken up, he'd've been dead in a matter of heartbeats.' She pulled the blanket away completely, wincing at the sound of the dried blood ripping away. The stench of voided bowels rose up to mix with the stale air. 'There,' she said, pointing at the black stains on the trousers.

'Bled like a pig,' Einar said. Although the smell clearly stung him, he didn't move away. 'Not a lot of honour in that. Do you have a knife?'

'No – why?'

'I'd like to have a look at the wounds.' Einar produced his own short, stubby blade from his belt and proceeded to cut away a section of the cloth. The skin underneath was pale and coarse with long, black hairs. 'Look,' Einar said.

Helga leaned closer. 'They're so . . .'

'Thin. Very thin cuts.'

'He won't have felt a thing.'

'Especially not after the third barrel.'

Helga's head spun. There was something here. *Something*— 'I know which blade made these cuts,' she said.

Einar frowned at her, looked at her face, searching for something that suggested her mood.

Blood thundered in Helga's ears and the words felt alien in her mouth. 'My mother's carving knife.'

Jorunn swung the hand-axe, split the log neatly in two and swept the pieces aside with a practised hand towards Sigmar, who stacked them into the rapidly filling woodshed. A swing, and the edge of the axe bit into the top of another log. They worked in rhythm, each confident in the other's movements.

'Did you do it?' Her voice was calm.

Sigmar chuckled. Then a moment later, he paused. 'What—? You're— *What*—?'

The axe swung down and the log split. The two halves tumbled towards Sigmar. 'Did you?'

Calmly placing the splintered logs on the pile, Sigmar paused before walking across to the splitting stump, narrowly dodging more flying wood. 'No,' he said. The axe was already airborne, and the log smacked into the stump by his knee. Sigmar didn't flinch.

'He was an arse,' Jorunn said.

'I know.'

'But he was still—' Before she could bury her axe in another log, Sigmar stepped in and held her tight. She struggled against the hold, but he didn't let her go.

'He was your brother,' Sigmar said, and the axe clattered to the ground. 'He was *family*.' Her eyes closed and her mouth twisted, but no tears followed. 'We will get to the bottom of this. Someone will crack. They always do.'

'I just thought – because I know what you used to—'

'That was another life, my love,' Sigmar said, his voice soothing.

'Another life, and another man. That being said, I held no great affection for your brother, but when have I ever done anything without your permission?'

Jorunn's mouth twisted again, this time into a small, reluctant smile. 'You're right, and only too right to remember it.' Her arms snaked out and met behind his back, returning the embrace. 'You know me well.'

'I do,' Sigmar said.

'So when I find out who did this, you'll be there to assist me and do what needs to be done.' Sigmar took a step back, released her and looked her straight in the eye. What she saw there made Jorunn smile. 'I married well,' she said, reaching for the axe.

'You are *not* saying that,' Einar said. He glanced again at Karl's body.

Helga swallowed. 'Of course not, you idiot. She told me yesterday that she couldn't find it. Sent me up to the new barn to look for it and everything.'

'So anyone could have walked past, picked it up and waited for the right moment.'

'Yes.'

'And all they needed was to be light on their feet and know where the veins lay.'

'Yes.'

'Which eliminates—'

'No one. Everyone. I don't know,' Helga said. 'I just don't know. They didn't use brute force. They moved unseen. Must have been one of the family because we would have heard the dogs.'

Einar shrugged. 'There's nothing here,' he said. 'I'll just—' He bent over, trying to shift Karl's body, and cursed. 'Heavy bastard,' he muttered.

'Get someone to help?'

'I don't know,' Einar said. 'They all got shipped out to do chores, quick as you like. Hildigunnur took Agla and Gytha down to the river, Bjorn walked his family up to the copse with axes and Aslak led Runa and the kids off to pick berries. Father went with Unnthor to mark the mound. I don't quite know how they are going to figure this all out.'

'That makes two of us,' Helga said.

The only sound in the little clearing was of steel biting into wood. Bjorn swung again, his reward a spray of splinters. On the other side, Thyri knelt by a fallen tree and busied herself stripping the branches. Volund, at her side, was doing his best to help.

'No,' she said under her breath, grabbing the boy's arms. 'Like this.'

Volund adjusted slowly, frowning. 'Here?' he said, scratching at the joint where the branch met the tree with his knife.

'Yes,' his mother said. 'Now pull the branch and saw at it.'

'But then it will break and come off.'

'That's what we want.'

Volund frowned. 'Oh,' he said, reluctantly slicing into the wood. Bjorn roared.

The sound bounced around the clearing and rose up, up above the branches, settling in the tree crowns as he spun, shifted the grip on the axe so that his big hand was just below the blade and stormed towards the fallen tree.

The colour drained out of Thyri's face as she saw her husband's fury. She raised her hands protectively above her head and cried, 'Bjorn – no! Please—!'

Three steps and the giant was towering over them. Volund stared up at him, lower lip quivering, mouth half open. 'Take the branch off. *Now*,' his father snarled, but the boy just stood there, staring, not understanding. In one swift motion Bjorn knelt down and swung, and the blade whistled towards Volund's head.

In an instant the branch was airborne, with only a straight line to mark where it had been connected to the tree.

'Next one,' Bjorn ordered.

Volund bent the next branch he could reach and started clumsily hacking at the join.

When she rose, Thyri was taller than her kneeling husband. She reached around and pulled his head in towards her breast, stroking his hair. 'I'm sorry he's gone,' she said softly. 'It is a sad thing.' Bjorn's muscular shoulders shifted, but she tightened her grip and shushed him. 'Just – let him go. We didn't kill him, and we'll find who did. Your mother's wisdom is deeper than the sea. She'll learn who took your brother, if she doesn't know already.'

Like a gentled bull, Bjorn snorted, a loud, wet sound. By his feet Volund had slowed down some, but he was still whittling away at the branch. 'We could leave him here and come pick him up in eighteen summers and he still wouldn't get it done,' he muttered. 'It took me months to teach him how to bleed a pig.'

Above his head, Thyri smiled. 'That just means he got my beauty and your brains,' she said.

'Hey!'

She bent down and kissed his brow. 'I jest, of course. He's not your son at all. I sat on a rock at the wrong time.'

Bjorn looked up at her. 'I married well,' he muttered.

Thyri smiled. 'And if you want to stay married, you'd better go and make some use of yourself.' She looked at the wounded tree. 'Your strong, hard-working son and I will be done with this one soon enough.'

As he rose, Thyri disappeared once again into his shadow. 'If the woman says so, then it is so,' he rumbled and set off, axe slung over the shoulder.

'I'll do it,' Helga said. 'I'll help you.'

Einar glanced at her. 'Sure?'

'Why not?' In fact, she didn't care. All she knew was that she needed to get out and she needed Karl's body to no longer be in her house.

'I'll get the shoulders,' he said, bending over Karl's body again, 'and you get the legs.'

She stretched over the dead man's feet, looked at the corpse and felt the stone at her chest heat up. There was something wrong ... something *missing* ...

'Are you going to help or not?'

Like a startled bird, the thought fluttered out of sight. Helga sighed and grabbed bony ankles, just past where the gushing blood had drawn a line on Karl's shin. The weight had to be all on Einar's side, but with the two of them lifting, the body started rising slowly out of the bunk.

'Got him?'

'I'm fine,' she said, but in truth, she was anything but fine. It wasn't the weight, that wasn't too bad, but the lack of heat in the body really bothered her. She'd carried an animal carcase or two in her time, but human legs were supposed to be *warm*, and these weren't.

'He feels like winter,' she murmured. 'I wonder how quickly we turn cold?'

'If you're just going to stand there and wonder you'll find out soon enough,' Einar said, huffing. 'He's a heavy bastard.'

They were halfway to the door when it opened and Hildigunnur entered. 'What are you doing?' Her voice was level, but taut.

Einar stopped in mid-step, awkwardly balancing the weight of Karl's upper body in his arms, and turned his head to Hildigunnur over his shoulder. 'We— I just— We—'

'We thought we should bring him out,' Helga supplied.

'Put him down,' Hildigunnur ordered.

Einar looked at Helga. 'You first,' he said, glancing at the ground, and once she'd lowered Karl's heels to the floor, Einar did the rest. Out of his bunk, the first son of Unnthor Reginsson looked smaller somehow – diminished, bereft of the tooth-gnashing fury that had fuelled him last night and all of his life.

Hildigunnur closed her eyes for a moment. 'A great wrong has been committed in my house,' she said. 'A great, great wrong.'

'Yes, Mother,' Helga said. 'And it's been done with your knife.'

Hildigunnur's eyes shot open. 'What did you say?' she snapped.

Recoiling from the venom in her eyes, Helga stuttered. 'It's – it's been done with your knife – the carving knife that Father keeps sharp for you.' She glanced down at the body. 'The cuts to the vein are so thin, you'd need a really sharp blade for it. He won't have felt a thing.'

The old woman took a deep breath, then exhaled slowly. Without speaking, she repeated the action. 'With my knife,' she said at last.

Helga nodded, and Einar did the same.

Hildigunnur looked like she wanted to say several things. 'Whoever did this,' she finally said, 'must have picked it off a table in here at least a day ago, because I haven't seen it since the first night.'

'Oh,' Helga said.

'Why "oh"?' Einar said.

'Because that means whoever did it planned to do it,' Helga said. 'And that's worse.'

Hildigunnur nodded.

'*Oh*,' Einar said.

'Carry him out into the yard,' Hildigunnur said. 'We'll cover him and take him out to the fields, dig him a cairn. It's the least we can do.'

'And then?' Helga said.

'Then we find whoever killed him,' Hildigunnur said. 'So we have to ask ourselves: many people had a reason – but who had the best one?'

*

Runa yanked on the branch of the bramble-bush until the berry came off, snorting in disgust as it squished in her hand.

'Maybe if you went a little bit more gently you could—' Aslak began, but Runa turned and glared at him: a look that could have cracked ice.

'Shut your hole,' she snapped.

'I was just—'

'I know what you were *just*. You have no idea—'

Aslak looked at her, smiling. 'I'll just be over here with my full basket of berries,' he said, sauntering away.

'Oh go hang!' Runa shouted after him. 'Is that what you count as an achievement? Picking fucking berries?'

Aslak stopped, calmly put down his basket and turned back to face her. Then he walked towards her, saying softly, 'No, but raising happy children who have a pissy mare for a mother? *That* is an achievement.'

Runa's jaw fell.

'Behaving towards you in the manner I choose, rather than in the manner you deserve? *That* is an achievement.'

She opened her mouth to speak, but Aslak's rising voice swallowed hers. 'Knowing that I could walk away any time and choosing not to? *That* is an achievement.'

He took half a step closer and firmly grabbed Runa's shift near the throat. Twisting it, pulling her face towards his, he said, 'Keeping this family *together* – with *you* in it – *that* is an achievement.'

She clawed at his hand but Aslak held firm, taking her by the wrist and pushing her hand away. 'You've always looked down on me,' he hissed, 'you've always thought you deserved something – some*one* – better. Well, I've grown tired of it.'

Wild-eyed, Aslak stared into Runa's narrowing eyes.

He never saw the fist.

Instead, his head jerked to the side and he let go of his wife's wrist, clutching his ear.

Runa rubbed at the reddening flesh on her arm. 'You pick a strange time to act like some kind of man, Aslak Unnthorsson,' she said, her mouth a thin line. 'And if you should ever think to dust off your manhood again, don't do it like that. Ever. Unless you want to wake up with your manhood in your mouth.' With that she turned and walked off towards the sounds of the children playing.

'When we wed I promised you that nothing would break our union,' Aslak said to her back. 'And now I've made sure of it.'

Runa slowed down by half a step as the words reached her, but then she hurried away.

'It'll all be better now,' Aslak said to the blackberry brambles. 'It'll all be better.'

When he looked up, Runa was gone.

The wood was rough under Helga's hands and her arms ached. She hadn't managed to find any comfortable way to get at the back of Karl's bed for a sustained assault on the blood-soaked boards and the stains were stubbornly resisting her best efforts. Still, the work was allowing her mind to wander.

When she imagined Karl, the first thing she saw was the anger: the fury of a rabid dog needing to bite something. Had he snapped at the wrong person? He'd bloodied Jorunn's nose – was that enough to murder someone for? He'd insulted Bjorn and threatened Sigmar. Then there was the way he'd looked at her. Even at the height of summer, even knowing he was gone, Helga felt a chill creep up her back and had to twist her shoulders to get her spine back into place. Had he looked like that at someone else? Someone's *wife*?

'They're coming back.' Einar's head disappeared as quickly as he'd popped it through the door to the longhouse.

'That's what got us into this mess in the first place,' she muttered. She leaned back and wrung her rag into the bucket. The drops were a fair few shades lighter now – they'd been dark red when she started, so that was progress, of a sort. Knees creaking, she rose and turned away.

The image crashed into her mind so hard that her knees buckled.

The pendant.

The bloody pendant.

When he was fighting with Bjorn, he'd tucked something in under his shirt. The light had caught on it when he was insisting on helping her put away the crockery. It was silver, a Hammer of Thor.

Helga staggered towards the door, suddenly struggling to breathe. This felt important.

Outside, the body lay in repose, now covered with one of Hildigunnur's cloths. The mastiff sat by his side, head hung low, looking miserable. Behind her, Helga could hear voices – Bjorn and Jorunn? – coming from the woodshed. She had to check, but quickly.

When she knelt by the body, the dog's head snapped up and it growled half-heartedly at her.

'*Ssh*,' she whispered. 'It's all right.' Quickly, she pulled the cloth away to reveal Karl's pale face, his neck – and nothing.

'What are you doing?' Hildigunnur was standing behind her.

Helga froze. 'I— *Um*—' She looked over her shoulder, narrowing her eyes to keep out the sun. 'I needed to check.'

'Why?'

'Because he had a pendant. And now it's not there.'

The sun at Hildigunnur's back turned her mother into a dark silhouette. 'I see.' Then, 'Get up, *quick*. They're coming.'

Helga rose, feeling uneasy. Had she discovered something important? Had she done something wrong? But her mother gave nothing away, communicated nothing. *How does she even feel about this?* Helga realised that she didn't know. Her mother had been shocked, then angry . . . but why? At the moment she thought it just as likely that Hildigunnur was angry at Karl for having the gall to die on the farm without permission. Looking out past the gate, she saw Aslak and Runa approaching. Even from a hundred yards away, she could see that whatever was between them was even worse than it had been.

'You could break rocks with those shoulders, they're set so hard,' her mother muttered under her breath as she glanced Runa's way.

Helga had to stifle a laugh that was part amusement at the precision of the observation and part relief that her mother was her old self again. 'How's Agla?'

'She was always fragile, but I think she'll recover.' Hildigunnur said no more, for Aslak and Runa were nearly within hearing range.

They joined them in a circle around the body, and the silence grew with each new member of the family, like snow on a roof, until Helga felt her chest squeezing. Nobody said anything; nobody looked anywhere but at the ground.

Only when they were all gathered did Unnthor appear, with Jaki and Einar at either side.

'We have marked out the site,' he growled. 'The necessary preparations have been made. The gods are not pleased about this.'

The gods are rarely pleased about anything, Helga thought, but she kept that to herself. Unnthor turned and stalked away, and like a flock of sheep they followed. No one talked, no one looked at anything but the broad back of the Farmer at Riverside. Without words, Jaki and Einar broke away and walked towards the shed to collect shovels and picks. A quick barked command and Bjorn swung by the woodshed, returning with an armful of lumber.

Helga found herself walking next to Gytha. Her face was still pale, and she looked tired and worn. A moment of doubt – of fear, even – then Hildigunnur's voice echoed in her head: *Don't be stupid, girl. You know what to do.* She reached out and put her arm around Gytha's slim shoulders. A captive breath escaped the girl's throat in a sob, then she was shuddering and clinging to Helga, holding her shirt in a death-grip. They walked awkwardly together at the back of the line of people, Helga muttering soothing words to the shaking girl. She looked at the backs of her family, heads bowed, all shuffling to the grave-site like lambs to slaughter. Almost without thinking, she touched the rune on the thong around her neck.

Images flashed before her eyes: the twinkling smile of the old man in the field. His whispered words, his voice stronger than his age suggested. *The rune of Nauth*, the wind hissed at her. *It will tell you about the wants, wishes and needs that flow in you all.*

'Worth a try,' Helga muttered.

'What?' Gytha sounded like someone half asleep.

'Nothing,' Helga said, 'nothing at all. Look,' she added, pointing ahead. 'We're nearly there.'

Chapter 11

GUILTY

Helga sat in the midst of her extended family, but she felt utterly alone. Around her, shovels cut rhythmically into the ground, slicing the turf – *like a blade through skin*. She took a deep breath and tried to remember how the smell of grass used to make her happy. She wanted to let her mind drift, lulled by the repetitive motions, but in the company of her family it was proving hard. To her left Bjorn was working at a steady pace, shoulders rising and falling with shovel-strokes that could easily lop the head off a man, shifting heaps of soil up onto the bank, out of the growing shape of the longship. Sitting by the side, Runa and Thyri busied themselves weaving bark into panels and shapes to furnish the grave. The whole family was working around her to create Karl's final resting place. Whenever a task finished, Hildigunnur was there to snap out new orders. She never raised her voice, but there was not a moment's respite anywhere.

'Get to it, Helga. Come on.'

She blinked at her mother's voice and resumed spinning the ropes. They felt rough in her hands. Helga imagined what they would look like lashed around bent and curved branches, holding together a cage clad with bark to form a shell just like Hildigunnur had described. She pictured it, upside down over Karl's body as it lay on the deck of the boat, protecting him from the soil raining down from above, getting him ready to sail to the world of the dead. As he hadn't died in battle he wouldn't go to Valhalla, but Unnthor had decided that his son should be buried like a rich man and a landowner, in the field of prayer, within sight of the stone table and the oak, so that was that. Helga stole a glance over at them and shuddered. She had only seen her father preside over a handful of ceremonies, but even he looked oddly powerless and *human* standing next to the stone and the oak. Even now, on a pleasant summer afternoon, they radiated menace like ill-tempered bulls.

The gods don't care about us. Looking at the tree, she was filled with a terrifying certainty. *We are summer breeze and sunlight. They are the tree and the stone.*

The hole was deep enough to reach up to the middle of Bjorn's thigh. Behind him Aslak was compressing the sides with a broad plank, strengthening the inner walls so they would withstand the waves of seas beyond this world.

The hole was taking shape and finding form before her eyes, thanks to Bjorn's work and Aslak's hands. As the woven panels of bark were finished, Jorunn jumped down into the grave and laid them out in the unmistakable shape of a longship. Above them all stood Unnthor, now a silent taskmaster, hand on the haft of his axe. He stared at them, unmoving and unblinking, daring any one of them to shirk their duties.

No one did.

When the sun started descending towards the horizon, the ship was ready.

It was time to lay Karl to rest.

Hildigunnur gestured silently to Bjorn and Sigmar and as the rest of the family stood looking down at their handiwork, the two men took hold of the blanket under Karl's body and hoisted him up before walking towards the stern of the ship, where the hole was shallowest. They walked carefully along to the middle of the grave before lowering the body gently down onto the bark in the bottom of the ship.

Gytha was standing silently beside Helga as her father's body was carefully laid out – then she caught a breath in her throat, as if trying to muffle her grief. As she started sobbing, Helga awkwardly embraced the shaking girl, and was rewarded with a bone-cracking hug.

Unnthor stepped down into the ship and stood by Karl's head. 'The gods will see my son for what he was,' he rumbled, and the world fell still around them. These were the words that should be spoken, and it was important that they be spoken right. Helga didn't quite know how they'd sound if they were spoken wrong – she had always believed her father. Looking down at the man by their feet, though . . .

'Karl was a Viking, true to his land and true to his gods. He roamed, he fought and he bent the knee to no man.' Clenched fists and pursed lips all round. Bjorn's massive chest rose and fell like that of an overworked horse. 'There were few who would wish to face him when he was awake and aware. My son died a warrior; whoever killed him lives an honourless coward.'

And stands by his grave, looking down on him, Helga thought. *You need some serious balls to do that.* She stole a glance round: Bjorn, Sigmar and Aslak were all stony-faced. Agla stood by Hildigunnur, chin tilted upwards, lips pursed, looking like a stone sculpture. Thyri stood by her gigantic husband, hand on his arm, glancing at his face, fear in her eyes. *What is she afraid of?* Helga had to work to keep the frown off her face. Runa was staring intently at Jorunn, looking like she was trying to draw her eye with will-power alone. *She's moved further away from Aslak,* she noted. *Why? What's happened between them?*

Strange.

'My son shall take with him the means to pay his way, wherever he's going,' Unnthor said. From the folds of his tunic he produced a pouch about the size of his fist and threw it down into the grave. It landed with a dull clink. It was quick, the glance that passed between Sigmar and Jorunn, but Helga saw it. 'And he shall take with him the means to defend himself,' Unnthor continued, and Karl's axe followed suit. 'And he shall take with him the means to travel where he needs.'

A horse whinnied behind them. Karl's mare was reluctant to go down, but she was well-trained, and Einar led her into the longboat, whispering calming words in her ear as he lined her up alongside to Karl, and—

—it happened so fast that Helga almost missed it.

Unnthor's arm moved, and suddenly the knife was in his hand, blade facing away. The swing connected with the back of the mare's head with a dull *clonk*, and the horse keeled over. Einar strained, yanking the reins until the mare that Karl had so prized was lying next to him. They looked peaceful together, almost like they were asleep.

'And he shall bring with him a faithful companion,' Unnthor said.

Jaki followed his son down into the ship, leading Karl's mastiff by the leash.

Helga tasted vomit in her mouth, and looked away. She knew what needed to happen, but that didn't mean she had to like it. There was a sound like someone stepping on a twig, and when she opened her eyes the dog was lying on Karl's other side, head twisted at an unnatural angle.

Unnthor nodded to Jaki and Sigmar, who pushed themselves up onto the bank and picked up the wooden structure they had built to house Karl on the next leg of his journey. They placed the shell over the bodies of man, horse and hound, then walked up out of the ship.

'Get going,' Hildigunnur said. 'Shovels, but careful.'

As one, the family got to work. The soil piled on the banks of the hole went back down, first sprinkled on top of the wooden structure, until slowly, the bark panels disappeared from sight, sinking under the still waves of the earth. Then, gently, the wooden struts were covered, leaving a hump above the ground.

By the time the last shovelful and the last handful of soil fell on Karl's burial mound, the sun was half gone.

They all knew it was finished. Gytha and her mother had no more tears to cry; Unnthor had no more words to say.

'Home and food,' Hildigunnur said pragmatically. 'I'm not digging holes for you lot as well.'

As soon as her mother's lips started moving, Helga's feet did too: she needed to be in the right place at the right time. Sure enough, Hildigunnur charged ahead, her stride determined, and Helga fell in beside her mother.

'Before you say anything,' Hildigunnur said without looking at her, 'you're helping me with the pots.'

A half-strangled laugh escaped Helga's lips. 'I should think so,' she said. 'I don't think I can outrun you yet.'

Half a step ahead, Hildigunnur's face was almost hidden, but there was the hint of a smile. 'You make an old woman happy, Daughter,' she said. 'Well, as happy as one can be on a day like this.'

'Let's hope Karl is happy fighting whatever he'll meet in the afterlife,' Helga said.

'He'll come back to haunt us,' Hildigunnur said, 'mostly because he'll annoy everyone wherever he goes and get kicked out.'

Now it was Helga's turn to smile. *Now. It had to be now.* 'I was wondering, though – should there not be runes? To guide his way?'

Hildigunnur glanced at her. 'What do you know about runes?'

'Nothing,' Helga said quickly, then corrected herself. 'Well, I mean, I've heard stories . . . aren't they magical?'

Hildigunnur snorted. 'About as magical as my arse. Scratch a bit of wood and see what happens.'

'Why – what can happen?'

'If you scratch the right pattern and you know what you want, something might,' Hildigunnur conceded. Then she smirked. 'Maybe a big bull of a man might come to your house, hit your father with a thighbone and sweep you away to a life of joyous rutting and troublesome children.'

'Mother!' Helga exclaimed, to chuckles from the older woman. 'Are you saying you bewitched ... ?' She gazed at her father striding along behind them, then Hildigunnur shot her a look back that very clearly said *I'm not telling*. There was a glint in her eye, but Helga couldn't help but notice that her mouth was set in a serious line.

Back at the longhouse, an uneasy silence settled, only occasionally punctured by a muttered request or the sound of blade on wood from the corner where Hildigunnur and Thyri were manning the pots. Helga tried her best to keep up, but the two women worked with almost impossible speed, and no matter how fast she peeled roots and passed along chunks of meat, there were always hands waiting to grab from her.

'Go and get firewood,' Thyri finally snapped. 'You're slowing us down.'

Hildigunnur said nothing.

Stung, Helga made her way out past Sigmar, who was sitting next to Unnthor and speaking in hushed tones. Volund was sitting by himself, his back to the wall and his hands in his lap, looking unhappy as he glanced aimlessly around the room. The only ones not affected by the mood were Sigrun and Bragi, who were playing some complex game in the corner involving three bones and a stick.

When she opened the side door the evening breeze welcomed her, caressing her cheek and drawing her outside. She thought of the angry people inside the longhouse. *It feels good to have a closed door between us.* The sky stretched above her, honeyed gold in the west, purple up above and black all the way to where the gods lived. *If I were a bird,* Helga thought, *I would be up there now, flying through the colours, fast and far, to foreign lands.* 'And getting no firewood at all,' she added.

'I'll help.'

She couldn't help it – the yelp, high-pitched and girly, escaped before she could stop it. 'Aslak! What are you doing out here?' she said, sharper than she'd intended.

The youngest of Unnthor's children looked back at her from his place in the shadows, just an outline against the deep blackness. 'I just . . . needed to step outside for a little bit. It's like a load off the chest, it really is.' He stepped forward and the moonlight caught on his cheekbones. *His eyes are so big,* Helga thought, and something changed inside her. Away from his brothers, alone and outside, Aslak looked . . . *different.* Thinner. Haunted, somehow. Like she'd always imagined Loki from the tales.

'Uhm . . . thank you,' she said, flustered, and annoyed at herself for being so. 'Help – yes, please. You know how she gets.'

'Oh, I do,' Aslak said, a small smile on his lips. He moved towards her – and Helga's heart didn't beat again until he was past and walking towards the woodshed. *What's wrong with you, girl? Get moving!*

She hurried on after Aslak, trying to push the sad, beautiful face in the moonlight out of her mind.

When they got back, the table was set and everyone was seated. Eyes kept going to Karl's place like a tongue to a tooth gap, but no one said anything. Helga half expected Runa to be shooting hateful glances in her direction, but she was curiously preoccupied, unable to take her eyes off Jorunn.

'. . . play,' Volund was muttering sullenly, down at the other end of the table.

'No, you'll eat first,' Thyri said firmly.

The spoon slammed into the bowl and a large chunk of turnip rose to meet Volund's mouth, disappearing in one gulp. Moments later, sounds of pain followed as the boy tried to eat and keep the boiling bit of vegetable out of his throat at the same time. '*Nngh!*' he managed at last, spitting the mouthful back into the bowl.

Bjorn turned and glared at his wife. 'Send the boy to his corner,' he said.

'He should eat, otherwise—'

'He's not going to eat,' Bjorn said wearily. 'And no one wants to see that. He eats like a pig.'

Helga glanced at Volund, but he hadn't appeared to notice his father's insult. Thyri thought better of protesting and waved the boy off to play. He shuffled back to his area, knelt down and stuck his head under the bed. Helga caught Bjorn glancing after him, a tired, pained expression on his face.

'On the way here, we heard stories,' Sigmar started.

Jorunn's mouth pursed in response. 'Sigmar, don't.'

'What? We should tell them.'

'Tell us *what*?' Unnthor growled from the top of the table. Unsettled by the menace in their grandfather's voice, Bragi and Sigrun hurried away from the dinner table and their mother's knee as quickly as their six-year-old legs could take them.

'We heard stories that Karl owed money,' Jorunn forced out between gritted teeth. 'A lot of money. Enough to send someone after him.' She looked at her father. 'Someone skilled.'

'A good piece of meat thrown to the dogs would have put them off the scent,' Sigmar added.

'And why didn't you tell us in the morning?'

Jorunn looked at her father and spoke gently. 'Because it would have made us sound very guilty indeed. If whoever he owed money to cared enough to send someone to walk the night, we would never have caught him anyway.'

Unnthor scowled, but didn't speak.

'And how reliable is this news?' Hildigunnur said.

'Oh, very,' Sigmar said. 'We buy and sell. People fall over themselves to tell us true, in order to keep us coming back.'

Unnthor glared at him, then at the others around the table. After some moments, he said slowly, 'It is possible, I suppose. There have been—'

The wail of pain came almost immediately after the fleshy thump, followed by a scream of rage and a small voice shouting '*Mu–u–u–u–u–um!*'

Every head at the table turned as one to see Bragi lying on the floor, sobbing, and his sister running back towards Runa. Volund, standing over the fallen boy, clenched his fist around something.

Instead of words, a loud keening rose in his throat, like the sound of an oak splitting.

Thyri was up immediately and charging at him. 'Volund—! What are you doing?'

The boy turned to see his mother approaching; a meaty arm shot out and he shoved her away, sending her spinning. With a shout, Bjorn was up and at the boy, but as he grabbed Volund's arm, he started struggling against his father and screaming at the top of his voice, 'Mine! *Mine!*' over and over again.

'I only wanted to see it,' Bragi cried, holding on to his mother's skirt. 'And he's a *meanie!* He *hit* me!'

'I know, sweetling,' Runa said, soothing the child. 'We'll have a talk about that later, shall we?'

'Get him out! *Now!*' Hildigunnur shouted over the din, and Bjorn shot her a glare.

The boy was deep in the throes of a tantrum, keening and thrashing about in his father's arms, until, grunting with frustration, Bjorn drove an elbow into his son's sternum, causing Volund to double over, winded and gasping in pain.

The light caught on something silver in his palm.

'*MURDERER!*' Agla's scream was easily as loud and far more piercing than Volund's.

When Helga turned to look at the woman, she struggled to recognise her for a moment: her face was crimson with fury, her eyes wide open and nostrils flaring. She looked like something come from Trollheim. A bony finger was extended as far as it would go, pointing at Volund in his father's arms.

'*MURDERER!*' she screeched again, and Gytha rose, her own eyes narrowed.

Dangling from the boy's hand was Karl's amulet: the silver Hammer of Thor.

'Give me that!' Gytha said, darting forward.

'MINE!' Volund bellowed again, snatching back his hand. Gytha dived for the dangling pendant and received a knee in the gut for her trouble.

Bjorn yanked Volund off his feet and walked backwards, half dragging the howling, flailing boy towards the door. 'Mine!' he cried out again in despair, '*mine!*' as Bjorn elbowed the door open and pushed him outside.

The moment the door closed, Agla rounded on Thyri. 'YOU!' she screamed, 'you owe us wergild for your idiot son! He *murdered* my husband!'

'Shut up, you horse-faced shrew,' Thyri spat, not backing down, even in the face of Agla's rage. 'You have *no idea* what you're talking about. Volund couldn't kill anything – he can't even hold a knife properly!'

'He did it! *He did it!*' Gytha was as shrill and furious as her mother.

Helga watched as another conversation took place across the table, silent but sharp. Runa kept staring at Jorunn, imploring her, asking for *something* – attention? But with no luck.

'Hildigunnur!' Agla implored, 'you saw the boy – he has a fury in him! He's *dangerous!*' Her face was drawn, twisted in pain.

'We will not decide on guilt under my roof until we are convinced.' Hildigunnur's voice could have frozen a lake. 'I saw no knife. I saw no blood. The boy could have found the amulet on the ground. And ask yourself – could he have *planned* a murder? He may be harmless, as his mother says.' She glanced at Thyri and nudged her head towards the door, as good as a command: *go and see to your family.*

A memory flashed before Helga's eyes: Volund, holding an axe, looking very like his father.

I'd break your head open.

Unable to harm? Bjorn had struggled to contain his son's wild strength. Unwilling, yes – but *unable*?

Agla sat back down, but she was still looking like a wolf about to pounce. After a moment's stillness, she asked, 'How do you *know*, Thyri? How do you *know*?'

Halfway to the door, Thyri stopped. She turned and looked straight at Agla. 'I am his mother,' she said. 'And he isn't easy, or perfect, but he is my son.' She didn't raise her voice, but her words fell heavy. 'My husband told me that this' – she gestured to the silent guests, seated around the table, then swept her hand towards the rafters – 'is family, and that family is the most important thing.'

It looked as if she was about to say something more, but she stopped herself.

As she turned back towards the door, it opened and Bjorn came back in with Volund in tow.

Agla opened her mouth to speak, but a sharp glance from Hildigunnur silenced her.

'He is calm now,' Bjorn said. 'And I know what you're thinking, Agla. You think he did it. But I can promise you' – he looked straight at her – 'my son is no killer. He must have found the necklace.'

'How can you know that?' Gytha snapped.

Bjorn's voice didn't rise, didn't change. He sounded tired and sad, Helga thought. 'Because the cuts were neat, precisely placed. They were done by someone who knows well how to handle a knife.' He rubbed his left arm and winced, before continuing, his voice patient, calming, 'And my boy is strong, make no mistake, but if he'd done it there would be very little left of my brother to recognise. He can just about work out which end of a knife to hold, but only if you show him every time.'

Curiously, Agla seemed to see something in this. 'He *might* have found it,' she muttered. '*Maybe.*' She sat down again, but once more she was eyeing *everyone* with suspicion until the strength of Hildigunnur's gaze pulled her back in. The old woman smiled tenderly at the widow, and Agla looked down, sniffling loudly.

'I know it's early,' Hildigunnur said, 'but I think it's time to get some rest. We all need to sleep on this.'

'Wise words, Mother,' Bjorn rumbled.

Unnthor rose without a word, still looking like something carved out of an angry mountain, and glared at the assembled family, which started off a chain of rising and shuffling as they all obeyed. Helga noticed movement towards her left: Runa had somehow managed to inch towards Jorunn, and the look on her face was unlike anything Helga had seen before. Discomfort? Begging? . . . Fear? Curiosity made her inch towards Aslak's wife.

'Can I have a word, Sister?' Runa said.

Jorunn looked at her. 'Why?'

'I— I—'

'We should be going to bed, my lovely wife,' Aslak said, swooping up behind her. Helga watched Runa freeze and fall silent. 'I don't think my sister wants to chat,' he added calmly.

Jorunn looked at him with a mixture of curiosity and annoyance. 'Whatever you say, Brother dear.' Aslak shot her a smile as he reached over, grabbed Runa by the elbow and started steering her towards their corner of the longhouse.

Helga looked around. Sigmar and Jorunn were already in their bunk. She could just about make out the shapes of Agla and Gytha, who had moved from the bed where Karl had died and were busy piling hay and blankets near the fire. Runa was lavishing an unusual amount of attention on her children. At the far end of the hall, Hildigunnur had pulled Unnthor, Jaki and Einar into a tight huddle for a hushed conversation.

None of this mattered to her, though; something else was bugging her, niggling at her, something that didn't fit.

She touched the leather thong around her neck, running her fingers along the rough material to the central stone, tracing the contours of the rune under her thumb. Half-remembered words skittered away from her glare.

Scratch a bit of wood and see what happens.

It was worth a try.

Helga waited and listened and waited some more until she was sure time had stopped and the sun would never rise again – but then she felt it: a particular silence in the longhouse, the almost imperceptible sound of steady breathing. She inched towards the edge of her bed. *I'm sleepy*, she said, not believing it for a second. *I've just woken up – No, I can't sleep.* She repeated it in her mind until the lie fit her face. Then she stretched her leg until she could feel the floor and levered herself up as quietly as she could.

A soft light fell from the candles that had been hoisted up towards the beams. Einar sat by the door, looking mortally bored. He waved silently at her. *Good.* Taking care to sleep-shuffle towards his seat, she waved back. As she moved past the table she grabbed a jug of water.

'Hey,' he whispered.

'Hey yourself,' she whispered back, taking up position beside him. 'Want some water?' He took the jug off her and took a deep gulp, then another.

'It's thirsty work, catching murderers.'

This far away from the candles, it was hard to see his face. His nose and mouth made an outline against the soft glow, but his eyes were dark. He must have heard the teasing note in her voice, but even in the half-light she could feel him glaring at her. 'Shut up. I'm bored, but I have to do this – probably so Hildigunnur can sleep. I think she's really scared.'

Helga scoffed, 'Her? Here? No – no way. She's *never* scared.'

'Maybe not. But I still have to stay awake half the night.'

'Maybe that isn't so bad, though.'

'What do you mean?'

'I wouldn't mind being awake when none of them are around,' she said, forcing a little smile into her voice.

'You're not wrong there,' Einar said, sighing.

Now. Had to be now.

'You still feel for her, don't you?'

There was a sharp intake of breath in the darkness. When he spoke again, his voice was colder. 'What are you on about?'

She reached out and touched his arm and it felt like he was fighting not to flinch away. 'I've seen you looking at her,' she whispered.

'And? It's a small house. Hard to look anywhere else.'

'How long has she owned your heart?'

A pause. Then, softer, 'Years. Since I was a boy.' Helga had been watching Hildigunnur tease the truth out of people for a long time now. It didn't matter how upset or angry they were, if there was something in there that wanted out, it could rarely resist filling a silence. Sure enough, Einar continued, 'She was always kind to me. She'd stop Karl and Bjorn from beating me too badly when we were kids. Then I started seeing her . . . differently.'

Helga bit the cheek that faced away from Einar and swallowed all the things she wanted to say. Instead, she held his arm firmly. 'And then?'

'She grew, faster than I did – and now she is a successful woman who is earning her reputation and married to a spineless, ridiculous, weak-wristed Swede.'

Helga thought about what she'd seen of Sigmar and had to admit that she didn't quite agree with Einar's assessment. But apparently the heart sometimes saw what the eyes didn't, so she decided to go with it.

'Why spineless?' she asked.

'Because he should have fought for her when Karl . . .' Einar's voice trailed off. When he started again, the passion was gone and the wall was back up. 'He doesn't seem to be a man with honour or respect.'

Acting on impulse, Helga reached out and embraced her half-yet-quite-not older brother. *There will be words later*, she thought. *Now, there's this.* The body next to her felt stiff, hardened by farmwork and made inflexible by anger and reserve, but she held on and eventually Einar loosened around the edges, softening into her arms, hugging her back.

'Thank you,' he whispered after a while.

'You're an idiot,' she whispered back. 'But you're my idiot, and that counts for something. If you want to go out and get some air, I'll watch over the sleeping wolves for a bit.'

Einar rose silently, reached out and squeezed her shoulder, then disappeared out through the door like a shadow.

The moment the door closed behind him, Helga sprang into action. *No time to waste.* She looked around, scanning the workbenches. *Nothing.* Tables. *Nothing.* Her heart thudding in her chest, she waited for either of the old men to wake up. *THERE!* The knife lay tucked under Einar's blanket: a short, stubby utility blade. It wasn't ideal, but it'd have to do. She leaned over and picked it up, momentarily transfixed by the way the metal caught the light, until a voice a lot like Hildigunnur's shook her out of her state: *And if they find you in the night, holding a blade? What then?*

Blushing, Helga rose and palmed the blade, taking care not to step on or bump into anything that might make a noise, moving at a slow but regular pace. If someone challenged her, she'd simply say she was going back to her bed, that Einar would be along shortly.

There.

Runa's bunk.

Kneeling, she felt for her rune-stone with trembling fingers. She could trace the shape of the rune with her fingertips, just like she could smell the sleeping woman's breath, maybe five inches away from her. She pulled out the blade and—

'Mummy?' A voice softened by sleep-fog.

Helga held her breath and tried to shrink into nothing. The body just by her shifted with the slowness of the near-unconscious. There was a muttered sentence, couched in a melody of some sort.

Einar will be coming back any moment now. And he'll find me lying on the floor by the bed of Aslak's wife, holding a blade. Someone may wake – how do I explain this away? I am the only one here who is not connected by blood or marriage.

Her thoughts raced ahead to Agla screaming at her; Hildigunnur, spitting in her face; Unnthor, her adoptive father looking saddened, wielding his giant axe over her neck.

People breathe differently when they're asleep.

The thought struck her just before she realised that the only sounds from the bed just above her were those of rhythmic breathing.

Quick as she could, she traced a very gentle line straight down, no longer than her thumb, then another diagonally from left to right across the centre. The rune of Nauth. *Wants, wishes and needs. It'll look like a scratch. Just a scratch! No time to think. Move!* Forcing herself to move slowly and carefully, she pushed herself to her feet and walked at a torturous, measured pace across the room, making sure to put the knife exactly where she'd found it.

She drew breath three times in Einar's chair before the front door opened again and he slunk in, silent and light on his feet.

'Anyone stir?' he whispered.

'No,' Helga said, 'nothing happened.' She was glad he couldn't see her face. The smell of warm bodies, sleep and Runa's breath still lingered in her nostrils. 'Nothing at all.'

Chapter 12

FIGHT

Helga blinked.

'Wake up, girl,' Hildigunnur repeated, 'you're sleeping the day away.'

Helga blinked again. The longhouse was just a shade less than night-time dark, but Hildigunnur was standing by her bed, fully dressed. 'We've got work to do.'

She knew better than to argue. 'I'll be right up,' she said in her head, listening to her mouth as it made some noise that sounded like *hwl b r'umph*. Moments later she felt the rough packed earth under her feet. Around them, the family slept still. *Like wolves in a den*. The thought was there, then gone.

'Come on now.'

'What are we doing?'

'New barn. We need to make sure we're ready for winter.'

'But I already—'

Hildigunnur's glare stopped Helga in her tracks. She started to mutter an apology, but decided silence would be smarter.

The air outside was cool and fresh on her skin. The familiar song of the river calmed her as she followed her mother on a brisk walk up the hill, away from Riverside. As the forest enveloped them, she felt herself gradually waking up. *Who did it?* The question sat there, a squat and ugly thing, a rat in the middle of the road glaring smugly at her. The smell of pine tickled her nose and she could almost taste the raw morning air. The sun would not creep up over the horizon for a while yet, and the breeze on her cheek stayed refreshingly cold.

Who, though?

Faces crowded in on her, followed by snippets of people shouting at each other and sentences half-snatched from memory. A snap of annoyance jolted her brain. *This needs to be tidied up.* In her mind, Helga imagined a jumbled storeroom with things scattered all over the floor and empty shelves on the wall. She quickly scratched lines on the shelves – one line for Gytha, two lines for Jorunn and three lines . . . Aslak. *No reason*, she told herself. *No particular reason at all.* She bent down and picked a dress up off the floor. A beautiful piece of craftsmanship, must have cost a small fortune. Folding it carefully, she placed it on Gytha's shelf. Wants to go to court; can't go. Overbearing, controlling father. *Does cruelty pass through the blood?* She thought of Unnthor's face, creased with rage, and shuddered. Add to that whatever Karl might have done while raiding . . . She thought of Gytha's face as she stormed out from the longhouse, mocked by her father and uncle, murder in her eyes.

Then she glanced down at the floor of her imaginary storeroom. At her feet lay a brown rag, stained with dark red dots. She felt the rough texture with her thumb, then lifted it to her nose. Blood: dots of blood, some large, some small. She rolled the rag up and placed it gently on Jorunn's shelf. Eldest brother: absolute bastard. Insults her, challenges her husband, elbows her in the face. What would that be like? Enough to cut him with a well-placed insult or two – possibly even to put enough rotten berries in his porridge to send his stomach into a twist – but to *kill*? The smile on Jorunn's lips as she waited for her brothers at the finishing line came back to Helga. Karl had been ahead of her for inheritance, and Jorunn Unnthorsdottir did not like to lose.

Behind her, the storeroom door creaked and Helga's heart beat faster. She could smell him, feel the heat of him behind her. *And what about me?* Aslak whispered in her ear. *Do I go on the shelf?*

Yes, she whispered. *You've been acting strange around your wife. Something happened, and now you're being different.*

The imaginary brother sauntered past her, turned and leaned against the shelf. *Am I?*

The light warped around him, casting his face half in shadow and carving his fine features more deeply. She wondered how she hadn't seen it before: underneath the beautiful skin, the youngest brother was an intriguing mix of his mother's edge and his father's fury. Helga's eye twitched, she sneezed, and the flash of embarrassment was enough to break the spell. The storeroom faded, taking the imaginary Aslak with it. The packed earth under her feet remained the same, though—

Barn. She was in the new barn.

'—and we need to turn the new hay as well, so it dries out properly,' Hildigunnur finished. Turning, she cast a critical look at Helga and her eyes narrowed. 'What did I just say?'

'The new hay,' Helga said as confidently as she could. 'We need to turn it.' She threw in a sage, agreeing nod for good measure.

Hildigunnur was not fooled for an instant. 'And what do we need to do before we turn the hay, my darling daughter?' She smiled like a wolf might.

'Um . . .' No further words came to her rescue.

'You were miles away,' Hildigunnur said. 'What's on your mind?'

'I don't know,' Helga said, registering her shock at the speed of her lie. 'The . . . what happened to Karl, I guess.'

A moment's pause. 'You are allowed to be afraid,' Hildigunnur said, her voice soft. 'Just because I'm an old witch and her brothers beat it out of Jorunn a long time ago, doesn't mean you have to hide your fear. In fact, it should tell you that you are smart. Not that you needed telling, mind.'

'Thank you,' Helga mumbled, looking at her feet to hide the panic in her eyes. 'I did need to hear that.'

The next thing she felt was a dry, warm fingertip gently touching her chin and raising her head. Even though she was a good half a hand taller than her mother, Helga still felt small in front of her.

Hard blue eyes surrounded by laughter wrinkles stared straight at her. 'You're safe here, my girl. I promise you.'

Despite herself, despite lying to her mother's face, Helga felt a wash of relief. She *had* been scared, even if she had tried to avoid admitting it to herself, and all too aware that she was sleeping under the same roof as a murderer. And even though her mother couldn't make that promise in any sort of faith because she couldn't know whose hand had wielded the knife, Helga did suddenly feel a lot safer. It was really easy to do what her mother told her, and if the order was not to worry, then that was what she would do. She reminded herself to figure out later – after the new hay had been turned – why she hadn't wanted to share her thoughts.

The summer breeze set the grass to swishing at Sigmar's feet. Up here it grew longer and thinner, but come the depths of winter the animals wouldn't care too much where their feed was from. They'd care greatly, however, if it wasn't there. He swept the scythe in smooth, even strokes, watching as the long stalks fell to the ground with a quiet whisper. Walking slowly about ten steps behind him, Jorunn busied herself stuffing the fourth sack of the morning. Even though they were a good quarter of a day's walk away from the farm, he still scouted around quickly before he spoke. 'Who do you think did it?'

The set of Jorunn's shoulders changed ever so slightly, but the answer took a while. 'Does it matter?' she said finally.

'To us?' The scythe started moving again, swishing through the green. 'Probably not. We've marked our course—'

'—and we're not changing it.' Jorunn's voice was firm. 'We proceed as we planned.'

Sigmar smiled as he swept the blade across the grass, watching as the green yielded before him. 'As you wish, Wife.'

'Shut up and keep working,' came the reply behind him, but there was a smile in the voice. 'Wielding a scythe does wonderful things for your arse.'

The rays of the morning sun caught on the thin, sharp blade sweeping rhythmically through the stalks.

'Can you see them up there?' Einar peered through the trees as he knelt by the post, holding on to the base.

'Who?' his father grunted, hefting the sledgehammer.

'Jorunn and Sigmar. Where did they go?'

'Hold it steady. Unnthor sent them' – *Grunt. Heave. Sound of wood smashing down on wood* – 'to make hay up by the ridge.'

'Huh.' Einar moved over to the next fence post. A line of them, evenly spaced, stretched back at least a quarter of a mile. 'Not much to be had up there, though.'

'There's enough,' Jaki said. 'Steady, now.' Einar lifted the post and placed the point in the ground just as the sledgehammer rose and fell. 'And you should keep your mind on the work,' he added. 'Don't you be worrying about where the family may or may not be going, or what they'll do when they get there. Mind where the hammer goes.'

Einar grunted again, kneeling in the soft grass. 'I don't care what they do,' he said, lifting the fence post and placing it point-down.

'Good,' his father replied. 'Not yours to worry about. Unnthor needs our help. Steady, now.' The sledgehammer smashed into the fence post and sent it spinning out of Einar's hands, smashing into his side as it fell.

'Ow! What did you do that for?' He jumped to his feet and glared at his father.

'I did nothing,' Jaki growled. '*You* weren't watching what you were doing. There's a stone in the ground and you put the point right on it. If you'd been paying any sort of attention to your work you'd have felt it.'

'Do you want to hold the next one, then?'

'Go home, boy,' Jaki said. 'Go and whittle or something. Carve out a love poem. You're no use to me.'

Einar scowled. 'But you'll be slow without me.'

'I've put up a fence or two before your time.'

'Fine,' Einar said. 'I'll go and fix some of the tools you old farts keep breaking.' But his father had already turned his back on him and gone to wedge the fence post in the ground. 'Stubborn old bull,' Einar muttered under his breath, only just resisting the urge to kick one of the newly erected posts on his way back to the farm. He glared towards the hill. 'Fucking stupid, going up there to cut hay.' He snorted. 'Maybe she went with him to make sure he didn't get carried away with the sheep.'

He marched along the row of fence posts, shoulders hunched and hands knotted into fists. He didn't notice the shape in the distance until the distance wasn't all that much. 'Oh, the gods are cruel!' he swore. 'What did I do to deserve *this*?'

There was nowhere to hide.

When Gytha looked up, she didn't wave or react in any way; she simply stopped and waited. There was no way around her.

'Morning.'

'And to you,' Einar replied. 'Where are you going?'

'Somewhere else.'

'Fair enough,' Einar said.

'And you?'

'Father sent me away. He can be a grumpy old, uh . . .' Einar's voice trailed off and he swallowed. 'Sorry. I didn't—'

Gytha raised her hand, palm up. 'Shh.' She looked at him, then smirked. 'What? Did you think I was going to burst into tears?'

'Uh . . .'

'You know who my father was, right? What kind of man he was?'

'Er . . . yes?'

'If he'd caught me keening like a bitch over his death he'd have made it a point to come back to haunt me.'

Einar blinked. 'I . . . um . . . Fair enough, I suppose.'

'I mean, I didn't want him to die, but he is dead now, and all the tears in the world won't change that.'

Something in the way she blinked . . . He made the decision before he could think about it or scream at himself. Two quick steps and he was close enough, then his wiry but strong arms were wrapped around the girl.

'What are you doing? Let go!' she said, but the stiffness in her body melted away almost instantly. Her cheek rested up against his chest and a sigh escaped her lips.

They stood close like that for a long time.

Einar finally broke the silence. 'We should go.'

'Yes,' she mumbled.

He dropped his arms slowly and stepped back, uncomfortably aware of the sudden absence of her heat.

'I'll . . . uh, see you,' he said.

Gytha looked down, suddenly shy. 'Thank you,' she whispered.

Lost for words, Einar nodded in reply. 'Tonight,' he added

awkwardly. Then he turned around and walked back home towards the farm, feeling her eyes on him as he moved.

The shadow of the longhouse roof drew a black line across the yard and Helga smiled involuntarily as she crossed out into the sunlight again. *Summer*, she sighed. The linen sack felt rough against her hands, but the spreading warmth on her bare fore-arms made up for it. The air felt honey-sweet with it. *Summer.* The moment in the new barn had passed as quickly as it had come on, and she'd worked in pleasant silence with Hildigunnur. Sometime later, when the gentle creaking of the wood around them suggested that the sun had started heating the barn, she wondered whether her mother hadn't dragged her out and up here just as much for her own benefit. It didn't matter much; things were as they were.

'Need a hand?'

Helga blinked. She hadn't heard Aslak, nor seen him. He was just suddenly there, standing by the corner of the hen fence. 'No,' she said, adding, 'thank you!' and kicking herself for how awkward it sounded.

'Suit yourself.' Those were his words, but his voice said something different. *I'm staying here*, it said. And she might be imagining it, but she thought it said, *I like to look at you.*

'Fine,' she blurted, 'if you could get the gate for me.'

He walked across to the fence and opened the gate for her with a smile and a look that said, *Will this do?* She nodded at him. Inside the shack she could hear scrabbling feet and the first clucks.

'Coming,' she said, trying to ignore the rising colour in her cheeks. The gate clicked closed behind her. The scrabbling in the small shack intensified, and when she opened the door the hens all but burst out.

'Hungry little things, aren't they?' Aslak said from the fence.

Helga reached into the sack and spread out the feed, trying to get the birds from underfoot. 'They are. They don't like to be cooped up.'

'I can't blame them,' Aslak said. 'No one likes that.'

She was stuck for words. 'I guess not,' she finally managed.

'You can do better than guess,' Aslak said. 'Guessing is weak.'

Helga choked down a rising dread that she couldn't quite explain. 'No one likes to be shut in,' she said with as much conviction as she could muster, scattering the final handful of feed and turning to the gate. Aslak was leaning on it, one hand on the latch.

She took two steps towards the gate.

He made no move to shift out of the way.

Another two steps.

Her eyes met his.

There was a spark to him, a crackle. 'No one likes to be forced into things,' he said.

Another two steps and Helga was standing by the gate, close enough to feel the heat of his body. 'No,' she said, putting her hand on the gate. She pushed – and he pushed back.

'You guess?'

Another flare, this time of annoyance. 'I *know*,' she said.

He did not break eye contact, but she felt the pressure on the gate disappear. He shifted to the side – not by much, but so that she could squeeze past him. Cheeks crimson, she pushed past and away. Completely unbidden, the image of the storeroom came to her. In her mind, she doubled the size of Aslak's shelf.

The scythe was balanced easily on Sigmar's left shoulder. Over her right Jorunn carried a stuffed sack of hay. They walked in comfortable silence, enjoying the sunshine sweeping across the hill. Below, the river sparkled.

'Precious stones on Khazar cloth,' Sigmar said.

'Ever the poet. But I will agree, if forced: it's a pretty place.'

'It has done them well. I think – hang on – who's that?'

Far below them, just at the foot of the hill, someone waited. Jorunn groaned. 'It's Runa.'

'This will be . . . interesting.'

'She's not coming to talk to you.'

'I know. Just . . . keep your head, will you?'

'When do I not?'

Five steps turned to twenty and they could both make out Runa's features now. She was turned towards them, hands clasped in front.

'Go.' Jorunn's voice was firm.

'Are you sure?'

'Yes.' His shoulders tensed, but he didn't look back at his wife; instead, he gripped the handle of the scythe harder and lengthened his stride. As the distance between them grew, he drew a deep breath. 'You have it your way, *Wife*,' he shouted, coating the word with contempt. 'We'll see who is right.' Moments later he passed Runa without so much as glancing at her concerned face.

When Jorunn reached Runa's spot she uncoiled visibly. 'Jorunn,' she said, her voice trembling, 'I – I have to talk to you.'

'Why me?' Jorunn snapped, slowing down as she passed but not by much, forcing Runa to turn on her heel and stride beside her to catch up.

'I—' There was a sniffle, then a clearing of the throat. 'I have something I have to tell someone, and I think I can tell you.'

The path led straight to the west fence at Riverside, but Jorunn didn't slow down. In the distance, Sigmar had rounded a corner and disappeared out of sight.

A few more long strides, then, 'Out with it, *Sister*. What is it?'

'It's about Aslak.'

'What now? You just saw how my husband *really* feels – and you want advice from *me*? I thought you were much better at all of that than I was.'

Hurrying in her wake, Runa tried to catch her breath. 'No! That's not what I meant – *never*!'

'And I didn't mean to be so cruel,' Jorunn said, her voice softening as she reached the gate.

'Wait!' Runa hissed. 'Please, slow down!'

Jorunn slipped inside the gate, held it open for Runa and smiled. 'Sorry. When Sigmar puts me in a mood I sometimes find it's best to walk it off.' She looked at the shorter woman. 'Now, Sister, tell me what's on your mind.'

Huffing, Runa looked up. A tear glistened in her eye. 'I'm . . . scared.'

'What's wrong?'

'I think – I think Aslak murdered Karl.'

Runa's head whipped to the side with the force of the blow. Eyes wide open in shock, she stared at Jorunn, who was squeezing the knuckles on her right hand.

'You are *not* part of this family,' Jorunn snarled, 'and you do *not* get to accuse my brother.'

'Why?' Runa's face had twisted into a sneer. 'Is that because *you* killed Karl?'

The first scream came from behind the longhouse. When the second followed, Helga realised that she was already running towards it. Heart pounding, she could see Einar out of the corner of her eye, along with Bjorn and Sigmar. When she rounded the corner, she couldn't quite believe her eyes.

'Hey!' she yelled, grabbing a water bucket – the thing nearest to hand – and sprinting towards the two forms wrestling on the ground. '*Stop!*' She twisted her body and swung, throwing the water over the fighters. She recognised Jorunn and Runa in one blink of an eye before she realised that the water was somewhat more slop-coloured than she'd expected.

The two shrieks came in unison and for a moment the women on the ground froze, catching their breath and blinking at the unexpected assault on the senses. Jorunn was first to recover; she used the opportunity to roll over, pin the shorter woman to the ground and deliver a straight right to her nose.

'Jorunn – stop!' Bjorn roared as he rushed past Helga, but his sister's fists were rising and falling, pummelling Runa's forearms as the smaller woman desperately tried to cover her face. When he swept Jorunn off she kicked out, flailing at the whimpering

Runa and trying her best to stamp on Bjorn's foot, though with little luck.

'*What is the matter with you?*' The big man held his sister half a foot off the ground easily.

'She's a bitch!' Jorunn snarled.

'I know that,' Bjorn said, 'but so are you, and we're not busy punching you in the face, are we? What happened?'

But Jorunn refused to offer any answer; instead, she just wriggled in his arms. 'Let go of me, you bastard,' she snarled.

Helga watched as Bjorn came to a decision and turned towards the river.

'Let go of me!' Jorunn shrieked. 'Let go!'

Silent as winter, Bjorn just kept walking.

'Helga!' Einar called, breaking the spell, 'help Runa into the house – we need to clean her wounds and stop the bleeding.'

To her surprise Sigmar bent down to help support Runa towards the longhouse. When he saw her staring, he snapped, 'I can't look at her just now. She's safe with Bjorn—'

A piercing yell cut off the end of his sentence, then it abruptly disappeared. Moments later Jorunn's voice came to them from the riverbank, screeching, 'I'll fucking kill you! You bastard! I'll—' The voice disappeared again.

'At least Jorunn will be clean,' Einar remarked as they led Runa to the longhouse, not quite managing to keep the smirk off his face. 'Why the slop-water?'

'I just grabbed the first thing,' Helga admitted.

'Served her right,' Sigmar muttered. Beside him, Runa was sniffling.

As they rounded the corner into the yard, Agla and Gytha came rushing towards them. 'What happened?' Gytha asked, her eyes wide.

'It's pretty obvious,' Agla snapped. 'Get her inside, you idiots.' Sigmar and Einar snapped to and, led by Gytha, half-carried Runa inside. *Like dogs at heel. So that's what he saw in her*, Helga thought, interrupted by Agla's gaze. 'You – get water.'

She turned around and started searching for the bucket of rainwater she now knew to be around the corner. Without shrieking women on the ground pummelling the life out of each other, the bucket was painfully obvious. From down by the river she could hear snatches of conversation: Jorunn's clipped voice and Bjorn's rumbling tones.

'—but she thinks *he* did it, Bjorn. Her *own husband*!'

'Everyone's on edge, and you more than most.'

'Well it's not my bloody fault, is it? We're sleeping in the same house as a murderer.'

'If you believe that, then maybe don't punch the murderer's wife in the face.'

Suddenly ashamed of her eavesdropping, Helga grabbed the bucket and hurried towards the doors of the longhouse.

When she got in, blinking to get used to the half-light, she heard voices: three – no, four – people all talking at once over Runa's whimpering.

'—she can't just—'

'But what happened?'

'—there's probably a good reason—'

Aslak and Thyri had arrived, and Agla and Gytha were busy carefully removing Runa's clothes and rooting around for something clean for her to wear. Helga gazed at Runa over the shoulder of her awkwardly hovering husband. *She looks so young*, she thought. *So small and . . . vulnerable.* The thought stuck sideways in her head. Helga could deal with a lot of things, but thinking of Runa as 'vulnerable' was not one of them. Wait – was that the tiniest hint of a smirk on her face? Helga blinked and it was gone and Runa was just an upset woman on the edge of her bed, being tended to by her friends. *As far away from being seen as a murderer as anyone could be*, Helga thought, and cleared a small space on the shelf in her stockroom for Runa.

'Something has to be done about her,' Agla said.

'You're patching her up, aren't you?' Sigmar said.

'Not her. Your wife,' Agla snapped back.

Sigmar hunched over, looking absolutely miserable. 'And why is that my job? This place is crawling with her family.'

Agla frowned. 'But . . . you're her *husband*.'

Sigmar just snorted in disdain. 'I'm more like—'

The door creaked, and conversation stopped. Everyone turned to look as the hulking frame of Bjorn entered, followed by his lithe sister. *Drowned rat, more like*, Helga thought to herself. Jorunn's clothes clung where they didn't droop, and the slosh of her shoes was audible all across the room until her steps came to a halt.

Helga became very aware of her heartbeats. *One-two . . . one-two . . .*

'There is no honour in you. Not a shred.' Aslak's voice was taut, level like a bowstring. 'You could have killed her.'

'You pick a strange time to stand up for that woman,' Jorunn replied.

'DON'T YOU DARE SPEAK!' Aslak screamed, suddenly furious. 'DON'T YOU DARE MOVE YOUR MOUTH OR I WILL BREAK ALL YOUR TEETH, YOU SLIMY LITTLE BITCH!'

'*Aslak!*' Agla exclaimed.

'Shut up,' Aslak snarled as he focused his stare on Jorunn. 'You *knew* that I'd finally fixed it, didn't you. You *knew* that I had provided for my family. You knew that we were going to be happy. And you had to go and ruin it. I'm going—'

It wasn't a big movement; it was more of a shift, but suddenly Einar was standing between Aslak and his target. 'That's enough,' he said, and Helga felt a cold chill. His voice had changed, and so had the set of his shoulders. It was less of an invite to stop and more of a promise of what would happen if Aslak didn't.

Out of the corner of her eye Helga caught a quick, exchanged glance between Agla and Thyri, and moments later Bjorn's wife was by Aslak, up close, a gentle but firm hand on his arm. She whispered to him, murmured soothing sounds. It was hard to tell the words apart, but the sense of it was clear: *Calm down. Calm . . . down.* It was working, too – under the combination of Einar's suddenly imposing presence and Thyri's whispers, Aslak backed down.

He's lost, Helga thought, suddenly. *Lost and confused.*

At the other end of the hall, Jorunn sneered, 'I'd have you in a second, you little shit. But at least you're a man, unlike *my* so-called husband.'

In the corner, Sigmar tensed up. 'Be careful, *Wife*,' he growled.

'Or what? You'll beat me when we're gone?' Jorunn snapped. 'You wouldn't dare. At least not while I could look you in the eye. You're limp.'

Behind her, Helga could hear Agla draw a quick breath.

'And you are a horror! Every day, snapping at my heels – nothing I ever do is good enough, no amount of money will make you satisfied and you are never, *ever* happy!'

'Oh – happy like you were at coming here and meeting my family?' Jorunn was almost screaming. 'You *never* wanted this! You never wanted *me*! You married for convenience – or maybe to hide something else – and now you're stuck with me. *And I know you hate it.*'

'I will not be stuck with you,' Sigmar said, and he shouldered past Helga to the side door. A swift kick, the door flew open and he was gone.

Behind Jorunn, the main door opened and Hildigunnur came in, followed by Unnthor.

'What in Hel's frozen armpit is going on here?' the old chieftain barked.

Jorunn's wail of distress was only half-human. She seemed to go soft at the knees first, then slowly leaked down onto the floor, sobbing.

'Jorunn!' There was a note of panic in Hildigunnur's voice that Helga hadn't heard before. Within moments her mother was at her side, with Agla hurrying to join in.

'He – *uh* – I can't—' The rest of Jorunn's words dissolved into tears and loud sobs.

Hildigunnur knelt beside her and stroked her hair. '*Ssh*,' she whispered. 'Breathe first, talk later.' As Jorunn shook silently in her arms, the old woman's head whipped round and caught Agla's eye. 'She's bruised. What happened?'

'Um . . . we caught them fighting. Her and Runa,' Agla stuttered.

'Why?'

'We don't know,' Agla said.

Runa rose from her bunk and started walking over towards them, moving gingerly. 'It was my fault.'

'Oh?' Hildigunnur's voice could have sliced through stone.

'Yes – she asked me a question and I said some things I shouldn't have.'

The old woman eyed up Aslak's wife. 'It can't have been too bad,' she said.

'How do you know?' Agla said.

'Well,' Hildigunnur said, 'she's still alive, isn't she?' With that she turned her attention back to Jorunn, stroking her hair and whispering gently. Helga watched from a distance. She would have gone to help but it felt wrong, somehow. *They're the same*, she thought. *They are all the same, and I am not.*

After a little while, Hildigunnur led Jorunn to a seat and gathered the family around her. Runa's face had started to colour, but she was surrounded by Aslak and her children. To Helga they looked closer than they'd been before, which stung a little, but in another way she was relieved. After his outburst Aslak had lost some of the edge she'd seen in him, some of the danger she'd sensed – a good thing, because judging by her father's face, Riverside had all the danger it needed.

'It was him all along. I'll find him and wring his neck,' Unnthor said. 'Like a chicken.' There was a calm to his voice that was utterly terrifying.

'You'll do no such thing,' Bjorn said. 'We will go after him and we will catch him and tie him up, and then we will convene a council and talk this over.' He paused. 'And then you may do whatever you wish to his neck.'

'Why the wait?' Unnthor said.

'Shut up and listen to your son, you big ox,' Hildigunnur said. 'He's being smart, for once. Jorunn, talk to us. Tell us about him.'

'He was ... good to me, at first,' Jorunn began. 'After ... you know ...'

Nods around the table.

What? What does everyone know?

'Karl said he'd sailed with him once, long ago. I won't say that he brought him to me all trussed up, but—' She smiled at the recollection. 'That was a fateful trip to the fair that day.' Helga only just noticed as Einar slunk away into the shadows and towards the back door. *Whatever they're remembering, he doesn't want to hear it.* Her heart ached for the young man she thought of as her brother. *Much more than this lot, anyway.* 'He was just ... different from the farm boys,' Jorunn continued. 'Quick on his feet. Quick with his tongue.'

'I bet,' Hildigunnur murmured, to a swallowed scoff of outrage from Gytha.

Jorunn ignored it. 'But he had to go east immediately – so I went with him.'

'And broke your mother's heart,' Unnthor said.

'She did no such thing,' Hildigunnur said. 'Just because she wasn't wooed in the traditional way—'

'—with a thighbone—' Aslak added, and despite his fury, Unnthor smirked.

'—doesn't mean she wasn't supposed to do what needed to be done,' Hildigunnur added. 'Wouldn't be my daughter if she didn't.' She reached down and squeezed Jorunn's shoulder affectionately, and for a moment they were both fifteen years younger.

Helga felt another pang in her chest.

'We went back. His father was ill – he died soon after we arrived. He left Sigmar a broken house and a barren farm, but there was a cart and two old horses, and a load of furs. We reckoned there was only one thing to do, so we travelled and we traded. And we were happy,' Jorunn continued. 'Turns out I have a knack for negotiating – *apparently*, I make grown men quake – no idea where that comes from!' She glanced at her mother, who feigned innocence. 'We went all over, down to the Danes, across to Rus, where we bought a boat. Then we sold the boat – we just kept moving. Somewhere along the way we found some pretty trinkets and gave them to Eirik, who liked the look of Sigmar and gave him some stuff to sell.' At her mother's quizzical look she clarified, 'Amber, grain, timber.' She paused. 'And weapons. And we took them away and brought back a profit, and for a while, everything was working very well indeed. But then—'

Jorunn looked down and took a deep breath. The silence in the longhouse was thick. She said quietly, 'He changed.'

'How?' Gytha asked breathlessly.

'He started going away on his own,' she said, 'just a day, two days, at first, and then he was inventing reasons for me to stay in Uppsala while he went away to sail. I found out that some of our so-called friends in Svealand didn't much care for us . . . I felt really . . . *alone*.'

Helga felt strange, hearing this. She felt . . . sorry for Jorunn. She must have been so lonely – just like *she* felt alone now, excluded from the inner circle of the Riverside family. That had to be why she felt a strange tingling in her throat, why her eyebrows seemed to want to tie themselves up in a knot. Very discreetly she inched back until she could feel cooling shadow on her face.

'You don't need to tell me,' Bjorn rumbled. 'Bastards, the lot of 'em.'

'And some of the men . . .' She swallowed. 'Well, they were all too happy to approach me when Sigmar was away. I was glad of the things you taught me, Mother – although turns out wives don't take kindly to their men limping back home with their knees closed, vaguely suggesting they may have tripped over a root. It quickly becomes—'

'—your fault,' Hildigunnur finished quietly. 'I've seen it too many times.'

Agla sniffed audibly, and both Runa and Thyri were angling closer to mother and daughter.

It's almost as if she's telling them their own story, Helga thought.

Jorunn sniffled and reached up to clutch her mother's hand.

'But when I got your message last year, I found my courage. I stood up to him: I told him what I wanted – what I *needed*.'

Complete with the suffering victim winning in the end. Helga felt the hairs rise on her forearms. *She is . . .* lying. *She's lying through her teeth!* The shock forced her to work hard to close her mouth, and she thanked the gods she was out of sight.

'You told him to come here,' Unnthor said.

'Yes.'

'Where he met Karl again,' Bjorn added.

It was like watching a spooked horse. It had torn free of its reins, gained its head and now it was picking up speed. *This is* exactly *what Hildigunnur would have done. What . . . had to be done.* She tried to remember what had gone on between the three of them, but too much was happening. *Later*, she thought. *Later.*

'Karl always brought home a take from the raids,' Agla said quietly. 'Even when I heard later that others had not done so well.'

'Because he was the quickest and the bravest,' Gytha added, like someone finishing a sentence. 'Because . . .' Her voice trailed off.

'The little shit,' Bjorn growled. 'He *sold* you. He took money to make you Sigmar's bride.'

'But you got your dowry, didn't you?' Hildigunnur said. 'Karl said . . .'

'. . . he'd hand it over,' Unnthor finished grimly. 'He was going on a ship to Rus anyway.'

This time the sniffles came from Agla, who had bowed her head in shame.

The family were silent then, everyone thinking their own thoughts.

Helga watched them, one by one, trying to imagine what was going on in their heads. Hulking Unnthor, furious about Sigmar, and Hildigunnur, standing over her daughter like a mother bear. Bjorn, lost in thoughts of his brother's dishonesty. His wife, standing close, hand ever on the giant's forearm. Agla and Gytha huddled together, shamed and shocked. Runa, oddly quiet and wary. She'd been very quick to forgive Jorunn. *What did she know?* And beside her, Aslak who had been so furious with his sister, was now looking deeply concerned.

And in the middle was Jorunn, *a liar*.

She was sure of it.

Nothing added up. She and Sigmar had been inseparable since they arrived – and now? All of a sudden he was a horrible man? The pieces didn't match – she didn't even know what all of them were, but she had the awful feeling that something wasn't right.

But just when she'd composed herself enough to start arranging the things she'd seen, her father broke the silence.

'So why shouldn't I go after this bastard?'

'You're the same size, but luckily one of you has my blood as well,' Hildigunnur said. 'Think about it. If a husband slays a wife's brother . . . ?'

'The union is void,' Unnthor said.

'And our sister walks away with a good chunk of Sigmar's pelt,' Aslak said.

'And then maybe,' Bjorn added, 'we can find a way for her to inherit the rest quickly, but without loss of reputation. The dogs of the world be less likely to paw at her door if they know she'll have their belongings and their name as well.'

Jorunn smiled at her loving pair of big protectors and Helga's stomach turned. *You'd stab them both in the back if you thought you could get away with it.*

'The two of you can go and fetch him,' Hildigunnur said firmly. 'We'll manage while you're gone, and probably sleep better too.' Some smirks around the room. 'This is the last place he'll show up.'

The door slammed as Jaki entered. 'It's Sigmar. He's half a mile down the road and approaching fast. And he's not alone.'

Chapter 13

STANDOFF

Helga never saw her mother reach for the knife. It just appeared in her hand, like it had always been there. Bjorn's wide frame was highlighted by the sun as he walked through the door, Unnthor and Einar on his heels and Aslak following soon after.

'Get the kids,' Hildigunnur barked at Agla. 'Take them out back. Hide in the woods.' She turned to Helga. 'Go with them – up the hill, then around.'

'And where are you going?' Helga said. It felt strange, listening to her words come out. It was almost like hearing herself speak through water.

'We've got visitors,' Hildigunnur said. 'It would be rude not to welcome them. Now go.'

'No,' Helga said.

'What?'

'I'm not leaving you.'

In a flash, Hildigunnur's face was inches from her. She could smell the old woman, all leather, heat and sunshine. *But no fear.* 'Run.' Her mother bit the word off almost before it was out there.

Something in Helga twisted, bent and stuck sideways. 'No.'

'They'll be lost without you.' Outside, the dogs had started barking, loud and angry.

'I know the woods,' Runa said. When Hildigunnur's head whipped round, she continued, a measure of her customary defiance creeping in, 'She wants to be with you. Let her.' She didn't wait for an answer but grabbed the twins and headed after Thyri.

Hildigunnur stared at Runa's back, then at Helga. For a moment, there was a twinkle of something in her eye. 'Fine. But stay behind me. If there's a fight, circle round, try to get at their backs.' Her mother was already moving towards the door. They could hear raised voices from the outside.

The doorframe felt rough on her hands. *What if this is the last time I leave the longhouse?* Her fingertips lingered on the wood. There was a definite emptiness inside her, something missing . . . *Fear.* She had no visions of swinging axes, no thudding in her chest, nothing. As the sunlight made her blink, Helga realised that she really wasn't afraid. Maybe she wasn't as far from Hildigunnur as she'd thought.

She stepped outside.

Her eyes adjusted to the light – and she blinked, twice, not quite believing what she was seeing: nine horses, all big, strong animals. On them sat five silent men, with Sigmar in front. Maybe it was just the angle, but looking up at him Helga couldn't help but think that a man looked very different on horseback. Sigmar seemed comfortable and relaxed. There was definitely something different about him.

He was carrying a sword.

The scabbard hung off his side so naturally that she hadn't noticed it at first. Behind him, the men all carried axes or other blades of some sort. Two of them had bows slung over their shoulders as well.

In comparison, the defenders of Riverside suddenly seemed . . . *human*. Bjorn was a big man, granted, but one kick from a horse's hoof would see the end of him. Standing side by side, Unnthor with his axe and Jaki with his club, her father and his sworn brother suddenly looked very old – and next to them, Einar and Aslak a lot younger.

'Unnthor Reginsson. I come to you with an apology.' Sigmar's voice was calm and measured.

'For what?' Unnthor growled.

Helga's breath caught in her throat as Sigmar moved swiftly – and dismounted. 'I left your home in haste, and I did not treat my wife as I should have.'

She could feel her mother tense up beside her as voices drifted towards them.

High-pitched voices.

Children's voices.

Agla and the women emerged from around the corner of the longhouse, walking slowly, in a tight group. *Herded*. Behind them, three armed men moved like sheepdogs, silent but dangerous.

'They were waiting,' Runa said, seething.

Good to see she's recovering, Helga thought.

'Sigmar.' Jorunn's voice was quiet, but somehow audible by everyone.

The effect was immediate; Sigmar looked deeply pained. 'My dearest wife,' he said. '*Please.*'

'Please what?' Jorunn said.

'Please forgive me.'

Jorunn stared at him and her mouth moved as if she was trying to form words that weren't quite coming out.

Helga looked around. Not a single person in the farmyard appeared to know what to think. Unnthor was still clutching his axe; Einar looked confused. Sigmar's men looked bored but ready, like they'd done this – or something like this – countless times before.

'I do not know what's going on here,' Hildigunnur said firmly, 'but here's what's going to happen. Sigmar, you and your men are invited to break bread with us, and possibly drink something cold too. While you are under my roof, you will have guests' rights. Jorunn – you are going to talk to your husband. If I see another blade out in the time it takes me to count to five, the wielder of same will be in serious trouble. Does everyone understand?'

The effect of her speech was immediate. *She turns men into boys*, Helga thought as she watched knives, swords and other implements of murder hastily disappear.

'Welcome to Riverside,' Unnthor boomed.

Sigmar's men dismounted, leaving Einar and Jaki holding nine pairs of reins. Bjorn stepped in to help, as did Gytha, and within moments the horses were being led to pasture as the newly declared guests headed to the longhouse. Volund sloped off after his mother, while Bragi and Sigrun immediately assaulted the newcomers with a barrage of questions.

'Come on,' Hildigunnur hissed, snapping Helga out of her dreaming. 'I told you. We've got visitors.'

The longhouse had filled up; the hastily assembled table was suddenly a lot more crammed. Hildigunnur conjured oatcakes from somewhere, along with loaves and butter. She rolled out a keg of ale, but insisted on pouring herself, so she could make sure it was reasonably watered down. Helga trailed around behind her, trying to find things to do; her mother was suddenly moving even faster and more efficiently than she'd ever seen.

The first thing Sigmar did was step aside with Unnthor.

'Tell me, daughter of mine,' her mother muttered under her breath as she buzzed about, improvising food for nine new guests, 'what are they talking about?'

Helga looked harder at Unnthor and Sigmar. 'It's impossible to hear' – Hildigunnur's contemptuous snort suggested that more detailed information might be needed – 'but the way Sigmar's standing suggests that he has something urgent to say.'

'And—?'

'Father is leaning back and tilting his head to the side.'

'Which side?'

'The right.'

'Good,' Hildigunnur said.

'Why?' Helga said.

'His left ear is better. That means he's listening. Keep watching. Watch *everyone*.'

Helga did as she was told, and all the while, her thoughts were racing: Runa got beaten to a pulp, then took the blame. Aslak fought for her. Jorunn lied. Sigmar left, then came back. Are they still married? Nothing made sense. She'd scratched the rune of need onto Runa's bed. *Does this mean it worked?* Out of the corner of her eye she saw Sigmar move towards the table.

'He's sitting down,' she muttered to her mother, who acknowledged her with the smallest of nods before swooping in with tankards of weak ale for the guests, then sitting down quietly next to her husband. Yet again Helga marvelled at her mother's ability to shape-shift as the occasion required. *The front keeps changing – but what's behind it?*

The question didn't stay alive in her head for long. She didn't allow it to.

Unnthor dipped his chin in thought, then looked around at his family and Sigmar's new additions. 'We can all agree,' he began, 'that whoever killed Karl cannot have come from the outside. The dogs would not have recognised them.'

Mute nods around the table.

'Sigmar's men, who were camped five miles down the road, have seen no one pass. And so it must be that the killer is in this room. Sigmar has graciously offered his trusted men as guards to make sure no one leaves before we find the knife and the murderer.'

Her stomach sinking, Helga glanced towards her mother, but Hildigunnur said nothing; she just sat and watched.

She's waiting for a reaction.

'And why should we trust him, Father?'

And there it was. Jorunn was sitting bolt-upright, staring daggers at the chieftain from Riverside. 'These men are also under my command. If I command them to leave and they don't do what I tell them to, are we not right to assume that they're sent here to finish his job and murder us all in our sleep?'

'Come now, Sister,' Aslak said. 'You shouldn't need to worry unless you have something to fear.'

'Am I wrong?'

'I've had about as much as I want out of you,' Hildigunnur said, a tone to her voice that made Helga involuntarily shift backwards. 'You' – she turned to Sigmar – 'and you, *outside*. Talk.' When neither of them shifted, she added, '*Now*.'

Sigmar was the first to rise. 'Come, Jorunn. Please.'

With a show of great reluctance, Jorunn got to her feet and walked towards the door, not acknowledging Sigmar in the slightest. Her husband followed, looking a little less like the leader of men he had been just a short while ago.

When she was almost by the door, Jorunn whirled and snapped, 'Why am I doing this? I don't need to go anywhere with you. I owe you nothing—'

Sigmar recoiled. 'What do you mean?'

Around the table, the guards were looking decidedly awkward.

'For a year you've kept me as some kind of decoration. You've kept me out of every market there was, you've created reasons for me to stay home, you've done nothing but evade and hide. I know some women live like that, and some women are fine with it, but that is not what we had. That is not what I want. And if that is how you're going to be, then I don't want you.'

Sigmar froze in his tracks. 'What—?' he breathed.

'Don't lie to me!' Jorunn shouted, tears in her voice. 'Don't *lie* to me! You should tell me things! You shouldn't – you shouldn't *hide things!*'

Then laughter bubbled up out of Sigmar, just a short burst, and he walked up to her and took her in his arms. 'Oh! No, my love, *no, no, no* . . .' He started whispering in her ear as she struggled against him.

Unnthor and Bjorn were half out of their seats when Hildigunnur spoke. 'Sit down, you oafs. They're fine.' And indeed they were, for what had started out as a struggle was now a tight embrace, and Jorunn's shoulders were shaking with either laughter or tears.

Around the table there were mixed reactions. Agla and Gytha wore identical, open-mouthed expressions. Runa was whispering to Aslak, who was eyeing the couple suspiciously. Bjorn sat back in his chair, his face somewhere between boredom and annoyance.

Helga studied Sigmar and Jorunn, trying to read in their bodies what was being whispered. She could not see much of Jorunn's body, nor her eyes, and for some reason, this bothered her. *I don't trust that woman. I don't trust her at all.*

Finally, husband and wife broke their clinch.

'Well?' Hildigunnur said.

'I . . . um . . .' Jorunn looked sheepish. 'I got it all wrong. Sigmar explained.'

'And?'

'Mother . . .' Her voice was barely a whisper. 'I am with child.'

This was noise of a different kind. Agla leaped up, ran to Jorunn and hugged her, but Bragi and Sigrun were fast behind her, shouting joyously, 'Where is it? Can we play with it?' Jorunn reached down and stroked Sigrun's hair.

'And you needed your husband to tell you this?' Hildigunnur said, to smirks around the table.

'No,' Jorunn said. 'No . . . We've only known for a few months and I'm not thick in the waist yet – but he's been travelling all around, finding me the finest of decorations for the child.'

'If it is a boy we will name him Unnthor,' Sigmar announced.

The hairs rose on Helga's arms. *Sigmar is in on it too. This is a* performance. *They're both—*

She noted movement out of the corner of her eye and the door closed behind Einar. As people were standing up around her, rushing to congratulate the beaming couple, she used the chance to duck out after him.

Even though it was near twilight, the sun was still up, with only a hint of the coolness of night. She saw Einar walking towards the tool-shed, shoulders slumped. Her feet decided for her, and she followed. The thought of staying in the longhouse, watching Jorunn spinning her tales, set her teeth on edge. *Why were they doing this? Did they murder Karl together, maybe?* She turned it over in her head. She'd heard that carrying a child did funny things to a woman's head, but *murder*? Apparently they screamed bloody murder when it came out, or so Hildigunnur had told her, but to take a man's life? A sleeping man who could not defend himself?

On the other hand, Sigmar had looked like he knew how to handle a knife. Maybe he had sliced Karl open on his wife's behalf.

That sounded more likely. She cleared a shelf in her stockroom for Sigmar. *It's getting crowded in here. Maybe—* The first metallic *clink* sent the walls of her imagination crashing down and brought her back to reality. *Shed. Einar. Right.*

The door swung open at a light touch and the noise of rhythmic but controlled hammering grew clearer.

Einar was bent over his workbench, right arm rising and falling steadily.

Helga cleared her throat, but nothing changed.

She tried again. This time, the hammer rested briefly on the workbench, but then the arm rose just like nothing had happened.

'Stop,' she said softly. 'It's just me.'

The hammer landed on whatever he was beating and stopped there. 'I know,' he said, back still turned to her.

'Do you need any help?'

'No.'

She watched as his back hunched, like he could retreat into himself and shut her out. What could she say? What would Hildigunnur have said? 'I don't think you're missing out on a big catch there.' For a moment she thought she could see the words leaving her mouth, like someone coughing up their insides. *What was that, you stupid girl? The love of your life is a lying whore? That's not going to bloody help!*

'What do you mean?' Einar had not relaxed a single muscle. Nor had he let go of the hammer.

'She – I—' *Anything.* 'The way she went for Runa,' Helga stammered. 'She doesn't . . . I don't think she is very nice.'

Einar's shoulders rocked back and forth once as he snorted. 'You've hardly been off this farm since you got here, and that was a lifetime ago. How would *you* know?'

His words stung: there was a sharpness to him, a willingness to hurt. 'What do you mean?' Helga said. *The door is just there*, she thought. *If I need to, I can—*

'How would you *know*? Your world is Hildigunnur and Unnthor. You think they're how all people are – but they are *not*. They're hard, both of them: hard as nails. They'd do anything to keep their place in the world. Jorunn is better than they are, and you will not say otherwise.'

Einar turned and Helga almost gasped. His face was twisted, somehow – there was only a hint of the friendly, open-faced boy she thought she'd known, and what had replaced him was something else, something *angry* – something holding a hammer like a weapon.

Someone who could do anything to anyone.

The realisation hit her like ice water. *And who would do anything for* her.

'I'm sorry,' she muttered, not taking her eyes off Einar. 'I just wanted to say something nice. I'll go.'

Einar's mouth twisted and the hard set of his face softened a little and she finally caught a glimpse of her brother behind the fury. 'You can stay if you want to, but I'll have to work. And I . . . um . . . I know. I know what you're trying to do. But sometimes talking doesn't work. You have to . . . *do* things.'

He paused and looked at her.

He is searching for words, she thought, *but they're not coming.*

Instead Einar turned, raised his hammer and brought it down on the worktop with force.

Helga retreated out of the hut, not quite daring to look away. There had been a set to his jaw that she hadn't seen before, a determination. *You have to do things. Had he . . . ?*

As she closed the door, the evening breeze played with the hairs on the back of her neck. She shivered.

Unnthor leaned back in his chair, Hildigunnur to his right and Sigmar to his left. 'I can't keep them here for ever. There's not enough space, and in a while there won't be enough food.'

'So the first one to leave is the murderer, then?' Sigmar said.

'That's weak,' Hildigunnur said. 'All they'd need to do is wait until your men killed the first poor soul to mount a horse.'

Unnthor snorted. 'My wife is wise. She is also able to think like a murderer, it appears.'

Hildigunnur smiled sweetly. 'That's what it takes to stay married to you, my love.' A brief titter spread around the table where they sat. 'But if no one confesses and we don't find the knife . . .'

'There is one thing we could do,' Sigmar said, and Unnthor and Hildigunnur both turned towards him. 'Bjorn's son had the pendant. We could ask the gods.'

Unnthor snorted. 'They won't listen,' he said. 'And if they did, they might not tell us what we want to hear.'

But there was a gleam in Hildigunnur's eye. 'That is an excellent idea,' she said, smiling at Sigmar.

'Why?'

'Shut up, Husband. Your next thought is that we could just

beat it out of them, and if that happens you'll have a house full of murderers. No, Sigmar is right. The gods will know.'

'So it is decided, then,' Sigmar said.

Unnthor nodded, his lip curling in distaste. 'It is decided.'

Had Sigmar murdered the man who'd insulted him? Had Gytha lost her temper? Had Einar's lost love driven him crazy? Helga's mind raced; any one of them was as likely a murderer as the rest. *Runa? She'd been strange and jumpy. Jorunn? She had lied – but for what reason?*

The faces of the family filled her head, all of them snarling and spitting, with darkness in their hearts and death in their eyes. She didn't notice the shape in the shadow by the corner of the hut until she nearly stepped on an outstretched foot. 'Oh!'

'Sorry,' Volund mumbled, tucking his gangly legs back in under his knees. 'Didn't mean to . . .'

'No, no,' Helga said hurriedly, 'you've done nothing wrong, Volund, really truly. But why are you out here?'

'Don't know.'

What should I say? What do—? Helga made a concerted effort and reined in the part of her brain that was racing ahead and allowed herself to just do the first thing that came to mind.

She sat down next to the boy and looked up. There was a delicious quality to it, just sitting down and looking up at the sky. They could hear muted chatter from the longhouse. Far away in the field a cow lowed plaintively.

'The light is changing,' she said.

'Yes.' A brief pause, then, 'It always does, you know.' He made a tiny sound, almost like someone trying unsuccessfully to clear his throat.

Helga glanced over at him and caught movement. The corner of his mouth was twitching.

'Are you . . . teasing me?' she said, incredulous.

The noise burst out of Volund like a brook breaking through ice, and he chortled, then started chuckling and blowing raspberries. 'Yes!' he managed at last, and hid his face in his shovel-blade hands as he shook with very badly concealed mirth.

Helga's chest ached, a pleasant, warm feeling. She could almost touch the love that flowed from the boy. 'Well, then, I'll just have to – *tickle you!*' Lightning-quick, she reached for the softness of his belly—

—and the force of the blow felt like it had shattered the bones in her forearm.

Volund was scrambling to his feet, pressing his left hand to his temple at an odd angle, his mouth frozen in a silent scream.

What have I done? 'Volund, I'm sorry – I didn't mean to startle you!' She rose to her knees and begged him, 'Please, sit down again. *Please*. No tickling, I promise.'

But the boy was already staggering away from her, tossing his head forcefully like a horse trying to shake away a cloud of flies.

She swallowed, trying to get past the lump in her throat. For some reason Einar's rejection hadn't hurt half as much as this.

The door of the longhouse announced her arrival with a loud creak but no one spared her a second glance, because all eyes were fixed on Sigmar, who was standing beside Unnthor and Hildigunnur at the head of the table.

'—and when the sun rises, we'll all go to the stone and the oak and ask the gods for advice,' he finished. Then he added, 'Until then, my men will stand guard.' He gestured to a wiry man with thinning hair and a hard turn to his mouth. 'Thorolf will answer to Unnthor.' The man presumably called Thorolf nodded curtly.

Helga glanced at her father, who was somehow looking younger – younger and more alive. There was nothing left of the tired old man who'd spoken to her before the guests had started to arrive. He looked completely comfortable with the idea of commanding men, for one thing.

'You heard him,' Hildigunnur said. 'We'll be sacrificing to the gods tomorrow. Until then, I need you lot' – she gestured at the women – 'to help me with all sorts of things in here. The rest of you – get out of my house!' The last command was given with a smile, but no less authority.

She speaks to their feet, Helga thought, for the men were up already and milling towards the door. It didn't matter who was what – chieftain or guard, they all knew who to obey.

When the men had all cleared out, Hildigunnur clapped her hands. 'Right. We're doing stew. You two, vegetables.' Agla and Gytha immediately headed to the workbench, moving with purpose.

'I need someone good with a needle.'

'I can do that,' Runa said.

'Good. Jorunn – over here.' Without another word, Hildigunnur sat down and waited for her daughter to sit next to her. A significant glance told Helga that her presence was requested too. When they'd all settled, the old woman had cast an eye over her assembled troops, pressed to work by the fireplace, then fixed her daughter with a bear-stopping glance.

'What's going on?'

'I – I don't know,' Jorunn stammered.

'Do I have to worry that your husband and his men will slit all our throats in our sleep?'

'*No!* I mean – no, I don't think – no . . .' Jorunn looked down at her toes then back up at her mother. 'I thought he was a bad man, Mother,' she said, her bottom lip trembling. 'I thought he'd found someone else.'

Helga knew the look wasn't directed at her, but she still felt her insides turn to snow under Hildigunnur's gaze. *How can she not see that her daughter is lying?* But apparently the Queen of Riverside could not.

Instead, the old woman sighed, then managed a smile for her daughter. 'When do we ever know?' For a moment, they sat there in companionable silence.

'Who did it, Mother?' Jorunn said. She looked younger, suddenly.

The smile disappeared from Hildigunnur's face. 'I don't know,' she said, 'but we'll find them. And when we do, they will get what they deserve.'

This appeared to put Jorunn at her ease. 'I have to go out for a moment,' she said. 'I'll be back, and then I want something to do.'

'Oh, don't you worry about that,' Hildigunnur said, smiling as she watched her daughter rise.

She's lying. She thinks you are a fool. She's involved in Karl's murder. The words were there, on the tip of her tongue, but Helga couldn't get them to reach Hildigunnur's ears – or even to leave her mouth, for that matter. Instead she just watched her mother, who didn't take her eyes off Jorunn until the door had closed behind her. It was impossible to guess what she was thinking.

'She looks very healthy,' Helga said at last.

Hildigunnur's mouth pursed. 'She does,' she said. 'And she was plenty quick running around the field as well.'

She could have sighed in relief. *It's not just me. Mother can smell the lie too.* Her mind was racing again, but still she had no answers. *What's going on? Why was Jorunn lying? And why is Mother playing along?* Then another thought pushed its way into her head. *What is my mother intending to accomplish?*

At last she said, 'What needs done?'

'Prepare to feed the family,' Hildigunnur said, then added, 'and our new guests.'

Helga thought about Sigmar's men. Some had sat silently and waited; others had engaged in muttered conversations; no one had attempted to talk to the family. Nothing had caught her eye. *They are just men.* None of them had looked particularly murderous.

Maybe one of them was.

Maybe they all were.

Her mother's voice was quiet. 'Don't think too hard.' Helga looked at her, but the old woman was busy studying the hem of her dress. 'Don't think, and don't worry. Head down, do what you need. You don't need to look for the killer: they will reveal themselves when the time comes – and when that happens we'll catch him.'

Or her, Helga thought – but she didn't say anything. Instead she went to the workbench and set to chopping up roots.

Jorunn exhaled as the door closed behind her. The sun was past the mid-point of the sky and there was a welcome touch of a cool breeze on the air. In the distance the dogs were yapping at each other. She measured her steps away from the longhouse, repeating, over and over again, until her voice settled, 'One . . . two . . . one . . . two . . .' She breathed out again and looked around at the familiar old buildings: the longhouse, the barn, the sheds, the fences.

'This fucking place,' she muttered.

To her left, a door creaked.

On impulse, Jorunn ducked in behind the cowshed, keeping the source of the noise in sight.

Moments later she saw a hulking shape by the corner that could only be Bjorn, though he looked far from his usual boisterous self. He checked all around before stepping out into the yard. In a blink his customary swagger was back, and he walked towards the longhouse.

Moving quietly, Jorunn slipped around the back of the shed, making sure that Bjorn didn't see her, and headed for the door of the cowshed he'd just left – the place where he and his family were sleeping.

*

Helga gathered up the wooden bowls. The smell of the hastily assembled stew still lingered; Unnthor had slaughtered a lamb to welcome the unexpected visitors, but he'd kept the blood for tomorrow.

The dinner table looked very different with Sigmar's men gathered around the far end. To a man they'd been well behaved, but there was an unspoken menace to their presence, like a promise of violence. She tried her best to ignore them, just as they were ignoring her.

Sigmar, sitting by Unnthor's right-hand side, rose and called for quiet. 'We thank our gracious hosts for the hospitality extended,' he started.

Unnthor stood up, half a head taller than the Swede. 'And we thank you for helping to keep us safe,' he said. Around the table there were nods and murmurs of assent. 'The sun is down but I don't think anyone is ready to sleep yet?'

'No!' little Bragi piped up before his mother could silence him, and there was smiling agreement from all the guests.

'So maybe it's time for a story,' Unnthor went on.

Like a river, the silence flowed from his seat at the head of the table.

'I heard this one last year,' he started. 'Two years back, Aegir Njardarson was sailing to the west – nothing new about that, of course, he goes regularly, and rumour has it his house is built on a pit full of gold. But this time he wasn't after easy loot.

'See, three years ago Edgar of Wessex had for some reason decided to stand, rather than pay the geld – he ambushed a fair few of Aegir's men, too. Aegir came after them, but he was too late. They say he stood on a hill and watched across a field full of men as Edgar cracked their skulls and dropped them in a hole, then stood over them and shouted something in their language about how important he was and how the White Christ would protect the crown of England.

'And Aegir didn't attack.

'Not then.

'Instead, he sailed away, back to the fjords. Some say his wife was a weather-witch. Some say he asked her for a hard winter. Well, whether or not he asked, he got it.

'And after that winter, Aegir had a full ship of hard and hungry men, and none hungrier than his son, Sigurd Aegisson. So they sailed out west. And some would have charged in, axes up, killing all they could.

'But Aegir didn't.

'Instead, he sent in his son and some of his friends, and they stole Edgar's crown – snatched it from his own bedchamber, and didn't hurt a hair on anyone's head.'

'What happened then?' Gytha's voice was taut with impatience.

Unnthor smirked. 'Aegir waited for the king's men to come to the beach. Then he threw the crown in the sea, right in front of them.'

There were exclamations and chuckles around the table.

'Edgar was furious – and he took it out on his men. He had the captain of the guard executed, and then when his family complained, he had them executed too, for "being in league with the Northmen".

'And then his own people stormed his castle and carried him out on a hay-fork.'

Because if you want to kill a man and get away with it, you'd better have a crown on your head, Helga thought.

'To Aegir!' Sigmar raised his mug.

'To the North!' Bjorn did the same.

'To headless kings!' Jorunn cried, to a round of laughter, breaking the reverent silence that had embraced Unnthor's story. Now it was gone, conversations broke out in the room as people rose from the table. Some told stories designed to top the chieftain's, and at least three of Sigmar's men claimed loudly that they knew someone who had been on that very ship, and Bjorn started telling a dirty joke about a raid on a nunnery.

Sigmar said something quietly to Unnthor and Hildigunnur and headed outside. They both smiled, but the moment he'd gone Helga saw her father approach Aslak, place a hand on his shoulder and, leaning in, whisper in the young man's ear. Aslak stiffened up, then shifted slowly towards the back entrance. She finished stowing away the pots, and when she looked around as Sigmar came back in, Aslak had gone.

The noise of the men's gently drunken conversation made Helga feel warm and soft as she lay tucked up under her blanket. It sounded a little like the babbling of the river, quick at times and loud at others, but always constant. The warmth was almost uncomfortable now, so she stuck her hand out from underneath her blanket.

The water cooled her fingertips.

Helga blinked and looked around.

She could feel the grass under her palms, lush and sweet-smelling. The sun was soft, hidden under a cloud somewhere, but the sound of the river was still there.

'It's a lovely day.' The old man was sitting there next to her. The brim of his hat drooped over one eye.

She didn't think she'd expected him to be there, but for some reason she wasn't surprised. 'It is.'

'And here we are, right on the riverside.'

'We are.'

'And what have you found?'

Helga thought. What had she found? 'I carved a rune.'

'Good. Did it help?'

She thought again. Had she seen Runa's needs and wants? 'Maybe.'

The old man leaned back, smiling like a cat in sunshine. 'Maybe,' he repeated. 'Good.'

Helga's mood suddenly turned. 'Why is that good? My foster-brother is dead, they're going to pin it on a soft-headed boy and I have no idea what's happening! For some reason Jorunn is lying, we suddenly have armed men in every corner and we might be stuck on the farm all together until we die of hunger or my father loses his mind.'

'And what are you going to do?'

'I DON'T KNOW!'

The old man touched the brim of his hat, almost as if he were reassuring himself that it was still there, then he looked up and stared into the distance. 'Yes,' he mumbled. 'Yes.'

'Yes *what*?' Helga snapped, although she was suddenly feeling awkward that she'd shouted at the old man.

'You need to ask questions.'

'*What* questions?'

'That's a good one to start with,' he replied with a grin that Helga wanted quite badly to wipe off his face with her elbow. 'You know what, where, when and how. You've asked why and who.'

'Yes.'

'But have you asked about the past? The future? The taste of blood and the smell of sweat and the sound of rutting in a glade?'

Helga flushed. 'I don't understand.'

'You will. Find what's hidden in a name and you will.'

The old man placed a warm, heavy palm on her sternum. As the river faded in her mind, Helga slowly became aware that something new weighed down the leather thong around her neck.

Unnthor watched Helga tossing in her sleep, his brow furrowed. He didn't look up as Hildigunnur approached, but said softly, 'Is she well?'

'She's sensible,' Hildigunnur said, placing her slim hand on his forearm and squeezing it gently. 'And because she's sensible, she's afraid.'

Beneath her fingers, Unnthor's muscles tensed as he clenched his fist. 'We need to end this. Whatever it takes.'

Hildigunnur stepped closer to her husband and embraced him. 'My husband is wise,' she said softly. 'And that we will.'

Chapter 14

NIGHT WORK

'Mother!'

The raw panic in the word jolted Helga awake immediately, just as the big door slammed open. A shape stood in the doorway – a lithe, female figure. A cool breeze from outside swept with it a smell that she *really* wished she didn't recognise.

Blood.

A piercing scream followed, from somewhere outside.

'MOTHER!' Jorunn's voice was taut, stretched like a rope on a billowing sail.

'Light the fires!' Hildigunnur's command was sharp, and moments later sparks from fire-steels appeared in the darkness. The first torch sputtered into life almost immediately after. 'Are you hurt?' All they could hear from the doorway was sobbing. 'ANSWER ME!'

'It's not me,' Jorunn said, leaning against a doorpost for balance. 'It's Bjorn.'

Helga was out of her bed and running towards the doorway, following the shape of her father. She wasn't alone; they were all moving now, rushing towards the exit, rushing towards the killer. There were indistinct shouts, the dogs were barking with excitement, Sigmar was bellowing commands in the yard – *I didn't see him leave – didn't see him inside* – and then they were all running as fast as they could towards the cowshed where she and Einar had built the beds for Bjorn and his family. The buildings were dark and straight in the flow of the moonlight. Calls for torches bounced around the farm, along with the barking dogs.

And then she saw him. He looked impossibly large, even in death. His body was lying just outside the door to his cabin. Thyri was sitting beside him, looking stunned. Helga stopped for a moment in shock and was unceremoniously shouldered aside by her mother.

'What happened?' The old woman slid through the press of men and knelt next to Bjorn's wide-eyed wife.

'I don't know,' Thyri said. Her voice was deathly quiet. 'We'd just gone back. Volund was in bed. Bjorn hadn't finished talking and drinking, so he was coming behind us – I must have fallen asleep, but I thought I heard voices . . . and then I heard him come in. He's always quiet when he thinks I'm sleeping . . .' Her voice sank to a whisper. 'But he didn't come to bed.'

Hildigunnur reached out and squeezed her arm. 'I know you're hurting, but you need to keep talking while it's still fresh in your mind. You thought you heard voices – did you hear them say anything?'

'No,' Thyri said, 'nothing.'

'But there were two people.'

'Yes.'

'You are sure of this.'

'Yes.'

'Two men, or a man and a woman?'

Thyri looked at her with confusion. 'I . . . I couldn't tell.'

'And then?'

'I woke up, because I felt a pain in my chest.' In the flickering torchlight, Helga noticed that Thyri's cheeks were glistening with tears. 'And I could hear Jorunn – she was saying his name, over and over, telling him to wake up. So I got up and came out and Jorunn was already running to fetch you because someone had—' Her words were swallowed by sudden, uncontrollable tears.

Hildigunnur rose and turned to her husband. 'No one moves,' she said. 'Give Einar and Jaki torches and tell them to go and search for tracks. We want to make fully sure that no one came in over the fence.'

'And then?' Unnthor rumbled.

Hildigunnur didn't reply but knelt down by Bjorn again, shooting Helga a glance as she did. *I hope I don't get used to this*, Helga thought as she joined her mother.

Hildigunnur grabbed her hand and placed it on the dead man's cheek. Bjorn's body was cold to the touch, but . . . *there*. A drop of warmth.

'He's not been dead long. But where—?' *Where is the blood?*

He was lying twisted, half on his back with his arm pinned underneath him. 'Help me find the wound,' Hildigunnur muttered, grabbing the shoulder of her giant son and pulling him towards them.

The back of Bjorn's shirt was sticky. 'There,' Helga said as the scent of earth mixed with blood and the smells of a dying man rose from Bjorn's last resting place and choked off anything else she could have said.

'Right between the shoulder blades. Must have gone through the heart,' Hildigunnur said through gritted teeth.

A thought gripped Helga. 'Where's Volund?'

'How in Hel's name should I know?' her mother snapped at her.

'He's inside,' Thyri said.

'And no one thought to fetch him?' Hildigunnur snarled something incomprehensible, grabbed a torch from one of Sigmar's men as she rose and stormed in through the half-open door of the cowshed. 'Volund?'

And then there was quiet, for heartbeat – after heartbeat – after heartbeat. The only sound was the gentle crackle of the lit torches. The darkness in the doorway to the shed spilled silence out into the world like an open grave. Within, Hildigunnur's flame was frozen in time.

Helga had the same idea as Unnthor, but he was half a step quicker.

Inside, shadows swayed on the walls. Hildigunnur was standing stock-still, standing next to Volund's bed, staring at the boy. The blanket had been swept aside.

They all stared at the polished bone hilt of a knife, half tucked under Volund's head rest.

Agla had taken Thyri away to sit by the fire. Gytha and Runa hovered nearby, offering silent companionship and contact, but Bjorn's wife just cried endlessly, silently, her face locked in a mask of suffering – hard cheeks, soft lips held together with force of will.

She did not speak.

'The boy?' Unnthor said.

'He must have seen his father slaughter animals at the farm,' Jorunn said.

'And then?' Hildigunnur said. 'He assaulted his father?'

'Who else? You found the knife in his bed. He must have snuck out – for whatever reason, I don't know – met his father and stabbed him when he turned his back.'

'I think we can see clearly that the halfwit did it,' Sigmar said, looking concerned. 'He has his father's size but none of the sense – and I can't see him denying it. But we should still ask the gods tomorrow,' he added. 'It is only right that they confirm our decision.'

Jorunn nodded. 'You're right. I— What is it, Ingi?'

The runty-looking fellow with hair that was thin on top and wispy on the side had taken three steps towards the group. 'We found tracks.'

'Where?' Hildigunnur said quickly.

Father isn't moving. Unease flooded through Helga's veins. *He knows something.*

'We found them by the northeastern corner of the fence – but they're not coming in. They're going away.'

There was a moment's pause. Then Jorunn said, slowly and quietly, 'Where's Aslak?'

Chapter 15

TRIAL

Helga scanned their faces. Jorunn's eyebrows made her look as if she were solving some complicated puzzle. Her mother looked like caged thunder. Sigmar couldn't quite keep the suspicion off his face.

'The boy had the weapon. He's a halfwit. He did it. Not Aslak,' Unnthor said.

'But—' Jorunn began.

'But nothing. It was not Aslak.' The old man stared at each of them in turn, daring them to challenge him. No one did.

'Then who?'

'Same as it was, Daughter: someone here. And everything suggests that it was the boy. He came to my house as a *guest*.'

Helga could practically see how bitter that last word tasted for her father. Guests' rights were *law* and you could not violate them. Hildigunnur had explained why, once. It was a matter of survival: if your host could not guarantee your safety, no one would travel and no one would trade, and without trade, survival would become that much harder. It even said so in the Havamal.

Unnthor would have to live with the shame of two of his sons murdered under his own roof – the only way he could recover some of his name would be if he could find the murderer and bring him to justice.

And now he had Volund, who had been made to sit by one of the big support beams in the middle with a man on either side to make sure he didn't run. Volund, who had no father to defend him. Volund, whose eyes she had felt following her across the room, silently pleading. Unnthor had his killer, and if Sigmar had his way they'd get an answer from the gods soon enough that would confirm his guilt.

Convenient.

She blinked hard to clear her mind. *No.* That couldn't be it. It *couldn't* be Unnthor. She looked at him again, to try and see a man who could murder in cold blood – and shivered. Oh yes, he was there: in the angles of the jaw and the shadow of the cheekbone, in the breadth of the shoulder and the set of the elbow. He was there all right. But if she couldn't trust her own father – *adoptive father*, her head reminded her – then who could she trust?

The walls of the longhouse suddenly felt a good deal closer.

'I need some air,' she muttered under her breath as she passed her mother. She didn't wait for a reply.

The night embraced her as she stepped out. There was no sound now, no men stampeding around the yard, chasing after a killer. There was just dark, and mostly quiet. She could hear the odd shout from one of Sigmar's people, and she could see the occasional flickering pinpoint of light in the distance, but she felt with odd certainty that they would not find anything that pointed to an outside killer.

No, it had to be one of them.

But who would stab Bjorn in the back?

She snorted when she realised her first guess would have been Karl, but he was very certainly dead and buried. So who then? Aslak? He'd vanished – but she was certain that had something to do with her father. Could they be in on it together? Hardly. How about the ill-tempered wife? No, oddly, Runa was much less combative than she had been at the start of this miserable visit, more content to hang back with her children. Her thoughts came back around to Volund. *Had* he done it? He'd shown her that his father did not treat him all that well – but did that mean *murder*? And anyway, why would he have killed Karl?

She looked up and for a moment thought that she was seeing one face from Riverside for each of the dots in the sky. The thought amused her. *They're all looking down on me.*

Helga drew a deep breath, then let it out slowly and turned towards the longhouse. More thinking would have to wait for tomorrow.

When she woke up, people were already moving about, doors creaking open and slamming shut and she could hear her mother bossing Agla about at the far end of the longhouse. Even through the fog of sleep she felt she could judge reasonably accurately how much trouble Karl's widow was in – not much, but increasing.

'Helga! Don't pretend, you lazy cow. I know you're awake.'

Well, if I wasn't already, I would be now. She swung her legs over the side of the bunk. A breath of morning air hit her shin and Karl's blue skin – his hairy legs, pale and white, cold to the touch – flashed into her memory. She shivered, but shrugged it off. *He won't get any more dead than he is already.*

'Come on! We need to get this done. The sun waits for no one, and we've a lot of work to do.'

Her limbs felt heavy as she rose, and her head thumped in rhythm with her heart. Reluctantly she pulled on her shirt and tied the apron around her waist. The smell of meat drifted towards her – there would have to be an offering for the gods. *Damn things eat better than I do.* She couldn't help but think that deep inside, Unnthor must be cursing his family for what they were doing to his rapidly declining herd.

Hildigunnur had put Agla to work with a spoon the length of her forearm, stirring the big trough full of blood. 'Your father slaughtered four lambs. The gods will tell us the truth – or I am never asking them for anything again. Now, take over from Agla, girl – her arms will be aching.'

'No need – I'm okay,' Agla said, but Helga could see that she was struggling. Not that it came as a surprise: the way Karl had described their farm, it sounded like she didn't have to use her hands at all.

'I know, but I have to put the girl to work. Leave her alone and she'll be sniffing around Sigmar's men next.'

Helga's cheeks flushed, but it was almost out of habit; there was no real outrage in it. She took her place on the high stool and accepted the spoon from Agla, who only barely covered a wince and her look of relief with a wan smile. As Helga set to stirring the blood, Hildigunnur said, 'Keep it nice and smooth. Your father will need to draw on the faces with it and it looks better if it doesn't clump.'

She looked down at the reddish soup. *How much blood is in four lambs? More than in Unnthor's two oldest sons? Or less?* It didn't matter now. It was out of the body and it would do no good. *The gods will tell us nothing.* As the thought flashed through her mind—

—she caught her breath with the intensity of the pain.

The skin on her chest felt like it was burning, a thousand needles stabbing into her, above and between her breasts, a red-hot line pulling on her neck.

'What's wrong?' Hildigunnur's voice sounded far away.

And just as suddenly, the pain was gone.

The relief washed over her so intensely that she was thankful that she was sitting down. Her scalp tingled and she had to struggle not to let her morning water go.

'N-nothing,' she said, recovering the strength to speak properly just in time. 'Just sleepy.'

'Hm.' Her mother glared at her for a moment, then went back to jointing the lamb carcase. Her heart thundering, Helga clutched the spoon and focused her mind on the stirring. Beneath her the blood swirled, death in a circle. The pain echoed in her skin.

What just happened?

'That's probably enough for a while. Go outside, breathe, drink some water. You didn't sleep well,' Hildigunnur said.

Helga could only nod, unable to form the words. When she got up from the stool, she felt lucky that her legs actually did what they had been told.

What is wrong with me?

The sun stung her eyes for the first couple of blinks, but she quickly appreciated her mother's wisdom. It was an absolutely beautiful summer's day – warm and dry, and covered by a blanket of blue sky. Sigmar's men were busy carrying planks of various sizes across the yard and disappearing behind the longhouse, no doubt taking them into the field. She could hear Jaki ordering them about, sounding perfectly comfortable in command. She glanced towards the tool-shed just in time to see Einar disappear out of sight. *He must be busy.*

Absentmindedly, she fingered the thong around her neck and stroked her rune-stones. The moment her fingertip touched the first one everything slowed around her and Helga felt suddenly dizzy. Quick as a flash, it cleared again.

Two.

She looked at the two rune-stones resting on her chest. The rune for need – and the rune for answers. Something was bothering her about this, like a rat crawling around in the back of her head, under the bed, inside the walls, invisible, but not silent.

She needed to ask some questions. *Questions . . . about names and time.* She needed time.

Changing course, she marched back towards the corner of the longhouse, nonchalantly scooped up a water bucket and started towards the slope down to the riverbank. As she walked, she tried to gather her thoughts. *Questions.* She knew she had to ask questions . . . questions about *something* . . . something that had happened in the past.

'But who?'

The words tumbled out of her. Trying to stop herself swivelling round and searching for an unwitting audience, she listened hard for some sort of reaction from the world.

Apart from a solitary raven *quorking* somewhere nearby, there was nothing.

Helga dipped her hand in the cold, flowing water. The chill of it helped clear her head. She dropped the bucket in and as she watched it fill up, she was imagining her head, like the bucket, filling up with ideas.

When she rose, she had a plan.

'They're beautiful.' Gytha stood close to her mother, gazing at the statues of the gods – Freyr, Thor and Odin – standing proud in the sun, dark wood glistening, soaking up the light.

The men had finished erecting a stage of sorts. The god-poles rose well above the heads of even the tallest there, as they should.

'They are,' Hildigunnur said, 'but you know what they say: the beautiful ones are rarely wise.' Agla and Runa, gathered around her, managed a smile. Thyri stood next to them, looking more like a walking corpse.

Such different women, Helga thought. *Thyri is destroyed, but Agla . . . She has recovered rather quickly, hasn't she?* She glanced at Jorunn. The daughter of Riverside looked in her element: relaxed and competent, the very shadow of her mother.

'No time to stand around, you old hens,' Jorunn said suddenly.

'My daughter is, unusually, right. Get to it!'

At Hildigunnur's words, the women dispersed to continue with their allotted tasks. Agla wrapped a slim arm around Thyri's shoulder and led her away, and after a moment, Gytha trailed after them. Jorunn and Runa walked over to where Sigmar was busy pointing and issuing commands.

Helga found herself standing alone with her mother. 'And what do we do?'

'We . . .' Hildigunnur paused, then smiled, a heartfelt smile. 'We wait. That's what we do.' She turned and unexpectedly embraced Helga. 'And though you are not of my blood, you are no less a daughter of mine,' she whispered in Helga's ear.

'Hildigunnur!' Unnthor's voice boomed across the grounds.

'. . . or we don't wait,' the old woman said, smiling ruefully. 'Our work is never done. Come with me – someone might have to hold his paw still while I remove the thorn.'

With that, Hildigunnur set off at a punishing pace, Helga hurrying behind. *They are one*, she thought. *She does for him what he can't do, and he for her.* The idea filled her with an odd, warm feeling. *That must feel good: to have someone you can trust like that.* She came back to the real world just in time to stop herself from crashing into her mother's back. They'd stopped in front of Unnthor and Sigmar.

'We have decided that the gods should be asked at sundown,' Unnthor said.

'Dark words for dark work. Makes sense,' Hildigunnur agreed.

'And Sigmar will be asking.'

What? Helga blinked, waiting to hear someone say that she'd misheard. When no one spoke, she glanced at Hildigunnur, catching the sanctimonious smile on Sigmar's face as she did so.

Her mother's face was very carefully composed, as were her words. 'That makes sense too,' she said, slowly but deliberately. 'He knows the words, and he is family but not blood.' She smiled back at Sigmar, who nodded graciously.

'That's right.' Her father sounded matter-of-fact about this, as if it was the right – no, the *obvious* thing to do.

But it makes no sense whatsoever! Helga wanted to scream. It was *Unnthor's* farm, *Unnthor's* idols, *Unnthor's* sons. He of all people surely had the right to an answer from the gods – and her mother would know all of this. So why wasn't she protesting?

You think Unnthor and Hildigunnur are regular people – but they're not. Einar's words rang in her ears, along with the sneaking feeling that a game was being played and she didn't know the rules.

'And after that,' Unnthor continued, but Hildigunnur interrupted.

'We'll see.'

Unnthor nodded solemnly – but there was a hint of a sparkle in his eye. Menace? Anger? Mirth? There – and now gone, as if it had never been there. His wife turned and walked towards the longhouse, gesturing for Helga to follow.

Helga heard the strands of conversation pick up again, but she couldn't hear the words. *Still*, she thought, *the plan holds.*

Just past midday, Aslak returned. They could feel it in the trembling of the ground, hear it in the baying of the hounds, see it in Sigmar's men shooting glances at each other and gathering behind their leader.

Helga glanced at her father and saw the shadow of a smile on his lips. *So that's where Aslak was – and that's why he didn't kill Bjorn.* She looked back at the youngest brother, who sat straight in the saddle and looked for all the world like the man who owned the place. Behind him, eight sturdy farmers sat astride their horses, looking stern. All of them, she noted, had some manner of weapon – axes, spears, the odd long-knife. *A match for Sigmar's men? Maybe not, but several of them would die.*

This changes things.

'Well met,' Unnthor said.

'Well met, Father.' Was there a hint of satisfaction in his voice? Helga was reminded of a dog sent to fetch a stick, dropping his precious cargo at his master's feet.

'Well met, Brother!' If Sigmar was worried, he did an expert job of hiding it. 'I see you've brought friends?'

'These are our neighbours,' Aslak replied. He was calmer and more assured than Helga had heard him before. More chieftain-like. *More like the* eldest *son.* 'They've come here for the sumbel. My brother was a big man, and his honour must be drunk accordingly.'

'Good!' There was only the faintest hesitation, but Helga caught it, and discovered there was something satisfying about feeling Sigmar squirm. 'We will start when the sun dips down.'

Aslak nodded. 'As we should. It's bad business, and the sooner we get the confirmation we need the better.' A soft wave of agreement swept the mounted riders. Helga tried to imagine them all being roused out of their beds. *My father has reaped his harvest*, she thought, *and he could reap it again, five times over.* In this valley any man would die happy knowing that his children could say he'd taken a blade for Unnthor Reginsson of Riverside.

'Come! We have things to discuss,' Unnthor said, motioning for the newcomers to follow him, and the men dismounted and walked past Sigmar's group without so much as a hint of menace. Behind them Einar and Jaki had appeared and grabbed the reins, leading the horses away. The Swede's face remained studiously cheerful, not changing at all, and looking, to Helga, incredibly false.

Once they'd gone she turned to Hildigunnur. 'There's going to be a sumbel?'

Her mother smiled. 'Of course.' She reached out and held Helga's shoulder firmly. Her bony hand was pleasantly warm through the shift. 'I'll teach you something here, girl. Men rule the world. They are chieftains, they are captains, they are kings. And they will make big decisions. And when they do, the woman who has poured ale down their throat and words in their ear gets to decide what those decisions are. Do you understand?'

Somewhere underneath, something stirred in Helga: a seed of suspicion that almost instantly blossomed into full-blown caution. She had to force herself to reply, squeezing in all the doubt and confusion she could muster. '. . . I . . . I guess.'

Hildigunnur smiled. 'I suspect you'll master all of this soon enough. Just do what I tell you, keep your eyes open and follow.' And with that, she turned away towards the longhouse to prepare a ceremonial drinking feast for the unexpected guests.

Or were they guests? What are Father and Mother planning? And why have I suddenly decided that it's important to play the part of the child? Unbidden, Helga remembered something Unnthor had taught her, skulking around in the forest with her bow when she was much younger.

It's easier to hunt if the prey doesn't know you're there.

Her mind racing again, Helga followed her mother into the longhouse.

The men came back sometime later. Whatever they'd needed to settle between them had obviously been settled – there was a different look about them, like dogs that had decided which way the pack worked. *Hard to be completely sure*, Helga thought, but her gut told her Unnthor had just about clawed back the high seat from Sigmar.

If the chieftain was thinking twice about the look of his great hall, it didn't show. Hildigunnur had pressed Einar into service and two new tables had been hastily assembled. Helga had watched from afar – her friend was practically bristling at her whenever she came close, so after a while she'd stopped trying. Had she said the wrong thing in the tool-shed? Had she pushed too hard? She'd never seen him quite like this before. He was even more miserable now than he had been – he was polite to everyone who spoke to him, but he wasn't *talking*; he said nothing without being asked. The tables had been assembled quick enough, though – he'd driven in each nail with a single precise and heavy smack of the hammer. Now they were all standing ready and laid, with almost every drinking mug and horn in the house set out.

Hildigunnur had asked Thyri to go and fetch a special small cask that had been squirrelled away in the back, hidden behind the regular barrels of honey-mead.

'Right,' Hildigunnur said now, waving a finely wrought pouring jug that Helga was absolutely sure she had never seen before; it had appeared as if by magic from some hidden storage space. 'Bring this to your father,' she said, producing another unknown item: a beautifully carved black drinking horn set with deep silver inlays. 'He'll be served first.'

Helga did as she was told. She recognised some of the men around the table from when they'd visited her father in the past, but their names eluded her, and the moment she saw two or three of them together, she forgot again. They all looked so alike, with solid bodies, thick necks, blocky hands and hard, callused skin. They might have gone into farming looking different, but as much as they'd tried to shape the land, the land had also shaped them.

Unnthor and Sigmar were seated at the top end of the table, but there was no order that she could divine to the rest; Norsemen and Swedes had been mixed up together with little regard to who was and wasn't important. Einar and Jaki had been summoned to sit down and join them, as had Aslak.

Einar wouldn't meet her eye, and Aslak appeared not to care about anything but his family.

Bjorn would have loved a seat at this table. I'd bet he'd be telling dirty jokes at his own send-off. Helga found she was missing the giant, and she spared a thought for Thyri. He'd been loud and annoying, for sure, but he'd certainly been entertaining company.

She set the drinking horn down by Unnthor's right hand, next to Sigmar. Her father shot her a brief glance and almost imperceptibly bowed his head – *thank you* – but immediately returned to the role he played so comfortably, sitting in his great chair, listening carefully to the men and dispensing quiet advice. There was no such thing as a king in these parts, but if a stranger had wandered in tonight he'd not have known that.

Next to him, Sigmar had a smile affixed to his face. At a casual glance he would have looked the happy right-hand man, but Helga knew better: the smile didn't reach his eyes.

So the game is still being played – and I suspect the rules are being written, broken and re-written as we go.

She could sense Hildigunnur moving behind her, and the men fell quiet as she advanced towards her husband.

'In this house you will raise your cups towards the seat of the Allfather,' she intoned.

'In this house we will raise our cups,' the men replied as one. The timbre of their voice sent a shiver down Helga's spine as she sat unmarked in her spot in the shadows; it wasn't an altogether unpleasant sensation.

Now at the head of the table, Hildigunnur poured a careful measure into Unnthor's horn. He waited for half a breath, then gestured towards the guests, and moving together, Agla, Jorunn and Runa stepped forward with jugs of their own and started filling each cup, their movements neat and precise. As soon as the men's mugs were filled, the women stepped back.

Unnthor raised his horn, and a beat later, the men did the same.

'Drink wisely, drink slowly,' Unnthor intoned, 'for tonight, we talk to the gods.'

The men followed his actions, carefully sipping the sweet-smelling ale. By the odd twitch of an eye or flinch of a shoulder, Helga guessed that her mother's brew was warming their insides. 'Now: Sigmar. Tell us a tale of Freyr, for we wish our crops to grow.'

'When the moon rises over the eastern seas . . .'

He fell easily into the rhythm of the skalds, reeling off an old story about the fertility god, a farmer with a lame leg and his buxom daughter. The men sat and listened politely, occasionally looking towards the chieftain at the head of the table. Not one of them spared the women a second glance.

But Helga noticed as the first one – it was Runa – quietly slipped out through the back door. Agla followed, then Thyri and Hildigunnur. When Gytha left as well, Helga hurried on after her.

Outside, the last rays of the sun were stretching across the sky. There was a particular quality to the light just before it left, Helga thought. It was the last chance you'd get for a while to see things clearly. The chill in the shadow of the longhouse made the hairs on the back of her neck stand on end, but she shrugged it off and followed the women, who were heading in a tight-knit group out to the big stone.

They hadn't waited for her to arrive and she walked into the conversation already started.

'—but the matter needs to be resolved,' Hildigunnur finished. The other women had shifted position and now everyone was standing next to Hildigunnur and facing Thyri, who stood before them like Helga imagined a beggar might at a queen's court.

Silence followed.

Hildigunnur said, 'You understand that, don't you?'

Trying her best not to feel like an intruder, Helga inched in towards the circle and stopped when she was just about a part of it, but not quite next to her mother and Agla.

Thyri looked back at Hildigunnur. 'Of course I do.'

'And?'

Thyri locked eyes with the old woman. Moments passed. 'Your son was murdered under your roof.'

This time it was Hildigunnur's turn to swallow the silence.

Thyri's features looked like they had been carved from the mountainside. 'And now . . .' The moment hung in the air between them. 'Now you expect me to . . .' It was warmer here, out in the falling sunshine, but Helga's hairs still stood on end. No one dared breathe.

'Four,' Thyri said at last, firmly.

Hildigunnur exhaled sharply. It could even have been a choked-down laugh.

'Each.'

Out of the corner of her eye Helga saw her mother's eyebrows rise. '*Four*? You have to be—'

'We both know the boy couldn't have done it,' Thyri said. 'You know it because you're smart, and I know it because I am his mother. But if you want me to give up my only child after I lose my only love, you'll be only too happy to pay me four men's worth for each of them.'

'Two.' Hildigunnur's voice had all the warmth of stones smashing together.

Thyri smiled. 'That's amusing,' she said. 'I thought the honour of the Riverside family would cost more than that. What do you think will happen to your trade when the story comes out?'

'What story?' Hildigunnur snapped.

'I haven't decided yet,' Thyri said, sweetly. 'If you say the gods want to take my boy's life, then so be it. But I will make up something delightful, something that the pig-wives will be all too happy to carry wherever they go. And when they do—?' Thyri looked Hildigunnur in the eye, and suddenly Helga saw all too well how this woman had managed to stand up to her huge husband. 'They'll charge double for what you buy and give you half for what you want to sell. They'll whisper behind your back, and they will certainly not come to you for advice, and your living husband's name will be mud. And that, to you, is worth a bag of gold?'

Two cats, squared off. Any moment now the claws will come out.

Hildigunnur's eyes narrowed. She took a deep breath, then another. 'Four for Bjorn. Two for Volund.'

Thyri swallowed hard. 'Done.'

The two women clasped hands and quick as a flash, Hildigunnur drew Thyri in and gave her a fierce hug as she whispered something in her ear.

Bjorn's wife shuddered, then with a visible show of force she stilled, and they separated.

'If she gets that, then so should I.' Agla's voice was thin, high-pitched, close to breaking.

'Mother!' Gytha hissed, but Agla would not stop.

'With Karl gone, we will be without any means of providing for ourselves within the year. She will have no dowry, and the name of your husb—'

Hildigunnur didn't even look at her. 'You will get thrice the blood-price for your husband.' Agla's mouth hung open for a blink, then closed. Beside her, Gytha stood red-faced.

Thyri just sold her son. The realisation hit Helga like a boulder in the stomach. *She just sold her . . . her unknowing son.*

'And this is how it's going to go.'

Helga managed to fight her impulse to run away, but listening to her mother's voice meticulously laying out a simple plan strengthened her resolve. *If no one will fight for Volund's life . . .* Her jaw tensed. *I'm going to have to do it myself.*

Behind her, the last fingerbreadth of the sun dipped below the horizon.

Chapter 16

SUNSET

Unnthor placed his empty drinking horn gently down on the table. 'It is time,' he said.

Sigmar looked round for Thormund. 'Take the men out. We will be with you shortly.' The gangly man rose and gestured at the other Swedes, who stood up in ones and twos and moved towards the big doors.

After a gesture from Unnthor the Norse farmers did the same and within moments the big house was empty save for the two men.

'So,' Sigmar said.

'Here we are.'

'Yes.'

'Did you kill them?'

Sigmar froze and stared at the big man. 'No,' he said eventually.

'I know what you are. No need to hide it. Did you?'

The Swede relaxed, and the right corner of his mouth twitched briefly. 'No. I didn't.'

Unnthor nodded, slowly.

'Did you?'

The big man's eyebrows arched. 'No,' he said.

'Good! Now that we've got that out of the way, let's go and ask the gods whether the boy did it.' They stepped back from the table, neither turning his back on the other, until Sigmar smiled and pointed at his bed. 'I'll be over here. You do what you need to do.'

The old man stood his ground, watching the Swede walk across the floor of the longhouse. Only when the younger man was standing by his own bed and reaching for a bundle of black cloth did he move towards the corner where he slept.

Helga watched the men leaving the longhouse. The procession was not particularly orderly, but there was an odd solemnity about it. They looked important and thoughtful. *And none of them knows that their little line of ducks means nothing. Everything has been decided.*

She looked over at Thyri, who was standing as tall as she could, her jaw jutting out in defiance, her lips pursed, looking ready to argue her son's life on the point of a knife. *Just like she has to.* The men had to rule; that was the way of the world. But women like Hildigunnur, and Jorunn . . . Helga looked at the assembled women. *Like every one of them, come to think of it.* None of them looked particularly like they wanted to be ruled by men. She thought back on all the big, important decisions she'd seen Unnthor make. Or think he'd been making.

Every time he'd done anything, he'd done it after long talks with Hildigunnur.

So who was the true chieftain of Riverside, then?

The doors of the longhouse opened. *Well, there's the one who looks like it.*

Unnthor, son of Reginn, stepped out in a dark blue shirt and black trousers. A massive black cape hung over his shoulders, pinned by a silver brooch the size of a man's palm. A triple line of silver crossed his right arm. Helga caught more than one man working hard not to stare. A chieftain measured himself by the rings on his arms, and while Unnthor had never been one for showing off, that had to be the biggest armband anyone in present company had ever seen. Standing straight-backed, he looked less the bent, tired old farmer and more a mythical warrior from the old tales.

Sigmar walked beside him, dressed all in black, his clothes simple but well fitting and made of expensive fabric. Hildigunnur had told her that unlike the spring or winter festivals, they'd be dressing to fit the occasion. *Well – there wasn't much cheer to it, that was for certain.*

She spied out Einar and inched close to him. 'The old man looks good,' she muttered, but Einar's only answer was a grunt. 'You're quite the sore bear today! What's the matter?' she asked, but Einar didn't respond. She gently placed a hand on his forearm, only to feel the contact between them disappear as he stepped away from her.

Not you too.

It suddenly felt like Einar would be the last person she could ever speak to, and now he too was moving away from her.

Tears welled up in her eyes. 'Talk to me,' she whispered. '*Please.*'

Einar swallowed, but remained silent.

She was about to scream at him, at everyone, at the world, but the procession of men had reached the big stone and it was time to be silent.

When the two men in black reached the stone, Unnthor unclasped the armband and handed it to Sigmar. It was a massive thing, thrice-woven. Clutching it, the Swede locked eyes with the massive Norseman and they dipped their heads to each other, then Unnthor stepped back to stand in line with the men.

Sigmar turned to the stone, and it felt to Helga like the world drew breath. Only the far western side of the sky was still bright with the last rays of sunshine, but Jaki had lit mounted torches that gave heat, warmth and shadow. The darkness crept over them from the east and was now reaching over the longhouse like a bear paw.

Unnthor's armband caught the light of the flames as the Swede raised it to the sky.

'I swear an oath upon the honour of Riverside!' he cried.

He brought the circlet down slowly, the silver sparkling in the torchlight, a dancing snake in his hand travelling inexorably towards its destination. The black surface of the bowl shimmered: a pool of darkness deeper and more forbidding than the night sky.

A gateway to the depths. Images collided in Helga's mind – claws breaking the clean line of blackness, sinewy limbs rising to break into their world, jaws distended in silent screaming as something rose—

The pictures shattered as the armband sank into the blackness. The light reflected from the slowly immersing silver showed flashes of red, circles spreading from the wound formed by the intrusion. Sigmar did not hesitate. The band continued sinking – half under now, then two-thirds – and his knuckles drew closer and closer to the blood in the bowl.

Helga couldn't stop herself wincing when Sigmar's hand clutching the end of the triple circle sank into the blood; she only breathed out when the descent stopped.

Sigmar's voice rang out. 'I swear an oath on Midgard!'

'MIDGARD!' The men's voices exploded into the sinking night.

'I call forth the gods of Asgard to give us wisdom!'

The whispering in the leaves above them gave a moment's warning before the wind swept up out of nowhere, tugging at clothes and pushing hair out of place – and then it was gone again. Wherever she glanced, Helga could see eyes widen and looks being exchanged.

The gods are listening.

Sigmar drew a deep breath and shouted as loud as he could into the skies, 'Tell us, Odin! Did you see Volund, son of Bjorn, murder his father and his father's brother with a stolen blade?'

The silence was absolute. One breath . . . two breaths . . .

If anyone had made any sound, they would have missed it . . .

. . . the sound of a drop, hitting a wet surface.

'L-look!' Hildigunnur shouted. '*Odin!*'

All eyes went to the carved idol of the Allfather. A dark line had formed in the wood, leading straight down from the one uncovered eye.

'He bleeds!'

'He *saw*!' That was Jorunn's voice.

'The gods have replied!' Sigmar roared. 'Asgard has spoken!'

Beside Hildigunnur, Thyri burst into tears, and Runa and Agla turned to her at once, hugging the distraught woman.

'My boy,' she wailed, but any other words were muttered into her kinswomen's shoulders.

That's right. Hide your face, woman. Helga was surprised at the heat in her breast. This was nothing but an elaborate song and dance to convince . . . *who*?

She looked around. This was the work of her parents – her *adoptive* parents – of that there could be little doubt. The men of the valley would carry it to their neighbours, how the fey giant boy murdered his uncle and then his father. But Sigmar and Jorunn? Did they believe this? Did Runa? Did Aslak?

Under Sigmar's chanting, the skies looked as if they were darkening quicker than usual. When he thanked the gods for their wisdom, poured the blood at their feet and said the blessings for fertility and survival, a cold wind blew in from the north, making Helga shiver. It was almost as if the gods were listening to him going through with this – this *whatever it was* – and were not impressed.

She felt woozy. It was all too much. Everyone and everything felt strange to her – Mother and Father were not like she'd ever seen them, and Einar . . . She felt a pang in her chest, then a wash of guilt as she remembered why they were there in the first place.

Volund.

What had happened to Bjorn? Who would tell her? What could she *do*?

Ask him. The idea was there, like a bird landing on a branch. *Ask the question.* She didn't move an inch; almost didn't look at it. *Yes. Something doesn't add up. Ask Bjorn. Go and look at the body. Go – do it now.* The urge to know almost pushed her off her feet and back down towards the shed where Bjorn rested, ready to be put in the ground the following morning.

Almost, but not quite.

Helga was still aware of taut muscles near her, of eyes trained on the gods far harder than they merited. She was becoming more and more certain that Volund hadn't done it – and that meant the murderer still walked among them, and would most likely not be very happy about her going to find out more about the killings.

She almost missed Sigmar concluding the ceremony. The silence lay heavy on the summer night, broken only by the occasional *snark* of a torch. Everyone knew what had to happen in the morning, but nobody was looking forward to it.

'We will sit at sumbel to think on this,' Unnthor said. 'Come, friends. The gods have spoken, and it is for us to listen.' He turned and led the way towards the longhouse. Farmers and Swedes alike looked all too happy to follow.

Helga drifted along behind them. There would be things to do – and somehow, she had to get out and find more information before night turned into morning.

The sumbel slowly but very surely picked up pace as mead went down and spirits went up. Thyri had retreated to spend the night with Bjorn's body, but the rest were happy to avail themselves of

Unnthor's mead. The barrel of strong had disappeared again – *my mother really must be part witch, the way she can do that* – but others had emerged in its place.

Her back to the table as she methodically scraped left-over stew from the bowls into a bucket for later use, Helga let the words wash over her.

'—King Eirik can't avoid going west for ever—'

'He will if he knows what's best for him! The west is best left to the Danes. They'll all disappear eventually, like Rollo.' Laughter among the men.

'Rollo just had the good sense to settle where the land is green, the women are soft and the men are both green and soft!'

More laughter.

The conversation flowed between the men; Jorunn and Agla participated, Gytha listened. Einar was somewhere else, and Helga found she didn't mind that. The boy had looked like a boil-arsed bull since . . . since . . .

Since Jorunn said she was pregnant?

The door to the storeroom in her mind creaked open, and Helga stepped inside.

Someone had killed Karl. And then someone had killed Bjorn. Most of them would have had a reason to kill the oldest brother – but only Karl would have had a good reason to kill Bjorn. So had Karl somehow reached out from beyond the grave? She chided herself and a voice suspiciously close to Hildigunnur's whispered in the back of her mind, *Don't be stupid, girl. Think about what Thyri said.* There had been not one but *two* voices outside. So who had been arguing with Bjorn? The work disappeared in her hands and Helga found herself with a head full of thoughts and nothing to do. As gently as she could, she drifted towards the door and ducked out.

The cooler night air was refreshing and invigorating, with a gentle breeze drifting in from the river. She could almost taste the cold, fresh water on her tongue, imagine it flowing over the smoothly polished stones. There were other smells, too – tendrils of warm animal musk crossed the yard, lingering where a horse had rubbed up against a fence post, wafting from a corner where a dog had marked its territory.

And, faintly, Helga could smell blood. Her heart thumped – *not another one, please, no* – but then she remembered the pillar with Odin's face, weeping right next to the torch, carved features like a gaunt ghost in the blossoming dark.

'What are you doing out?'

She started at Jaki's voice, but there was enough warmth in it to calm her down immediately. 'Hello, old man.' She could hear in her own voice how tense she was, and tried to breathe herself calmer.

'It's a good night.' He must have been able to hear it too. Jaki's voice was soothing, like when he dealt with skittish animals. 'How are they getting on in there?'

'I don't know – and I don't know that I care.' The ease with which the truth flowed out surprised Helga, but she wasn't lying. Suddenly, she didn't care any more. *So what if whoever it is kills all of us? We've all got to die sometime.* The thought was equal parts thrilling, exhausting and sad. 'They're in there drinking, and they've just decided to slice open a boy's throat tomorrow morning.'

Jaki stepped closer, and Helga took a good look at him. *How do our people become so old? Only last year you were impossibly big.* She could see how Unnthor's right-hand man must have been built like his son once, but old age had worn him down like water does the rock. He was sunken, somehow – almost all of his life spent, and on what? Lugging timber and mending tools.

'The gods spoke.'

'Of course they did,' Helga all but spat. 'And they gave exactly the answer that everyone wanted: we get to pick out the weakest in the group – the only one who can't defend himself' – her tears flowed free and hot – 'and meanwhile whoever *really* killed Karl and Bjorn walks away. They walk away free, and everything goes back to the way it was.'

'I know,' Jaki murmured, comfortingly, 'I know. They're a funny lot, the Riverside folk.' He looked around. 'Come with me. We have some time – let's sit and look at the water. It helps sometimes.'

Helga felt the gentle, warm touch on her elbow as his heavy, leathery hand nudged her along. She fought the urge to dry her tears. Maybe he hadn't noticed. For some reason, that became the most important thing in her world at that moment: that old Jaki didn't think she was soft.

'I love this river,' Jaki said.

'Why? It's just a river.'

'Maybe. But if you listen to it—' He stopped talking, and they both focused on the rippling water. 'Hear that? It's laughing. The water is laughing at us as it floats past.' He guided her to a well-worn spot on the riverbank and took a seat nearby. 'And when I was young that used to make me angry. "How dare you laugh at me!" I'd growl, and I'd grip whatever tool I was using, real good, hard enough to smash a skull, and I'd work furiously. And then . . .' The old man paused.

I can hear him smiling. 'Then what?'

'I'd wake up in the morning, aching and sore, and the water would still be laughing at me.' Below their feet there was a splash in the darkness as the river agreed. 'And I thought to myself that maybe I mattered less than I thought. And if I did, maybe so did everybody else.'

'So you're saying Volund's life doesn't matter? Not really?' Helga felt her throat tighten in fury.

'No, no, no – I'm not saying that at all,' the old man replied, with warmth in his voice. 'I'm saying that sometimes you have to move on, regardless. There are always more things to get done.' In the silence they could hear a muted shout from the longhouse, followed by a wave of laughter. 'I'll tell you a story, though. You came here, what? Five winters ago?'

'Eleven,' Helga said quietly.

'Eleven! Loki's balls but that is a long time,' Jaki muttered. 'Well. So this must have been a good fifteen summers back.

'Jorunn was growing up to look exactly like her mother, so the old folks told me. A slice of summer, they always said. She was light on her feet then, too – and she had to be, because every boy in the valley and the next three over was finding some excuse to come here with various bits of nonsense – wood for the carts, hay for the horses, supplies for the household. Unnthor told me he remembered lending out about half of what was returned to him that summer. Even back then everyone thought highly of Unnthor of Riverside, and it would have been a great match for any family to have wed one of theirs to his daughter.'

Try as she might, she struggled to imagine the guests as people her age, let alone her adoptive parents without white hair.

'Anyway, his name was Dreyri. He was a horse trainer at Oakfell in Skidal, and a fine-looking specimen he was too: strong and lean, and blessed with a pretty face. They met at a market fair down on the plains, and Jorunn made her mind up pretty quickly that she wanted him, and because he had eyes in his head and half a brain to match, he wanted her.

'Only the gods didn't smile on the match. Jorunn asked her mother for counsel; she asked Unnthor, and Unnthor . . . well, he said no.'

'Why?' She was almost twitching with the need to hear the rest.

Jaki smiled at her impatience. 'Because the boy had no land, no family and no history. There was no sign that he could offer Jorunn any sort of life other than as a huskarl's wife, and that at best, so Unnthor decided that it wasn't going to happen.

'Oh, there were tears and screams, and a hurled axe or two, but the old man stood firm: he said *he* made the rules, and that there would be no negotiating.

'So Jorunn decided to take matters into her own hands.

'The boy came here under cover of darkness, with two horses, and they stole away in the middle of the night. Unnthor was furious, of course, but nowhere near as mad as Hildigunnur – truly, I thought she'd kill us all. She didn't say much – she never does when she's that angry – but I made sure to stay well away.'

'And then what?'

'Jorunn came back two days later, looking like she'd been in a fight – which she probably had, come to think of it. She didn't want to talk about Dreyri – and neither did anybody else.'

Helga frowned. 'Why not?'

'He was never found,' Jaki said. 'Not ever. And keep in mind that your father and mother know a lot of people in these parts. They'd certainly have heard about the passing of the man who almost stole their daughter.'

'That's true,' Helga said.

And it works both ways: every one of their friends in the area would hear of their wise solution to their minor murdering problem . . .

'But I looked after the horses then, and I know that someone rode out after her.'

Suddenly, Helga was more than aware of the cold on her skin and a growing heat around her neck where the rune-stones lay. Fragments of images flashed through her mind – a rider in moonlight, a hunter quietly stalking prey, screams, the face of a beautiful boy up close, terrified, and then broken. She felt the weight of him, dragging through the forest behind an unseen attacker. She saw the ground come closer as the hunter bent down and touched a paw-print.

Left for the animals.

'Jorunn was furious – she was her mother's daughter, after all – and she swore she would never look at another man. Hildigunnur said fair enough, no doubt expecting time to heal the wounds.

But now there were whispers,' Jaki continued, 'and some of Jorunn's suitors were turning bitter at the constant rejections, and more and more fathers were seeing the lack of a wedding as a declaration that no one in the area was good enough for Riverside. Unnthor didn't care – he was never much good at doing what other people wanted.' She could hear the fondness in the old man's voice.

'Luckily, he married well. Hildigunnur could see the storm on the horizon, and so she pulled Karl aside and told him to find the girl a husband.'

'And he did.'

'What boy ever says no to his mother?' Jaki said. 'Of course he did. He left immediately to go a-Viking, without so much as a word to anyone. Cost him a wife of his own, too.'

'Oh?'

'Didn't you know?' Helga frowned, but didn't reply, and Jaki said, 'He was supposed to be married to Runa, but after she'd waited for him for half a year she decided on Aslak instead.'

Helga could feel the cold air gently streaming into her wide-open mouth. Absent-mindedly, she reached up and pushed her mouth closed. *Runa was—*

The thought crashed into all the others in her head, and she felt dizzy. 'I did not know that,' she managed.

'Worked out well enough,' Jaki said. 'Hildigunnur played for time, bought a couple of friends in the valley and beyond with generous gifts come harvest-time. A few months later Karl arrived, talked to the parents, and off Jorunn went. You couldn't argue with Swedish nobility, after all.'

'*What?*'

'Couple of lines down, maybe, but Sigmar is second cousin to Eirik the Victorious.'

'That . . .' A small giggle burst out of her as she thought of all those self-important farmers of the valley, standing in the Riverside yard like landed fish. 'You're right, you can't. And there are clearly *many* things I don't know about the family.'

'You'd be surprised,' Jaki said. 'The family at Riverside rarely stops to dwell, not if they can move forward. Now, even though your kin are more dog than cat, and more wolf than dog, are you ready to go back inside?'

'I guess so.'

'Good.' The old man paused. 'You've got spirit, Helga of Riverside. I . . . I never had a daughter,' he said, haltingly, 'but if I had, I hope she'd have turned out like you.'

Helga bit her teeth together so hard that she half thought they'd crack in her mouth. Instead of speaking, she wrapped her arms around Jaki's solid shoulders and squeezed him for all she was worth, absorbing the warmth and the smell of him, storing the comfort he had given in a locked box next to her heart. 'Thank you,' she whispered, only reluctantly letting go before heading back towards the longhouse.

When she was halfway there she looked over her shoulder, but he'd gone. There were always more things to get done.

After the darkness and the cold air of the riverbank, the warmth of the longhouse was stifling. The guests were not yet drunk, but they'd definitely increased both the speed of drinking and the volume since she'd gone out – and someone needed to refill their cups. Helga fell into her routine quickly, swooping in between men's thick bodies to slosh the amber liquid in the mugs. She'd heard stories of girls having to keep one hand free to fend off grabbing paws at all times, but that kind of thing didn't happen at Riverside. *Mother would have their head.* No, the men largely ignored her, just continuing talking among themselves.

'—and I've heard that the Rus are moving further south.'

'What? Again?'

'Not enough space, they say.'

'Maybe Vladivar has just finished fighting everyone he knows and needs a new friend,' someone chimed in, and there was laughter at that, rough and choppy. She'd heard something about this Vladivar, she thought: a fierce warlord somewhere to the southeast. The men obviously found the idea of him having a friend very funny. The Swedes and the locals were mixing freely now, all tribal ties forgotten. *Or that's what it looks like, at least.* These days it was increasingly hard to know when the knives would come out.

On one side of the table, Jorunn had engaged two of Unnthor's farmer friends in conversation. She couldn't hear what they were talking about, but the old men were hanging on the young woman's every word like dogs with their master. There: a moment – and then a loud bark of laughter from one, immediately followed by the other. They were practically eating out of her hand – but was there an ounce of truth in whatever she was telling them? Helga found that Jorunn's lies sat uneasy with her. There was no doubt in her soul that the woman was lying – but *why*? Did the reason have anything to do with Karl?

Following that thought, another six or seven tumbled in and Helga had to squeeze her eyes shut in order not to shout.

One question. She needed just one question.

Who did it?

The buzz and clatter of the longhouse intruded on her thoughts again, and she caught the gimlet glare of Hildigunnur's eyes across the room. She stood next to Sigmar, who was deep in conversation with a heavyset, greying man who looked like Unnthor without the hill-troll heritage. Helga knew that look: *Work, girl!* And so she did, swinging by the table that held the mead jug and picking a route towards Hildigunnur and Sigmar that set her floating past Jorunn's little circle.

'. . . and I only just managed to sneak the eggs out of the way before he sat down. The king had no idea!' Gales of laughter. 'Can you imagine?' Helga walked away as the rest of Jorunn's story rolled off the tongue. Very much Hildigunnur's daughter, that one – the rehearsed tale skipped along merrily, and while entertaining the men Jorunn would be measuring them, drawing conclusions, arranging them into groups: trusted and not trusted – no, soft or hard. *That's how the Riverside family sees the world, isn't it? You're soft – or you're hard.*

Her mother was definitely in the latter category. Helga had seen her play the game before, talking so no one else got a word in while weighing up options and deciding who to favour. *Control.* It was all about control.

'You look thoughtful, darling daughter,' her mother said once Helga was close enough. The mead was honey-sweet on her breath.

Helga smiled. It felt weak on her face, weak and false. 'Lots of people,' she muttered.

Her mother smiled back and Helga felt the familiar thin but warm hand on her forearm. 'One day you'll have a home of your own to run.' Was she slurring ever so slightly at the edges? 'A husband to give you children, and children to give you nothing but trouble.' For a moment, the old woman paused. *What is she thinking?* She looked like she wanted to say something else, but then she thought better of it. 'And you'll be able to make this' – she gestured across the hall, where guests were standing and talking, mixing with new people and having good-natured arguments – 'happen without so much as an extra heartbeat of worry.'

Beside them, Sigmar stopped swinging his arms to make his point for a blink of an eye, and Helga refilled his tankard with a swift motion, taking care not to spill a single drop. She fought back a frown. She knew what awaited – husband, house and children – but . . . *this?*

I have to leave Riverside.

The impact of the thought was such that she only just managed to keep the smile stuck on her face and add a feeble, 'Yes.'

No.

Absolutely not.

How long have I known?

Still smiling, she walked away from Sigmar and the big farmer, neither of whom had so much as acknowledged her presence. *Must be nice, living in a world where your mug fills up without you noticing.*

But there was no room for anything else in her head because the new thought was there, like a bear in a cage, thrashing about.

I have to leave Riverside.

She saw it now. The place was cursed. Anyone who grew up in this corner of the world was doomed to a life of violence. It wasn't the world out there that had turned them bad – they were bad to begin with. She had to go and see other places, escape the shadow of the longhouse.

The thought of dropping everything there and then was pulling at her like a dream of sunshine and honey.

If I leave now, I'll always remember him. I can't let them get away with killing an innocent boy.

The memory of Volund's eyes was cold water on her head. There was something rotten in Riverside – but what was it?

And who?

Chapter 17

HUNTER

The smell of mead, breath and sweat pressed down on Helga. *Out. Now.* She caught her mother's eye and gestured towards the water butt, then the jug, then the door. All she got in return was a shrug. The door beckoned and she slipped out as quickly as she could without actually running. The air outside was like cold water on a hot day. She drank it in, feeling her mind clear with each gulp.

Who did it?

The question nagged at her, biting at her heels, buzzing around the inside of her head. She walked towards the river again and started making a list in her head. 'No,' she snapped out loud, 'that's not it. No list.' Instead, she tried to *remember*: Karl, lying flat in his bed, greyish-blue to look at, cold to the touch. The wound that killed him – two thin lines, one on each groin. Bjorn, dead. Lying half on his back, half on his side. Stabbed in the back, with force. The wound that killed him was . . .

Helga squeezed her eyes shut and tried to remember. *Come on!* She imagined Bjorn's shift, his bunched muscles, the sticky spot on his back where the knife had entered, between the shoulder blades, probably straight through the heart on the first blow. It had either been very skilled, or lucky, and delivered with great strength or great fury . . .

But why couldn't she remember the wound?

In her mind she could build a picture of Hildigunnur, looking at the body, then going straight into the hut – and then they'd found the knife.

We never saw the wound.

For some reason she couldn't quite understand, this annoyed her tremendously. But before she could start thinking what she could do about it, her feet had decided for her.

The hut where they had put Bjorn's body until the sun rose sat in the corner of the yard like a squat lump of rock dropped by a giant. It was an inglorious final resting place, but it was the only place that made sense after the god-speaking had decided. Unnthor would not want others around for the burial. The men had been talking about it at length, discussing the merits of various buildings – and they'd have taken half a day to get to it, too, except for the fact that Hildigunnur had inched her way into Unnthor's field of vision, caught his eye and glanced towards the old hut. It had been easy enough work for Einar and Jaki to clear sufficient space to lay Bjorn down, and a lot harder for six men to lift and carry him to his resting place.

Helga put her hand on the latch.

'Who's there?'

Her heart stopped for a moment and her throat seized up in

cold terror. *Get a grip on yourself!* Her ears caught up and as she recognised the voice, she silently cursed her mother's kindness. Out of consideration Hildigunnur had asked them to make space for Thyri to sit by the corpse of her dead husband.

'Who's there?' A rising note of fear.

'It's me,' Helga said to the door, as softly as she could, 'Helga.'

Silence. Then, 'Oh.' The door creaked open and a small bubble of soft warm light spilled out. Thyri had lit a candle inside. 'Come in.'

Steady. There was a faint smell that came with the light. It was hard to detect at first, but it was definitely there. *Steady!* Slaughter season . . . stale blood . . . death.

SPEAK, YOU HALFWIT!

'Thank you,' Helga said, still keeping her voice down. It looked like the big man on the bier was just sleeping, and she was suddenly horribly afraid that she might wake him up and he'd start being loud again. *Don't be a fool*, the voice in her head snarled at her. She grasped for words, weighed up choices and inched into the cramped space. Thyri reached past her hip and closed the door. Her body-heat added to the sensations – not unpleasant, but too close.

Everything in here is too close.

The hut wasn't big to start with, and Bjorn's body filled the length of it. On his other side, building materials had been stacked haphazardly around a broken cart and a load of sacks each about the size of a child. She struggled to make out the shape. *Wool?* Hard to tell – *also, not important*, she chided herself.

The square that Jaki and Einar had cleared for Thyri was no

bigger than half a sleeping bunk, but they'd provided her with a footstool to sit on, and she'd found a place on some boards to melt a candle onto.

It's a den: a den with a dead animal in it. The cave where the bear crawled to die—

Quick. Say something.

'So,' she tried, cursing herself for how weak she sounded – what would Hildigunnur have done? *Get her talking.* 'How . . . are you feeling?' The light was soft, but not soft enough to hide the flash of contempt on the older woman's face. Helga watched her bite down on it, swallow it down, replace it with kindness.

'I'm . . . surviving.'

'Sometimes that's all we can do.' She tried to leave the sentence on a pause, like she'd heard her mother do – gently nudge the door open for Thyri to start talking – but nothing was forthcoming. *It was going to take more.* 'Have you spoken to Jorunn?'

'No.' The reply was clipped. If Helga was trying to open the door, this was a very real attempt to slam it shut again. She felt an unexpected flash of delicious, combative pride.

Do you not know who I am?

Do you not know where I am from?

I'm from Riverside, woman.

You cannot brush me off that easily.

'It must have been hard for her as well, to find her brother like that.' Thyri huffed, but there was no immediate rebuttal. *Time to cast the net.* 'They had looked happy to see each other.'

'He liked Jorunn.' There was a husky note in her voice.

Helga reached out and placed a hand on Thyri's forearm. She

felt the flinch, but Bjorn's wife did not pull away. 'He seemed to like most people.'

'Huh. Most, yes.'

'But not Karl.'

'Oh, I don't know,' Thyri said, 'I think he maybe liked him more than he let on. Karl was a bastard, but you always knew where you stood with him. They went through some things together, and I think Bjorn will . . .' Her voice trailed off, then she swallowed and finished, 'I think Bjorn would have fought for his brother in any kind of circumstance.'

'Oh, absolutely.' *Not a chance.* 'They must have been quite a pair when they were younger.'

'They were,' Thyri said, and her voice warmed with memory.

Helga looked down, partly to hide her smile. *In the net you go, little fish.* 'I bet you know some stories.'

'Oh, I do. But you've probably heard them all.'

'Me? No – you know Unnthor and Hildigunnur, they're always thinking forward, always wanting to get to the next year, next harvest, next lambing. They're not big on old tales.'

'So have you heard nothing of your near-brothers in their youth?'

'Not really, no,' Helga said. *So this is what a hunt feels like. Careful, now.* 'There was one story I heard, just recently.'

'Which one?'

'About how Jorunn ran away with a pretty stable-boy?' She could sense tension rising in the woman across from her and forced a light note into her voice. 'She must have been about my age, maybe? Headstrong and ready to go out into the world?'

'That was a bad business,' Thyri said. 'I saw the boy, and he truly was a beauty to behold. No wonder she jumped him. But he had cruel eyes. He'd have left her pregnant in a fishing village somewhere before moving on to the next one – rumour had it he'd already done so twice, and that was why he was up in the valleys.'

'And did Bjorn and Karl go after him?'

'No,' Thyri said firmly.

Then who did? The question bounced around in Helga's head, but she managed to hold it back for a moment. 'So does anyone know what happened, exactly?'

'No,' Thyri said, 'but Aslak disappeared shortly after Jorunn did, and they rode back together. I can only assume that the boy ran away down to the coast or something.'

For a moment, Helga felt like she could feel her skin crawling away from her. Aslak's carved face stared at her from inside her eyeballs, grinning like a nasty mouser in an old barn. *Sure he did.* That boy was buried in the woods. 'Imagine that,' she said, stopping just short of pulling the corners of her mouth up by hand. 'But I reckon if Bjorn had just cleared his throat at the right moment, he could have scared the lad straight.'

'I know what you might think,' Thyri said, 'but despite what he looked like, Bjorn wasn't actually like that. Had Karl been near his size, he might be king now.'

'So Bjorn rarely had a fight?'

Thyri looked down on the prone body with deep affection. 'Barely needed to. They'd take one look at him and get a real need to be somewhere else. And I wouldn't have let him fight, anyway.'

'How so?'

'When we met, he was . . .' She swallowed. 'He was always in the middle. People were drawn to him because he was loud and funny and hard to lose sight of. And girls would throw themselves at him, ask him to lift them up and fondle his arms.' *Oh. So that's it.* In the darkness, Helga's eyebrow arched. You could skin a deer with the sharpness in Thyri's voice. Suddenly the idea of this tiny woman ordering the giant Bjorn around didn't sound too far-fetched. 'There was one – Alfhild, her name was – who found him after I'd laid my claim. She was absolutely sure that he'd drop me and choose her, just because she was rich and pretty.'

What do I say? Helga went with a vaguely sympathetic '. . . Oh! What happened?'

'She fell on a rock.' A satisfied pause. 'Four times.'

'He was smart not to stray, then.'

'Yes, he was.'

Or something awful might have happened to your husband as well. Helga looked at the other woman with as much focus as she dared, but the sharp words had taken the wind out of her sails somewhat. She looked deflated and was pursing her lips in some discomfort.

A chance. Take it – take it!

'It must be hard to sit the vigil all by yourself,' Helga said.

'It's been much better, thanks to you.'

'It's one thing, being lonely . . .' What had she seen Hildigunnur do? And how? '. . . and another being absolutely fit to burst.'

A tiny burst of laughter popped out of Thyri, and for a moment her eyes twinkled in the candlelight. 'You're not wrong, daughter of Riverside.'

'I can sit here for you, if you need a couple of moments to . . . um . . . appreciate nature.'

Thyri's smile was conspiratorial. 'Thank you,' she said as she rose with some urgency.

Three . . . two . . . The moment the door closed on Bjorn's wife, Helga moved. 'Right, big boy,' she muttered under her breath, 'time for you to tell me a secret.' The body was uncomfortably cold, like a massive slab of meat laid out for carving. She pushed her arms under Bjorn's side and heaved. 'And the fact that you weigh about as much as an ox isn't one of them,' she grunted. The body shifted slightly, then sank down on the bier again. 'Come on!' she hissed, heaving again. This time she managed to lift his side a half-hand off the table, but then her arms started to ache and she couldn't possibly shift him to his side. *Think, girl. THINK.* Looking around, she grabbed a fist-sized block of wood. 'Last try,' she muttered, and heaved. She knew his weight now, and it was ridiculous – but still, she managed to pull and create a little space to wedge the block in under his shoulder blade. *Quickly, now!* Moving the candle as close as she dared – burning down the vigil would probably be unpopular – she peered at Bjorn's back.

Shit.

He'd been dressed in a new tunic.

Moving quickly, Helga stepped to the left and found the line of his trousers. Tracing his spine with her fingers, she worked her way upwards to where she could feel the wounds, touching the point where his skin had split under the blade.

And at that moment, she knew.

There was no way the wounds had been made with the same knife.

She didn't even need to see them to tell. These had a thick, split edge to them where the flesh had been ripped out. Karl's wounds had been little slits, a thin wedge cut into the flesh. These were *holes*, punched by something broader and much heavier. So there had to be another knife, and—

Footsteps.

Straining, she lowered the massive weight of Bjorn down as gently and quietly as she could, sat down and took a deep breath, calming her thudding heart just moments before the door opened and Thyri entered.

'Thank you so much,' she said as she sat down. 'I really needed that.'

'You're welcome.' Helga tempered the smile on her face. *Just enough, no more. I've done nothing wrong.* She could feel the coldness of Bjorn's body on her fingertips and she wondered, in an idle, detached way what Thyri would have felt about her dead husband being touched by another woman the moment she left the hut.

'You're kind.' Thyri paused. 'There's something good in you. And around here, that's . . . unusual.' Her voice trembled slightly at the edges. 'So you should go now, and do what you do every day, and wait until all of this is over.' *Fine.* Even though she'd discovered big, new things, Helga still felt oddly hurt by the woman's dismissal. She rose and started to leave.

The touch on her arm was so light that she almost didn't feel it. In the flickering light, the older woman's face looked haunted. 'Be safe,' the widow whispered.

The outside was colder than she'd expected.

The journey from Bjorn's final resting place to the longhouse suddenly felt like it could take her for ever. *Two killers.* The thought went round and round in her mind. *No, not necessarily – but two knives.* Still the idea of the two killers wouldn't go away: one furious and rough, the other measured and calm.

Two killers.

'But why?' she asked no one in particular. The words felt good, liberated from her head. 'Why? Why steal Mother's knife for the first one if you had a perfectly good one yourself?' She stopped and looked at the longhouse, her home for the last eleven years. Light seeped out from the cracks around the door, escaped into the dark sky through the air slits, chased by chatter and bursts of laughter. She suddenly felt sick, so she turned on her heel and strode off towards the new barn. *Anywhere – anywhere but here.*

But the thoughts wouldn't leave her alone. *Who was the killer?*

Sigmar, with his forces? Sigmar could have done it. He could have snuck in and slit the veins in Karl's legs. 'That works,' Helga mumbled, easing past the gate and making sure it didn't creak. 'That works.' He looked shifty, he'd run away, and there was something about him that suggested he was quite able to handle a knife. But *why*? If it was just about whether Karl was a bit of a bastard, they could all have done it. And did he kill Bjorn? And what about Aslak? If Karl had had a thing with Runa back in the day, that would explain why she fought with his sister. Had Aslak killed Karl out of fear or jealousy? And who then killed Bjorn? Thyri? Sigmar? Sigmar's men? Any of the others? Had it been all of them, again? Who was the last to speak to Bjorn – and why hadn't they said anything?

Helga bit down on her lip until she couldn't take the pain any more. She had no words – just a growl of frustration. Stopping halfway up the hill, she turned and looked down.

Riverside lay before her, the house and outbuildings and fence, the river catching the night sky and reflecting it back at her. *It looks so peaceful*, she thought.

And slowly, ever so slowly, the fire of her rage died down and, from within, a forged purpose emerged.

Let's go and change that.

Chapter 18

HUNTED

Gytha leaned in towards her mother. 'When will this end?' she whispered, her voice barely audible through the chatter in the longhouse.

'When the last two men fall asleep,' her mother replied through teeth clenched in a smile. 'Now, make yourself look beautiful.' She turned halfway back to a conversation between two big farmers and a Swede, ably controlled and guided by Hildigunnur.

'What – for these old farts? I don't *think* so.'

Before the girl could blink, her mother's claw-like hand was around her wrist, pulling hard. Almost without moving, Agla shifted backwards so she was just out of earshot. Under her breath she hissed, '*You* do not get to choose. *You* do not get to play princess. After all I've done for you, do *not* treat me like your servant.' She turned, twisted and squeezed the wrist in her grip and looked at the girl's face contorted in pain. 'And don't you dare cry – I spent some of my best colours on making your eyes look nice for tonight. Your father is gone: do you understand me? *Gone*. There will be no one to threaten on your behalf, and no one to collect whatever you think you're owed, so you had better learn to be a woman, starting right now. And the first lesson is that you'll have to know how to pretty your way through boring conversations. Do you understand me?'

When Gytha nodded, her eyes wide, she let go. 'Good. Go and get yourself a drink.' She watched as the girl rubbed her wrist. '*Go*.'

Helga watched Gytha scuttle away, bowed under her mother's glare, and inched towards the water barrel. Sure enough, she made straight for the drinks. *Out goes the net.* Helga looked away so no one would see her put on the soft, friendly face. When she turned back towards Gytha, she looked kind, sympathetic.

'Hey.' The girl didn't notice her at first. Perfect. 'What are you looking for?'

A tilt of the head suggested that she had been heard and recognised. The stiff neck and shoulders told her she'd picked a good target. 'Nothing,' Gytha mumbled into her water jug.

'I'll tell you a secret.' She leaned in, exactly like she'd seen her mother do when she needed to bring someone on board: *This is just for us.* 'The next attractive man I see in here will be the first,' she whispered.

A half-laugh, half-sniff hissed out of Gytha, followed by the merest hint of a smile. 'Thank you.'

Helga could feel the girl turning towards her, creating a little secret ring of their own. 'But let that not stop us in finding you a husband,' she said, lacing her voice with bite. 'How about him?' She glanced at a broad-shouldered, thick-bellied farmer deep in conversation with Sigmar.

'A fine choice,' Gytha said, taking the offer and playing the game.

'Thorfinn Breechwetter, of the Breechwetter clan.' She could feel Gytha stifle another giggle. 'Found in nature, raised by a family of wild boars. Good for warmth in the winter, great at finding roots.'

Laughter was bubbling in the girl now. 'Stop,' she hissed, her eyes begging Helga to do anything but.

'Although he hasn't seen his own root in thirty summers.' A sharp jab in the side of the arm. Gytha's eyes were sparkling with delight now, and Helga allowed herself a smile too. *Though we're not smiling about the same thing.*

'So maybe not. The world will have to supply its own piglets. How about him?' Across the room, Sigmar's right-hand man was busy discussing something with Unnthor. They looked very serious. 'Agnar the Stick.'

'Ooh!' Gytha said, feigning interest. 'Tell me more!'

'Agnar the Stick is famous for his stick-shape, and the shape of his stick.' She could hear Gytha swallow a breath and see out of the corner of her eye how she pursed her lips to keep from bursting out.

'Explain . . . ?' she managed.

Helga waited. She needed to time this just right. 'Apparently Agnar's cock forks in the middle.'

Perfect. Gytha spat the water that she'd been intending to drink back into her mug. 'What?' she sputtered. 'Where do you even—?'

'Which has made him a very sought-after suitor, because women have figured they can use one till he's pleased and then move on to the next one till they are.'

Gytha giggled. 'You have a very warped mind, Sister!'

Helga smiled at her. 'And now you're smiling, so I'm going to say your mind isn't any less warped.' Gytha's smile faded just a little at the corners, and Helga knew that feeling all too well: a cloud drawing over the sun. An argument with the mother? Entirely possible. The fish was in the net; now she just needed to bring her in gently.

'And just so you know, I know neither of those men.' She winked. 'Although the Swede . . . who knows? I've heard they're *interesting* over there.'

Gytha's back straightened and her chin rose, just by half an inch. 'Mother and I will be going to the court now, since Father is dead.'

'Oh wow – you must be really excited!'

'It will be lovely, I'm sure.' The glint in Gytha's eyes belied the modest words.

You can't wait, can you?

'I can't imagine – It must be very hard for your mother to take on all of Karl's wealth.'

'Yeah, uh – she said – we'll be okay, and then we'll inherit his share of this place.'

Right, little fish. Let's see how well you do on dry land.

'Oh,' Helga said, looking at Gytha for an eye-blink, then looking away.

'What?'

'I thought you knew.'

'Knew what?'

'Apparently Runa told Unnthor that she and Aslak were quite

poor and that because Karl was so rich he should give up his share to them and their family.'

Gytha's fragile happiness crumbled in front of her. It started in the forehead, her smooth brow wrinkling, then her pretty little nose twitched, like an animal smelling a predator. The lips wobbled, but Helga could see the effort of will to straighten them out. There they were: the in-drawn breath, the slow exhale, the wan smile.

It was a thing to watch, the breaking of a dream.

And now I need to—

Helga didn't have time to finish the thought. Gytha was very much her parents' daughter and the fury bounded forward like a wolfhound after prey. She leaned in. 'Tell me *exactly* what she said.'

The feeling of success was so intense that it felt almost uncomfortable. For a moment Helga felt like everyone was watching her, sharing in her triumph, but she dismissed it. In their little bubble of girlish secrecy, she busied herself with the first part of her plan.

Runa balanced the jugs, two in each hand, and turned from the drinks barrel. Half a step – and the elbow hit her low on the rib-cage, hard enough to smart, but not enough to knock the drinks to the floor.

'Oh,' Gytha said, 'I'm very sorry.'

Runa inhaled. 'That's all right,' she said, forcing a smile.

'I was turning to look for my mother and I just didn't see you there.'

'I said it's fine. Now, step to the side.'

'Sorry – what?'

'I asked if you could please step aside and allow me through. I was bringing drinks to the table.'

'Oh. So you want me to step aside just so you can have what you want?'

'What are you talking about? I'm carrying drinks.'

Gytha smiled sweetly. 'Oh, that shouldn't be hard for you. Just like no man ever gets hard for you.'

Runa's eyes widened. 'You bony little whore,' she hissed. 'You're your mother's get and no mistake.'

The slap rang out across the longhouse, followed immediately by a shriek and the clatter of mugs on the floor.

Helga had been careful to turn away and just listen; it wouldn't do to be caught smiling when everyone else would be shocked. The moment Gytha had thought she'd found out that Aslak and Runa would inherit the farm she was spoiling for a fight, just like her late father. *It probably wouldn't have mattered that it isn't true*, Helga thought. Some people were always ready to believe the worst.

Within a blink, male voices had joined the shrieking and Helga turned to see big bodies rushing over to what could only be described as a pile of limbs on the floor. It was all she could do not to laugh: a gaggle of large men hovering at the edge, not quite daring to touch the two spitting, hissing girls on the floor.

Men fight like bears, her mother had told her: *big, slow and lumbering. Women fight like forest cats – fierce, quick and deadly*. None of the men looked to be in a hurry to stop Runa, who had twisted Gytha to the floor and landed at least one good punch.

Someone shouldered her to the side, and Helga frowned: a strong shape, moving quickly.

Sigmar.

The Swede pushed through the crowd, carrying something—

—the water barrel.

Luckily, it was less than half-full, but it was enough. The water went over the two women and in the moment that Runa blinked and gasped, catching her breath, Sigmar barrelled into her, sweeping her off Gytha's prone, howling form and she instantly disappeared underneath the Swede. A hand clutched around blonde hair was the last thing Helga saw, and then Sigmar had her pinned.

Gytha scrabbled to her feet, coughing and crying. She set her feet, poised like a cat, ready to propel herself at Runa, but arms grabbed her from behind; she strained, but Hildigunnur had appeared at her shoulder and was muttering in her ear, her lips moving fast.

Gytha's face crumpled, and she went limp.

'Carry her out for fresh air,' Hildigunnur snapped. 'Agla!' Karl's wife appeared at heel, like a dog; she listened to a few very terse commands, then walked out behind her daughter.

'Get off her!' Aslak pushed through the men and punched Sigmar in the shoulder.

The Swede was up and two steps back almost instantly, hands up in the air.

Aslak offered Runa a hand and pulled her up. Blinking rapidly, looking visibly shaken, she muttered something to her husband, who hugged her, then without a word, they turned and left the longhouse.

And that's that. It was odd, feeling like the hunter and the prey at the same time, but the murderer, whosoever he was, would be a little less certain about what could and could not happen tonight – and that was something. Everyone made mistakes. Sometimes they just needed a little help. She kept her eyes on her target, blocking everything else.

Time for the next step.

She watched them settle like a flock of birds stirred by a long-departed hawk. Before long Agla had cornered her daughter and kept her, soggy and fuming, by her elbow. Hildigunnur had started conversation again with a well-timed and rather rude joke about wet girls, and now they were drinking from the barrels, singing the songs and doing the things they always did. No one was paying her any special attention.

She reached in under the crates, where she knew her mother kept the smelly stuff. *We'll see how well your best homebrew goes down, Mother.* Her target was sitting at the far end of the hall, perched on a barrel and looking like a thundercloud. He'd been there since he came back in after calming Runa, clutching a mug and frowning at the world. She took a moment to enjoy just looking at him. There was something pleasing about Aslak's face, even when he was angry. Was this what it meant to *want*? Was this how that started? She grabbed that thought, put it in a box and stashed it away. *Something to figure out later.* She wove through the guests, pouring jug in one hand and two cups in the other, unaware of the eyes following her.

Aslak blinked and winced away the taste. 'I mean, why is it his business anyway?'

'Exactly,' Helga cooed. 'More?'

'No. Shouldn't.' Brief pause. 'More.'

She flashed an earnest smile at him as she raised the jug of her mother's vicious brew and sloshed the cloudy liquid into Aslak's cup. 'Here you go.'

'Thank you.'

You probably shouldn't thank me. 'You're welcome. I just think you need the support.'

'Why would I need s'port?' Slurring at the edges, but still spiky.

'I mean – we all saw him.'

'Who?'

'Sigmar.'

Unintelligible, angry mumbling.

'His hands were all over your wife.'

'He had to—'

'Oh, he did more than he had to. We all saw it. If anything, he owes you payment for your honour. More?'

Aslak didn't reply; he just stuck out his cup. When she'd filled it, he downed it in one. 'He's a rotten coward,' he growled.

'And he's old.'

'Yeah. *Old.*' The young man's lip curled in distaste.

'And he has no right to treat a son of Unnthor like that, and at Riverside too. It's a slight to your father's honour.' Helga watched as Aslak's grip on the cup tightened. *Good. Now, sadness.* 'I don't know what you could do, though.'

The rangy young man rose. If he was aware of her, he showed no sign.

'I'll go and get us some more,' Helga said quietly, just in case he was still listening.

He wasn't.

She managed to put most of the guests between them before Aslak's voice rose over the chatter.

'Sigmar Goransson!' One by one, the men's voices trailed off. 'Sigmar Goransson, I declare you a coward and a white-bellied bitch!'

That should shut them up. Helga watched as eyes opened wide among Sigmar's men. Shock? Amusement? Anger?

Over by Hildigunnur and Unnthor's group, the Swede turned slowly. 'Who said that?' – then a masterful pause, until just as Aslak was about to speak – 'I thought the children had gone to bed?' Roars of laughter from the men, and behind Sigmar's head, she caught a glimpse of her mother's face. She looked mildly annoyed. *You couldn't have done that any better yourself, could you, Mother?*

'Fine words,' Aslak said, unperturbed, 'but that is all that old men have.'

Oohs and exclamations from the men: *fighting words.*

'Oh, the puppy barks,' Sigmar said. 'And he is right, of course.' If Aslak had any sense, he'd be looking at the faces of the Swedes in the room. *They are all too amused by this.* 'Fine words, fine wool, fine women.'

For a brief moment Helga felt a pang of guilt. She had egged Aslak on, set him on the path – had she underestimated the Swede?

'I'll put you on your back like a woman,' Aslak growled.

'Oh, will you, now?' The timbre of Sigmar's voice had changed. He was no longer talking to the room – his eyes were focused on the youngest of Hildigunnur's children. Aslak stepped forward, and a space magically cleared around him. The tiniest of gestures – Unnthor shifted his weight towards the two would-be combatants, then stopped. The gentlest of hands on his forearm – just for a moment – and then Hildigunnur eased back again. Helga frowned. Why would her mother allow Aslak to go up against Sigmar?

She doesn't know who the killer is either, so she's creating tension.

We're playing the same game.

For some reason that didn't reassure Helga at all, but she had no time to puzzle it out. Aslak roared and dived for the Swede, who sidestepped quickly and delivered a firm slap to the back of the young man's head.

'I'm not down,' the Swede said.

'Not yet,' Aslak snapped back. This time the approach was more careful, arms spread out wide. *He can't have had much luck wrestling either of his brothers, but he'll have learned by watching,* Helga mused.

A quick grasp for hold – another lightning-quick chop from Sigmar, this time down onto Aslak's outstretched arm, and the young man retreated, holding his wrist and wincing. *He hit the spot where it hurt the most.* It was all too easy for Helga to see Sigmar leaning over Karl's prone body, slicing with a slim blade.

'I'm still not down,' Sigmar repeated, louder this time.

'Shut up, *coward*!' This time Aslak approached slower still, but he kept his hands close to his body, not reaching across; his hands at the ready to hit out at Sigmar as he moved his feet an inch at a time.

The Swede just watched him, a trace of a smile on his face. 'Are you waiting for me to fall to the floor of old age?'

Two steps, and Aslak was upon him. Then he was moving swiftly backwards and up, and not of his own volition. The thud when he hit the floor was followed by an 'ooh' from the guests; there was a wheeze as Aslak tried desperately to catch his breath.

'Maybe this is how you put your woman on her back,' Sigmar said, to laughter and catcalls. Then with a glint in his eye, he leaned down towards Aslak's ear. He whispered—

Farmers and Swedes alike had stopped shouting at each other. Through Hildigunnur's hard work, order had been restored again, but the carefree talk had vanished and been replaced with surly glances over the brims of mugs that were not staying full for long.

Sigmar sat in the corner, his back to the wall, scowling and clutching a sodden rag to his cheek. 'That little *shit*.'

'I agree.' Helga refilled his mug.

'Hel take him and wolves feast on his face – the little bastard *bit* me.'

'Mm.'

'Anywhere but here, he'd be taken outside and taught a lesson.'

'Mm.'

Sigmar glared at the backs of Unnthor and Hildigunnur. 'I should have known.'

'What?' *Keep him talking. They love the sound of their own voice.*

'That I couldn't say that.'

'What did you say?'

A wicked glint in Sigmar's eye once again. 'I told him Runa liked it just fine when Karl did it to her.'

Quickly, laugh. She forced a giggle, hiding the falseness of it behind her hand. 'He won't have liked that.'

'No,' Sigmar said. 'They're heavy on the pride here. Even Jorunn wasn't quite on my side for this one.'

'Well, I don't think you did anything wrong.' *Gently does it.* 'He insulted you, so you insulted him. Unnthor is very serious about his name, so why shouldn't you be? Fair's fair.' Helga frowned, as if she was thinking carefully.

'Absolutely.'

'A man should be allowed to stand his ground.'

A cloud passed across Sigmar's features. 'Yes,' he said, glancing over her shoulder.

That'd be Jorunn, then. In the net you go, big fish. 'And a man should get what rightfully belongs to him.'

'Yes, you'd think so.' Still scanning.

He needs to think that I'm making a decision. 'It's not right.' She paused. 'My father hoards his gold, but it's here, you know. For restitution.'

That got his attention. Sigmar looked at her for the first time, and Helga felt her stomach sink. There was a coldness to this one, something unblinking and unerring. She felt suddenly relieved that the Swede had been on his best behaviour. 'So she was right. Find me proof and you will be rewarded.'

'I will,' she said. The smile on her lips was only half forced, and she took her excuse to get up and go gladly, absolutely certain that if she looked back she'd catch his eye again. *Just enough time to convince him that I know where it is, and then . . .*

The sounds and smells of the house pushed at her, but she ignored them. The cold thrill of the game made her forearms prickle.

Once outside, she stopped in the yard and drew a deep breath. As she exhaled, she gazed up at the white dots in the sky. The sounds of a summer night were like a soft whisper after the racket of the house, mixing with the thudding of blood in her ears. '*Sssh,*' she whispered to her hand, resting above her heart. '*Shusssh.* Just a couple of moments.' Where on earth would she find proof of a buried treasure? Her plan, she realised, had been half-cooked.

Force someone to do . . . something.

She could hear someone starting up a song inside, rising suddenly in volume, then getting quiet again. It sounded almost like someone had opened a door—

—a strong, rough hand grabbed her by the arm just above the elbow and yanked, hard. Another on her neck was dragging her forward. Her breath caught in her throat as she stumbled, and in a panic she tried to force her feet to catch up so she didn't end up on her face in the dirt. It took her a few heartbeats to realise who the shadowy figure was.

'Oi! Let go of me—!'

'Shut up,' Einar snapped. Something in his voice sounded different, thicker, but as she was being half-dragged, half-hauled behind a shed she couldn't put her finger on what it was. As they rounded the corner he spun her around so she was facing him.

Moonlight caught on his face, sparkling on tear-stained cheeks.

'It was *me*, Helga.' She could hear it now, the lump in his throat. '*It was me.* I stabbed Bjorn in the back. I killed him – I killed him like a coward.'

She looked at the boy she'd grown up with and searched for the truth in his eyes.

No, you didn't. You're as strong as an ox and you would have left nothing to chance.

She had to shift her weight in order not to keel over. 'Calm down,' she murmured, reaching out to touch his forearm, but Einar jerked his arm away as if she were made of fire.

'No,' he hissed, 'don't touch me. I'm telling you. I killed him. I murdered big Bjorn Unnthorsson, and now I must have my head cracked – not that idiot boy. It was me.'

Her heart thudded and she grasped for the words. 'Einar . . . why are you telling me?'

'Because I've been watching you all night. You've been asking questions, pushing people – and you would have found out eventually.'

'And why did you do it?'

Hesitation. Just a moment, but it was there. 'Because he should have— Because he shouldn't have killed Karl.'

And how do you know he killed Karl?

But for some reason the question didn't fly out. It almost escaped her lips – but the sight of the boy she called her brother, chest heaving and tears streaming down his face, stopped her tongue and instead, the unanswered question just sat there, unspoken. Suddenly her heartbeats felt miles apart, and everything that had been bothering her came back.

Who was the other person speaking to Bjorn?

Who knew that Bjorn killed Karl?

Who are you protecting?

Helga closed her eyes ever so slowly. When she opened them again, she knew and understood.

'You know I have to tell Hildigunnur.'

'Yes,' Einar said.

'Don't go back to the house. Go to your shed. She'll not want this done in front of the guests.'

Einar nodded.

'We will talk about it. There will be something to be done.'

He nodded again.

'Now go,' she said, shooing him away like she'd done a hundred times before, forcing a little joy into her voice. 'You've told me, I'll tell Hildigunnur and we will get this right.'

As he sniffled and moved off, she saw a ghost of a smile on his face. He looked like a little boy. She shook her head and smiled. Even though the danger was greater than it had ever been, she felt satisfied. The dam had burst.

It was time to let the river flow.

It hadn't taken her long to get used to the noise of the house. They were singing in full voice now, red-faced and happy, eyes on each other and the mugs. She'd found Jaki and whispered in his ear, and to his everlasting praise Unnthor's man hadn't asked any questions. Instead he'd nodded and even smiled at her, impishly, like she was asking him to pull a prank. Now she just needed to find—

There.

Helga gently snuck past her father and two of his friends from three farms down and found Jorunn. She made sure she caught the young woman's eye and held it. Then she leaned in close.

'I know what you did,' she whispered, smiling. 'I know why, and I know where Father's hoard is, and I want my share or I'll tell them everything and you will not walk out of here.'

She was her mother's daughter, so Jorunn Unnthorsdottir's smile didn't even falter. Instead she tilted her head ever so slightly and nodded, a twinkle in her eye. 'Lovely. We could maybe talk about this somewhere more . . . private?'

Helga matched her, twinkle for twinkle. 'Of course. Follow me.'

She turned and headed towards the exit, all too aware she was being followed intently. Once out, the door didn't even come close to swinging shut on Jorunn's striding form. Helga made sure to lengthen her step. *Let the bitch run to catch me.* Past one building – another – and then—

Helga ducked into Einar's tool-shed. The speed of her appearance made the young man whirl and put up his arms as some sort of protection.

'I thought—' He didn't have time to finish the sentence. The door slammed open and Jorunn burst in. The words tumbled out of him. 'I told her, Jorunn. I told her I killed Bjorn.'

'You useless little boy,' Jorunn snapped. 'She knows you didn't.

In fact, this bitch knows way too much.' The knife was in her hand suddenly – and very comfortably, Helga noted. Stubby little thing, thick blade.

It'll match Bjorn's wounds. And this is the end. I'll be murdered on my own farm.

'What?' Einar moved towards them. 'No, my love – you can't.'

'My *love*?' The young woman's face twisted in gleeful fury. 'You think you *love* me? Get this shitty little brat to milk you until you get rid of that idea, boy.'

Helga looked at Einar, whose face had drained of all colour. 'But – you said—'

'"*You said*",' she replied, mocking him. 'So what did I say, then?'

'You said Bjorn had planted the knife in Sigmar's bed and that we just needed to place it back with Bjorn and that'd be that.'

'And you couldn't find your balls for even a moment,' Jorunn hissed. 'You kept keening like a little bitch, saying we should go and get the old folks – which would have been a *great* idea.' Her voice dripped with contempt. 'Because they would *definitely* have sided with my husband the Swede against their own son. And then what did you do? *Eh?*' She was squaring up to Einar now, her knife not quite pointed away from him.

He stood there, terrified, like a surprised deer.

'That's right,' Jorunn purred, moving towards him, a snake about to strike. '*Absolutely nothing.* That's what you did, you big, strong boy. And because you took so fucking long to search for your dick' – she was spitting now, snapping the words off, hurling them at him like stones – 'my darling brother showed up and you did *absolutely nothing* about that either. Did you ever stop to think about who killed Karl? And why Bjorn would have had the knife? He slit my brother's veins and tried to plant the knife on Sigmar, who I was *never* supposed to marry, and so he had to be taken care of. And when I'd done *that*, you had no ideas, none at all, so *I* had to slip the knife into his idiot son's bed.

'And after all of *this*, you think I *love* you?' She looked him up and down, and now there was a note of pity in her voice. 'There is *nothing* to love about you, or this place, or anyone in it.' She surveyed her captives and seemed to settle. She'd won, and she was going to enjoy it.

'We are just here for the treasure, pure and simple. You see, I have a problem. I deal mostly with rich old men who have the time to lounge on King Eirik's bearskins, look down on people like me and withhold the best parts of their business. To them I am an outsider, and I always will be. The only thing they'll understand is gold. I thought I could get Karl to force the issue by paying an old salt to pretend to be Havard Greybeard, but that didn't work. I thought I could squeeze some sympathy out of Mother with marriage troubles, or training Aslak's scab of a wife for him, but that didn't work either. So listen, here's what I am going to do. I am going to gut this bitch here, and then I am going to run crying to my mother and tell her you tried to force yourself on me, that she found you and you stabbed her – after all, you've already murdered my poor brothers. Karl and Bjorn are dead to advance your own cause. I'll give you a head-start – pray that you know the woods better than my father. Worst comes to worst? They'll split the treasure between me and Aslak – and then I'll accidentally lose the baby before it becomes apparent that I may not be all that pregnant. Now, stand back, or I'm going to gut you too.'

'No, you're not.' Unnthor's voice through the wall was calm and steady, with only the hint of a growl.

Helga remembered to breathe.

'But if you step out of the hut, now, and throw the knife on the ground, I might just let you live.'

Jorunn looked like she'd been hit with a club. She blinked, and her mouth opened and closed.

She's probably trying to guess how much he heard, Helga thought, then she wondered, *Can she lie her way out of this?*

'Out. NOW.'

A slow smile spread across Helga's face, quite against her will. *I guess that's a 'no', then.*

The outside of the hut was awash in torchlight. The farmers of the Dales suddenly looked quite different, much more like Unnthor. Some held torches; all held weapons. Helga remembered what her mother always said, when someone stopped by to borrow something or for a chat or a bit of advice: *This valley is full of old friends.* And when they were gathered behind Unnthor, all united in a single purpose, it wasn't so hard to imagine them thirty, forty years ago, sailing together to the west, testing themselves against the world. Sigmar and his men stood tightly bunched together, by their horses but without their weapons. She looked around for Jaki and found him leaning casually on a barrel full of spears and axes, grinning, his hand resting nonchalantly on a club the size of a giant's thighbone.

'We *all* heard,' Unnthor said.

Jorunn opened her mouth, but her father's massive palm, upraised, stopped her. 'And enough blood has been spilled on my land. I do not wish to exact the blood-price from the two of you' – the animal within Helga cowered, curled up and made herself as small as possible under her father's gaze, but the fury in his eyes was reserved for Jorunn and Sigmar – 'but I will if I must. The treasure you seek – my "hoard" – will go to paying the wergild for my sons, for Karl and Bjorn. It will pay for your life – and we never want to see either of you again. Now get on your horses and ride.'

'Where do you—?' Sigmar started, but Unnthor raised his hand again to stop him.

'I don't care where you go,' the old chieftain said, 'but if you ever set foot in these Dales again, you will be hunted down like vermin, hung from a branch and skinned.' He paused, and his voice was not loud, but everyone heard every word. 'I will keep you alive for days.'

After that, nothing else needed to be said.

The Dalesmen stood behind Unnthor and Hildigunnur like the trees of a dark forest as the Swedes mounted up. More than one of them glanced at the barrel of weapons that Jaki had stolen from them, but they knew better than to ask.

Jorunn and Sigmar rode away in silence.

Chapter 19

LEAVING

After the long night came the painful morning.

Time passed in a haze. Jorunn and Sigmar's departure had left a void, like drawing a spike out of flesh, and nobody quite knew what to do with themselves. The occasional cloud drifted across the sky, showing no care whatsoever for the business of the people milling about below. Regular farm work resumed, after a fashion, but no one's heart was in it.

They walk as if asleep, Helga thought. *Like they don't want to wake and remember what happened.*

By mid-morning, Aslak and Runa had got the children organised and their goods packed and were ready to go. The residents of Riverside walked them to the gate.

'Come to visit. Please.' Hildigunnur's hand on her son's forearm was gentle but firm. Behind her, Unnthor loomed sympathetically.

'We will,' Runa said, and to her surprise, Helga believed her. Something had changed in the angry woman during the visit. What, she couldn't quite figure out – but something had, something important.

As the gate closed, the men returned to their chores, but Hildigunnur lingered and watched the little family growing smaller and smaller in the distance. Helga debated and decided that staying would be kinder. The fact that it gave her a reprieve from her chores was neither here nor there.

'That's my only son now,' Hildigunnur said softly.

There was nothing to say, so Helga hugged her, hard.

They stood there together, watching the road that led from Riverside to the world for a while.

Agla and Gytha were also ready to go now. The new widow enveloped Hildigunnur in a crushing embrace, and sniffling loudly, even managed to shed a couple of tears.

Ugh. There wasn't even a word in Helga's mind, just a vaguely face-twisting feeling not dissimilar to berry poisoning. She'd noted the identical looks on their faces when Hildigunnur handed over the wergild for Karl – the joyful greed, the lust for gold – and now they stood there, just past the gate, two women who, but for the age difference, looked and sounded just about the same: mother and daughter, suddenly awash in the world.

The moment they mounted, though, Gytha transformed: she sat up straight on her horse and looked down at her grandparents, her lips tight.

Oho, Helga thought. *Somewhere out there a princeling is in want of a future queen.*

'Goodbye, all,' Agla said. 'We will be sending messages wherever we end up, and we too will be aiming to visit.'

'Make sure that you do,' Unnthor rumbled.

Gytha was the first to spur her horse; the mare responded enthusiastically, bored after days turned out in the meadow, and the two women bolted down the road.

Helga looked at Hildigunnur, who was not trying to hide the cold smirk on her face.

'"Wherever we end up" indeed!' she said.

It took Helga until noon to summon up the nerve.

In a rare moment of quiet, Hildigunnur had found a spot up against the longhouse wall where she sat spinning flax, the rays of the sun playing on her skin.

Helga approached gingerly. 'Mother . . .'

'I know.'

'W-what?'

The old woman squeezed her eyes almost shut and made a visor of her hand, peering up into the light at her. 'And I've asked, and it is fine.'

Helga searched for words, but they wouldn't come.

'What's fine?' she blurted at last.

'You want to leave. You *need* to leave. You need to find out who you are and where you belong in the world.' Hildigunnur looked like she was about to say something more, but checked herself. 'You can go with Thyri and Volund as far as their farm. You'll work there for a spell, and then move on – they'll need the help while they're selling and scaling down. They're ready to leave when you are. And stop looking like a stranded fish. People will think I raised a halfwit.'

No words came to Helga then, nothing but a pure physical urge.

She fell to her knees and wrapped her arms around her mother's neck, squeezing for all she was worth.

'What's this? A strangling?' Hildigunnur managed to cough, but there was a smile to her voice.

Hot tears flowed down Helga's cheeks, and when she felt a hand on the back of her head, smoothing and stroking, she could feel her lips trembling like a babe's. *Stupid girl. Stupid, stupid girl.* But she didn't care. This was everything, this woman and her fierce love for her family, her loyalty and the safety she'd provided, everything that Riverside had meant to her. And so she cried.

'We'll meet again, my child,' her mother whispered. 'I know it. I don't have much more that I need to do here, and when I'm done, I'll come and find you, see how you're doing out in the world.'

It took all the will she could summon, but Helga managed to let go. She clambered clumsily to her feet. 'Thank you,' she sniffled, her voice hoarse. 'I need – what do I have to—?'

'*Pssh.*' Hildigunnur dismissed her with a wave. 'I packed your things while you were out fetching water. Go and talk to Thyri. We'll be ready to say goodbye to you in a moment or two.'

The road felt odd under her feet, like she didn't know it as well as she thought she had.

It's different, walking a path for the last time.

Her thoughts swirled as Volund plodded beside her. She had come to learn to recognise when he was quietly happy, and this was one of those times. *Was this how the others had felt?* She thought about Agla, arriving at full gallop with Karl and leaving without him. How had *she* felt? She thought about Thyri, silent even when there was no Bjorn to tower over her.

She thought about Jorunn.

The woman had murdered her brother, just to get to gold that might not even have existed – what had gone on in her mind? Did she have any regrets? She'd never get answers to those questions now, but it felt oddly satisfying to at least know what had happened to Bjorn, and in turn, what had happened to Karl.

'It's a long trek,' Thyri said. Her voice was matter-of-fact.

'I know.'

'I won't be going back.'

Helga swallowed a sudden lump in her throat. 'I . . . I don't think I'll be doing that either.'

'They may say that my Bjorn did it,' Thyri said, her voice full of defiance. *These words aren't for me. They are for herself.* The realisation was stark, and Helga watched the woman in fascination. 'And maybe he did – he was acting strange.' Thyri drew a deep breath and bit through the words. 'But if he did, *someone* put him up to it. He would *never* have decided to kill Karl on his own.'

What do I say? Lost for words, Helga turned around for one last glance at Riverside, her home for more than half her life. The figures at the gate were still visible, but only just: a hulking bear of a man, and in front of him, a willowy woman.

'Someone *told* him to do it.'

The woman who defended her family's honour and her husband's name to the death. The woman who raised her children to do right, and was furious when they disobeyed. The woman who dealt with potential trouble quickly and decisively.

And then the words came back to her, whispered with the wind from the hills, written in the very foundation of Riverside, a place of honour and dignity, the home of a family who had fought hard for their name, and Helga saw Bjorn, standing by the longhouse, head bowed, taking the command to kill his brother in his sleep and pin it on Sigmar, and she knew who had made him do it.

What boy ever says no to his mother?

Acknowledgements

Without spoiling anything for the people who read this bit first (and without suggesting they reassess their approach to reading), I think I can safely say that this book is a bit of a departure – or possibly an arrival, depending on where you stand.

It would not have been picked up without the savvy of indefatigable agent Geraldine Cooke, Renaissance Woman and all-round legend.

Nor would it have been published without the belief and tireless work of inimitable publisher Jo Fletcher, who has very patiently watched me flail and figure out how to solve a story *without* inventing a monster or killing another fifteen Vikings and then fixed it when I got it wrong.

It would not have been any good without the support of Nick Bain, who taught me how to do this whole writing malarkey in the first place.

The good people at Merchiston Castle School have been nothing but positive about my writing. Julia Williams gets special mention here for being a splendid librarian, as does Paul Williams for being one of the most impressive and terrifying readers I've ever met. Stephanie Binnie has given me more support than I could have hoped for, Gail Cunningham has supplied timely chats and Dr Naomi Steen has been a constant source of encouragement. Furthermore, I wish to thank my students for their optimistic and repeated questions about writer earnings, sales figures and every other detail of my life. When I inevitably earn as much as J.K. Rowling and go on *Live at the Apollo*, I will bring biscuits.

Family and friends have been crucial, as they always are. Allan and Helen have supplied wit, wisdom and a regrettable lack of stewed fruit. My dear Mum and Dad are nothing like Unnthor and Hildigunnur. Honest. You're not (except in the good bits, of course, which are entirely based on you). In fact, the author would like to state that all similarities with big family gatherings in Iceland are purely coincidental. Ailsa and Chris (and Anna and Flora), Andrew, and Sarah and Steven have supplied an almost endless stream of positivity, hope and glorious meals. My dear friends – you have made moving to Edinburgh a wonderful thing.

But none of that would matter a jot were it not for my wife, alpha-reader and companion in all things, Morag. She likes to solve murder mysteries so I wrote this book for her.

I hope you enjoy it as well.

Helga's got another mystery to solve in

COUNCIL

Helga Finnsdottir Book II